D1311019

Published in this series

JOANNA RUSS
The Adventures of Alyx
The Female Man
Extra(Ordinary) People
The Two of Them

SALLY MILLER GEARHART
The Wanderground

JANE PALMER
The Planet Dweller
The Watcher

NAOMI MITCHISON
Memoirs of a Spacewoman

SUZETTE HADEN ELGIN
Native Tongue

JEN GREEN & SARAH LEFANU, eds
Despatches from the Frontiers of the Female Mind

JOSEPHINE SAXTON
Queen of the States
The Travails of Jane Saint and Other Stories

CHARLOTTE PERKINS GILMAN
Herland

JODY SCOTT
Passing For Human
I, Vampire

RHODA LERMAN
The Book of the Night

MARGARET ELPHINSTONE
The Incomer

DORIS PISERCHIA
Star Rider

JOAN SLONCZEWSKI
A Door Into Ocean

MARGE PIERCY
Woman on the Edge of Time

MARGARET ELPHINSTONE

Margaret Elphinstone lives in Galloway with her two daughters. Her stories have appeared in *Writing Women, Women's Review*, and in the science fiction anthology *Despatches from the Frontiers of the Female Mind* (The Women's Press, 1985). She is co-author of *The Holistic Gardener*; this is her first published novel.

MARGARET ELPHINSTONE

THE INCOMER

The Women's Press

sf

First published by The Women's Press Limited 1987
A member of the Namara Group
34 Great Sutton Street, London EC1V 0DX

British Library Cataloguing in Publication Data
Elphinstone, Margaret
The incomer.
I. Title
823'.914[F]   PR6055.L

ISBN 0-7043-4070-4

Typeset by MC Typeset, Chatham, Kent
Printed and bound in Great Britain by
Hazell, Watson & Viney Ltd., Aylesbury, Bucks.

We shall not cease from exploration
And the end of all our exploring
Will be to arrive where we started
And know the place for the first time.

1

The crossroads was the reason for the village. The village happened because of the travellers crossing from one town to another. There were four towns equidistant from the village, with nothing between them except tracts of moorland and forest interspersed with complicated water systems. The burns flowed down unexpectedly, here to the north, there to the south, as if someone had taken the watershed and turned it topsy-turvy, flinging the countryside for miles around into a confusion of hillocks and lochans. A curious intricate country, lying at the foothills of the mountains that dominated the north-west horizon in long rounded contours, visible from the little cairn-topped hills that sheltered the houses below. The slopes west of the village were steepest, anticipating the mountains beyond the humping back of the ridge that kept the main force of the west wind off the settlement. These hillsides were forest-covered, blanketed with thick cover of oak and ash, chestnut and rowan, beech and birch – huge forest trees extending through the years to slow maturity. Near the village the woods were carefully forested, the young saplings and the dead wood being thinned out year by year, so the land was accessible and open. It did not seem to be an old forest, or perhaps it was merely the renewal of something which had stood much longer, because the forest itself appeared so much older than the trees.

The road from the south wound through patches of this forest which converged on it from the west, sometimes engulfing it as it dipped down into hollows and circumnavigated outcrops of rock-strewn hillside. The town which lay about ten miles south of the crossroads was just above the sea, and though the sea itself was untouchable the houses still huddled above the harbour, and occasionally ships crossed the empty water to islands and countries beyond. The road from the south began as a winding path through fields and woods and hamlets, following the vagaries of a brown burn that flowed down from the hills ahead. As the road began to climb uphill, the burn beside it grew noisier, and white waterfalls appeared amidst rapids of broken rock. The land grew wilder, and the trees denser, a little threatening to a solitary traveller.

On a particular day in late November, a traveller, muffled in a hooded jacket and scarf, wearing thick boots and woollen leggings, walked purposefully northwards along the road from the south. The reason for haste was apparent enough; it was late afternoon, and the sun was dipping towards the south-west in a flame-coloured sky. Already a dimness was settling over the trees, the outline of the hills was indistinct and greyish, except to the north, where the reflection of the setting sun tipped the crowns of the hills with fire. It was growing frosty: the wayside grass was already white and scrunched underfoot when deep brown puddles forced the walker to leave the track. A few stars appeared, and suddenly the eastern sky was dark. The traveller's pace quickened. The road skirted a hill, then dipped down towards yet another burn. The traveller hurried after it in the fast fading light. An owl rose like a ghost from a small copse of trees to the left, and flitted across the path in silent flight.

With the drawing in of the dark the forest changed. A group of larches converged on the path ahead, their spiky winter branches silhouetted against the dimming sky. The traveller experienced that sudden realisation of darkness in which the perceived world begins to dislimn and merge into a shapeless presence of something other, no longer sky and trees and clear road, but merely a surrounding sense of place. The unknown nature of it pressed upon the stranger, who hurried on, with quickening footsteps sounding sharper in the fast freezing twilight air.

There was a denser patch of dark ahead, where a great fir tree cast its shadow across the road, or perhaps it was only the impression of shadow, for already the substance of the tree was losing itself in the dark. The footsteps wavered, and stopped. It was impossible to see anything, if indeed there were anything to perceive. The stranger hesitated, apprehending some sense of form, or lack of form, a possible obstruction in the path ahead. As if the very notion of obstacle could create one, the darkness in front seemed to grow more substantial. The presence of the tree brooded over the road, and the place where the track skirted it was impenetrable, opaque and secret.

2

Disconcerted, the walker turned. But the road back was shrouded in night, and the crisp outline of the larches had vanished as if it had been only the matter of a dream. The traveller turned again, glanced down to the ground which had echoed back the solid sound of footsteps. But there was only the enshrouding dark, no earth, no self, no body. The night closed in, the whole weight of it concentrated on the stranger who had been overtaken in its midst, and with it came the terror of the unseen.

There was a sound to it. A high-pitched sound like a scream that echoed on, piercing the night, which seemed to wrap it round, muting and changing it until it was perhaps only the wind in the trees. But it was not that, and the traveller knew it. It was more insistent than that, terrifyingly familiar, finding its echo in the very flesh and blood of the human being who stood on the road, arms stretched out to the dark, as if seeking deliverance from the terror of being alone. Or perhaps pleading to be left alone, not to be reabsorbed into this forest which was so frighteningly recognisable and demanding, ready to take back whoever thought themselves to be different.

There was movement ahead. Nothing precisely visible, merely a shift in the pattern of the dark. A faint stirring of sound upon the road, a hint of rustling, a motion among the drifts of restless leaves in the night wind. The watcher stared with straining eyes, as if the dark could be pierced by power of concentration, or fear. For a moment the night did seem to be subdued, for the demand of the watcher was met with an answer. Eyes reflected back eyes, or perhaps it was only a trick of the light, or a mind caught off balance. There was a momentary gleam, a will o' the wisp of light, green as young leaves in summer, fresh as the sun in spring, a splinter of light as though a door had been forced open into a hidden world.

There was a small sound from the traveller which might have been a sob. Then running footsteps and a cry in the dark. A gust of wind shook the fir tree. The dead leaves were blown again, flittering across the darkness in the road. There was only the dark left under the trees, a mild empty darkness now, with the last pale tinges of daylight still fading from it, and the frost of November raw in the air. The stranger was left standing on the deserted road, shivering with sudden cold, still half blinded by green light shining out of season on unaccustomed eyes, and the ache of loss lingering like a faint scent of summer grass on the freezing air.

The forest was silent, blank and untenanted. Then the small familiar noises of the night reasserted themselves: rustlings of hunting creatures in the undergrowth, flitting of night birds through bare branches, slight stirrings of the wind out of the north. The road was clear and reassuring, with the impression of passing humanity strong and comforting upon it, like a lifeline of known things threading its way through a wilderness which lapped at its shores but did not submerge it. The traveller was aware of ordinary things, winter air on chilled skin, numb feet and hands, and the weight of a pack. The road beckoned, offering humanity, shelter and possibilities. The stranger set off briskly into the night.

The burn was crossed by a small stone bridge, and the traveller followed, assailed by a sudden sound of rushing water. Then the road went straight uphill again, and the sound was gone, muffled by thick trees. The traveller passed between them, skeletal branches almost meeting overhead. At the top of the hill the trees opened out and a soft light glowed, framed by a square window. A few steps further and there was another, and then more. Low houses, their outline merging into the dark from the hills, each showing a square light, surrounding the place where four roads met at the top of a little hill.

The traveller stopped, relief flooding in like light, considering which was the right house to try, where to go next. The road was closed and dark now, the night moonless, but it no longer mattered. The crossroads was reached.

One of the houses, just to the left of the crossroads, boasted a painted sign hanging above the door. The inn, obviously. This village had always had an inn. Indeed it began with an inn, because every crossroads should have an inn. The traveller crossed the roads, knocked firmly on the door, and walked in.

A long low room, with a log fire burning, and two settles beside it. It was warm, and the scent of woodsmoke hung in the air, wreathing under the low ceiling so that a pleasant haze hung over everything like a gentle twilight. The warmth made the stranger's eyes water, and was soft on the breath after the sharp tang of frost outside. The place was still empty of customers, but behind the counter stood a boy polishing mugs and laying them in a row upside down on a white cloth. He was too short for the counter; his head and shoulders appeared over the top like an attenuated gnome. He stared at the visitor with round brown eyes, but apparently decided not to call anyone else. He waited, watching, while the newcomer undid her hood.

'This is Clachanpluck?' Her voice was low and rather breathless, as if she had been running.

'Ay.'

'Can I stay the night here?'

'Ay.'

'And have supper?'

'Ay.'

The boy put the last mug down, and unhurriedly looked the visitor over. A tall woman, whose clothes looked as if she had done much travelling on winter roads. He watched her unravel a long multicoloured scarf, and take off her thick jacket which had a rainbow embroidered across the back. A woman with thick red hair and cheeks nipped red by the evening frost. Without her old brown jacket she was quite startlingly dressed in patched and tattered clothes in the brightest of colours, yellow and orange and purple and crimson, all as bright as her hair which stuck up round her head in curls. She carried with her a most peculiarly shaped bundle which had been tied across her back with a frayed rainbow-woven strap and was now dumped carelessly on one of the settles. The boy regarded it speculatively, then turned back to the woman herself and frankly stared his fill.

'You don't see many strangers?'

'Ay,' he said, and the words *but not like you* hung on the air between them. He looked a nice little boy, ordinary and gap-toothed, but with thoughtful eyes. He could only be about seven, but he looked as if he were able to take her seriously if she talked to him.

'It's a strange road,' she remarked, observing him closely.

'Which one?'

'The one to your village.'

'There's four.'

'The one from the south.'

'What about it?' There was a guarded look about him. Perhaps he thought she was criticising. It was a very isolated place this, a long way from any other habitation. The inn parlour seemed normal enough, comfortable and homely. But the boy's brown eyes were definitely wary. She had no desire to trespass.

5

'Tell me about the forest,' she said, leaning casually against the counter. But her eyes never left his face. He wriggled, and fiddled with the immaculate mugs in front of him, not meeting her eyes.

'I don't know,' he said. 'It's just the forest. There isn't anything else.'

The woman stood up straight again and sighed, and the boy withdrew into his needless task of polishing and repolishing. She frowned at his downbent head. His hair was thick and black, unusual in this part of the world. His hands were still soft and childish, small brown hands, very neat with the mugs. She seemed to be searching for some point of contact, but he never looked at her.

At last she said, 'Does anyone play music in this village? I'm a musician.'

He looked up swiftly, and in spite of himself his face was animated. 'Are you?' he said eagerly. 'And that then? In the box? Is that what you play?'

'That's my fiddle.'

'Oh.' He stared at her again, with a revival of his first curiosity. 'I'll tell Bridget. What music do you play?'

'Anything you like,' she said, as though she could give him the moon if he asked for it. 'Do you know any music?'

He thought. 'I know about it,' he said eventually.

'How do you know about it?' she asked, as if his answer puzzled her.

'Oh,' he said again. 'Only stories. You know.'

'What kind of stories?'

He seemed to find her questions very complicated. She watched him searching about for an answer, as though she had set him a real problem. Or perhaps it was simply that the answers were obvious to him, and he couldn't think why they were not to her. It was often that way, in places where people were not used to strangers.

'About the forest,' he said at last. 'What you said before.'

'It doesn't matter,' she said. 'But I'll play to you after supper if you like.'

'And Bridget,' he said, apparently satisfied. 'I'll go and tell her now.'

He was already turning to the door behind him when she spoke to him again. 'My name is Naomi,' she told him. 'I come from over the sea, to the west.'

'Alan,' he replied. 'Alan of Clachanpluck.' He spoke proudly, as if this village were more than a chance huddle of houses around an ancient crossroads.

'Alan,' she repeated. 'And what happens in Clachanpluck?'

That question didn't seem to confuse him. 'Everything,' he said matter-of-factly, and left her, closing the door softly behind him.

2

In the beginning there was the forest. The forest covered all the land, and the land became alive with the creatures of the forest. Everything that lived was part of the forest, and each being knew that the forest was not complete without every one of them. The people also belonged to the forest. There was nothing within the forest which was hidden from them, and nothing of the people which was not also part of the forest. But then the people found a small clearing in one part of the forest, and they camped there. Then after a while they began to say to each other, 'This is not part of the forest. This is our own place, and it is different from the rest of the forest. We will make it bigger, and better for us than the forest itself. It will be unlike everything else because it will be ours.'

The people made the clearing bigger and better, and after a while it began to be separate from the rest of the forest. Different things happened there, different plants grew there, and no animals came except the animals which were attached to the people. The creatures of the forest saw that the clearing was not for them. They began to be afraid, and avoid the mystery that lay within.

And the people in the clearing began to see that the forest was different from their clearing, and that creatures unlike them dwelt within it. They began to be afraid, and avoided the mystery that lay within.

They became so filled with fear that eventually they built a high wall around the clearing, and they made a strong gate in the wall, and they prepared weapons to defend themselves against the world that lay outside.

But the creatures of the forest did not understand. They saw the people locked in behind high walls. They saw them imprisoned by the stout gate. They saw the weapons that prevented anyone passing out of the enclosure into the free living world. They were filled with

8

compassion, and said, 'It is true the people have been foolish and afraid. It is true they have brought this fate upon themselves. But clearly it has made them very unhappy, and it is not right that any being should not know happiness when it stays for a little while in this world.'

So they consulted together, and they decided that they would bring the people within the clearing a great gift which would make them happy until the end of time. They created a gift which would break down the imprisoning walls and reduce them to rubble, so that the people could be free.

When they were ready they approached the high walls around the clearing, and stood before the stout gate. They called out to the people within, 'We have brought you a gift. A gift out of the heart of the forest that will break down your walls and make you happy, and you will be free forever.'

The people within were terrified when they heard of the threat to break down the walls that protected them from the danger of the world, and they cried out, 'No, we do not want your gift. We put our trust in our stout walls and we will not let you break them down. We are safe here from the forest, and we do not know you any more. You are a danger to us, and we will not allow you even to exist.'

The beings of the forest looked at each other and said, 'They are wrong. But we can see that they are unhappy, and we know that in their hearts they are longing to be free. Do we ignore their words and bring them their gift, or do we melt away into the shadows and leave them to their chosen death in life?'

Some thought they should do one thing, and some another, and they debated for a long time. Meanwhile the people inside the walls were busy, strengthening their defences and sharpening their weapons against the world.

But at last, just as the sun was setting, a decision was made. The beings of the forest took out the gifts which they had brought, and they formed a procession and began to move in a slow circle, to tread moonwise in a ring round the stockade. Twice they circled the walls, and the people stood at their defences and watched them silently, with much fear and misgiving.

When the third slow circle was completed, the beings of the forest took the gifts which they had brought. They began to pluck the strings, blow the horns, beat the drums, to sing and to chant and to dance. With all the strength that was in them they danced around the *walls and made the first music that was ever heard in the world.*

The music reached right in over the walls. The gate had no power against it, and the weapons of violence could not keep it out. The walls around the clearing were flung down, the gate was broken open, the weapons dismantled, and the people came out and joined with the beings of the forest and made music.

And since that day, though stockades have been built and defended, and weapons have been forged and wielded, and the gates have been closed against the wilderness, there has never ceased to be music in the world.

Before Alan came back, the outside door opened, bringing in a draught of freezing air. Either it had got much colder, thought Naomi, or the warmth had permeated her already. She shivered, and, looking round, saw a woman enter. She must have been working on the land, for her boots were caked in mud and there were mud stains on the patched knees of her trousers. She kicked her boots off at the door and looked across the room. She started when she saw a stranger.

'Oh,' she said. 'I didn't know anyone had come.'

'I just arrived.'

'By which road?' came the quick question.

'From the south,' said Naomi, wondering.

'I see. Well,' said the other, recollecting herself, 'welcome to Clachanpluck. Is Bridget about? Or anyone?'

'Alan was here. He went to find Bridget.'

'I'll go through.' The woman strode round the counter as if she owned the place. Perhaps she did. She disappeared through the door behind. Naomi sat down again on one of the settles by the fire. She took off her outside pair of socks, one green, one scarlet, and hung them on the fender, watching the steam rise gently from them. When the woman came back she removed them again, in case they smelt.

'She'll be back,' said the woman of Clachanpluck, and came and sat down opposite Naomi, on the other settle. 'Have you travelled far?'

So she was disposed to be friendly. There were villages where strangers were definitely unwanted. Alan hadn't given her that impression, but coupled with earlier events she wouldn't have been surprised to have met with anything. But this woman was looking at her almost with enthusiasm. She really wants to hear, thought Naomi. She smiled back at the stranger, and found herself liking her. A woman about her own age, nearer forty than thirty, with thick dark hair with a touch of grey to it, and blue eyes that regarded her with candid interest. A woman with a sense of power about her, in spite of, or perhaps enhanced by, her mud-stained baggy trousers and patched working jacket. Naomi seldom had cause to work the land, except to give a hand wherever she happened to be at harvest time, but she respected those who did. This woman had a toughness to her that Naomi knew she lacked herself. Her hands were rough and engrained with earth, not musician's hands at all, but large and capable. She looked as though she could work the sun up and down again, and like it. But I'm not sure I'd like to have to keep up with her, thought Naomi, and was aware of a sudden instinct of caution like a hint of warning. Independence was everything, and Naomi reminded herself that she was glad to be alone and was afraid of nothing.

'Only ten miles today,' she said, with an easy friendliness that was habitual to her. 'I came up from the south.'

'By sea?'

'Originally. But I've been travelling a long time. I came west by the coast road. But the sea depresses me too much, so I turned inland.'

'I can understand that.'

'And you? You live in Clachanpluck?'

'Yes.' There was a pause. 'My name is Emily.'

'And mine, Naomi.'

'Are you planning to stay in Clachanpluck?'

'It depends.'

'On what?'

'Whether Clachanpluck wants what I bring.'

It was very easy with Emily, thought Naomi. This was an old game for her, fishing for interest, making people want her, encouraging them to think they had chosen to take what she offered. But Emily seemed quite ready, even eager, to be fascinated. Naomi wondered what she was seeing, this woman so unlike herself, so unaware of the impression she created that she was dressed like a scarecrow, yet who expected and obviously got all the attention she deserved. She's probably quite unaware, thought Naomi, that her sleeve is ripped right open, and there are four fingermarks of damp soil smeared across her forehead where she's pushed her hair out of her eyes. But Naomi liked it, because it was so different from herself. True, it was part of Naomi's calling to be fantastical. Wherever she went she must always be a performer, and she would never have chosen to be different. But she liked the way Emily failed to think of making any impression at all. Yet there was nothing of the bumpkin about her. She has a dignity about her, thought Naomi, and her immediate thought was, I wonder if I could copy it?

'And if we want what you bring, you want to stay with us?'

She's not going to ask the obvious question either. 'Is there much to stay for?'

'Oh, very much.'

Was Emily laughing at her? Naomi frowned. She wasn't used to that, either. She found herself speaking directly. 'I'm a musician. I play the fiddle. I'm looking for a place to settle for the winter, but Clachanpluck is obviously a bit small. Only . . .'

'Only?'

'I don't know. I don't expect to find this an ordinary village.'

'Why do you say that?' She had none of Alan's wariness. Indeed, she was leaning back on the settle now, apparently quite relaxed, her socked feet steaming in front of the fire. Obviously she didn't care if they smelt or not. But the question mattered. Naomi answered carefully.

'I don't know. I'm a stranger here. But there is the forest.'

'There is always the forest.'

Emily seemed to regard the subject as dealt with, for she sat up suddenly and looked towards the door. 'I thought Bridget would be here by now.' She turned back to Naomi, and said, 'You're staying at the inn tonight?' The question was definitely authoritative, almost imperious. Naomi answered with easy politeness, but a little cautiously, 'That's my idea. I thought I'd have a look round tomorrow. See what people want, and play a little in the village, if it's good weather.'

Emily stood up. She was tall, at least as tall as Naomi was herself. She stood with her back to the fire, apparently thinking the matter over. She thinks as transparently as she does everything else, thought Naomi. She's wondering what to do about me. Definitely a woman with a household of her own, and probably a mother. Certainly a person of influence. Naomi glanced up at her speculatively.

Emily's appalling jacket had fallen open, revealing an ancient jersey and a glint of something lighter, like a sudden gleam of spring sky. Naomi gave a small gasp, and half sat up. But it was only a blue stone that had caught the lamplight, a blue stone set in gold, hanging round Emily's neck on a finely-wrought chain that also looked like gold. As Emily moved it caught the lamp flame again, and there was another splinter of light like a piece of blazing sky that dazzled winter's eyes. Then it was gone, and there was only a heavy stone of dull blue. But the goldwork was fine and intricate, a suggestion of something quite other than this village woman who smelt of the dung she'd been spreading all day over the empty fields. Then who is she, and what is she thinking about me now?

Emily was thinking simply that it would be a fine thing, something quite exceptional, to have a musician here all winter. She desired music, and her affliction was that she had no way of making it herself. She couldn't sing so much as a single tune, and though all the songs she loved were clear enough in her head she could not repeat a single one of them, or share it with anybody else. Did this woman sing, she wondered, as well as play the fiddle? She liked the look of her. A woman as tall as she was, which was unusual enough, with thick red hair, almost chestnut colour, like leaves in autumn or clouds reflecting back a winter sunset. A good colour to touch. Emily laughed at herself, to be thinking of so much so quickly. She looked like a traveller, this musician, dressed as she was in thick red trousers still stained with the mud of the road, and a bright woollen jacket knitted in all the colours anyone could gather from begging ends of wool across the entire country. Her hands were brown and delicate, thinner than Emily's own, unscarred by work. Hands to play music with, not to cut wood or dig soil.

'Do you sing as well?' asked Emily.

'Yes, and I can play the banjo and the harp. But obviously I can't carry them about with me.'

'We have both in the village. You must tell Bridget that.'

'Does she play?'

'Not at present,' said Emily, and once again she changed the subject abruptly. 'If you're looking for a place to stop the winter, I'm surprised you turned north. There's nothing north of here, except villages, for a hundred miles.'

'I don't want to go back where I came from,' said Naomi, 'And west would take me that way. I just travelled from the east.'

13

'You've been away a long time?'

'I've nothing to go back for.' Naomi spoke flippantly, but she could see Emily pondering her words, and felt uncomfortable. 'One can stay away too long,' she explained. 'I've got used to being alone now.'

'It's a strong thing,' remarked Emily, 'to live without family.'

It could have been a compliment. Naomi tried not to look surprised. 'I find others like myself sometimes,' she said. 'In a way it's more important.'

'You mean other musicians?'

'Yes,' said Naomi, and because she didn't want to exclude any experience before it was even offered, she added, 'No.'

'I am thinking ahead,' admitted Emily. 'It's a habit of mine. There are musicians in this village. Not me, unfortunately. I can't supply any need of yours, but maybe there are those who can. I'll say no more just now, for fear of saying too much too soon. There is time enough. But I think you should consider staying for a little while in Clachanpluck.'

'I would like to. I was intrigued by what Alan said.'

'What did Alan say?'

'Almost nothing,' said Naomi, 'But when I asked him . . .'

The door opened again, and a third woman appeared, a round, curly-haired woman carrying a sack of logs.

'Bridget,' said Emily. 'Have you met your guest yet?'

Bridget came over to the fire and dumped the logs beside it. Naomi stood up to let her pass. Bridget was very like Alan, with the same round face, but her hair was light brown and curly, not black and straight. She seemed preoccupied; friendly, but without the childlike interest of either Alan or Emily. If Bridget ran the inn she must see plenty of travellers passing. 'Welcome to Clachanpluck,' said Bridget. 'I hope someone welcomed you. Have you eaten?'

'Not yet.'

'Then what are they doing?' cried Bridget. 'You must be hungry. You came up from the south, did you?'

'How did you know that?' asked Naomi sharply, before she could stop herself.

'Why, you were seen on the road, of course. Patrick told me you'd passed. He saw you cross the bridge by the burn. Were you not feared you'd be benighted, coming so near to dark?'

'No,' said Naomi, still rocked off balance. 'No, I wasn't.'

14

'They'd have told her where to find us. It's no more than ten miles from the sea,' remarked Emily, looking at Naomi more closely than was comfortable. Naomi recovered her usual assurance and looked her in the eyes.

'I'm used to the roads and the dark,' she said. 'I'm not afraid of what I may find. But I like to understand.'

'Yes,' said Bridget reassuringly. 'Of course.'

'She's a musician,' said Emily abruptly. 'We could do with music, don't you think, Bridget?'

Naomi saw the glance that passed between them, and looked down. There was a decision being made about her. Better not seem too interested.

'I'd like you to come to my household and play for us,' said Emily. The words were kindly spoken, but it could have been a command. 'I can't play anything at all myself, and I would do almost anything for anyone who can make up for that a little. You can win me over very easily, if you play good tunes.' Her tone was light, but Naomi didn't think she'd say anything she didn't mean. How did she dare to be so vulnerable? She must be very sure of her own power.

'I'd be happy to come,' said Naomi.

'Good. But you'll be tired tonight. Tomorrow? After dark? We'll be working all day.'

'Thank you,' said Naomi. 'Where do I come?'

'Alan will show you,' said Bridget. 'He'll want to hear. You'll probably find half the village turns out.'

'That's what I've come for,' said Naomi lightly.

'Of course.' Emily turned back to Bridget. 'I'll go now. I only dropped in to see about the books. But that can wait.' Another glance passed between the two women, some communication from which Naomi knew herself excluded. 'All right?' asked Emily.

Bridget nodded slowly. 'All right. But give it time, Emmy. Give it time.'

'You think I wouldn't?' They both laughed. Emily nodded a perfunctory good night to the incomer, and was gone.

3

Clachanpluck by daylight was much like any other of the villages at the edge of the hills. It was small, being merely a double row of houses with a cobbled street between, going north from the crossroads. The cultivated land was directly behind the houses: walled gardens for soft fruit and herbs, orchards and long rigs of vegetables behind. The land beyond had been cleared to make a patchwork of fields, separated by thick walls of the stones laboriously cleared off the ploughland. The fields were still unploughed, rough with darkening stubble and bright with puddles, for the autumn had been wet. On the stubble grazed thick-haired cattle, brought down from the summer pastures. Naomi regarded them from the wall opposite the inn. They looked up from their morning turnips and gazed ruminatively at her, as if they too sensed a stranger in the place. Their breath rose in a gentle steam in the grey morning air, and they smelt of mud and warm hair. Naomi leaned on the gate and looked over their backs to the hills beyond. The land to the east was open and only sparsely covered with copses and patches of woodland in the hollows between the hillocks. Otherwise it was open grazing, with rush grass still bright green along the line of the overflowing burn, and veins of grey rock mottled with mosses and lichens. The air was laden with gentle mist, and slow droplets of water had formed on the still trees. It settled in Naomi's hair, so that when she squinted she could see beads of water shimmering in red curls.

The hills were uninviting enough this morning, though it must be a pretty place in summer. Naomi left the gate and squelched back towards the inn. The door, which she had carefully shut behind her, was now open. Two children stood in the yard, each chewing a crust of warm bread, surveying the prospects and the weather. Naomi knew one of them. 'Hello Alan,' she said.

'Hello,' said Alan gravely. 'This is Molly. She'd like to hear you play the fiddle.'

'Then she shall,' said Naomi. 'Now?'

'We've got to get kindling now,' said Alan.

'Yes,' said Molly to Naomi, ignoring this spiritless remark. She was a sharpnosed little girl with straight mouse-coloured hair and no front teeth. She was extremely dirty, but under its coating of mud her jacket was thick and lined with fur around the hood, and her boots were stout and new. This village could evidently afford to feed and clothe its children. Naomi looked down at Molly, who was gazing at her with hopeful blue eyes. 'Can't you come and hear me play tonight, if you're supposed to be busy now?'

'Of course I'll be there tonight,' replied Molly. 'It's my mother that asked you. But I wanted to see the fiddle before my uncle Davey does.'

So this was Emily's daughter. Naomi considered the blue eyes, and detected a resemblance. 'And does your uncle Davey play the fiddle?'

'Of course he does. He's the best fiddler in Clachanpluck.'

'I should have known,' said Naomi humbly. 'I'm sorry.'

Alan glanced at her sharply, but Molly had no notion of being laughed at. 'Where are you going now?' she asked.

'To look round the village,' said Naomi. 'I think I should do that, and you'd better get your wood. Is Bridget in the kitchen?'

'No,' said Alan. 'She and George took the cart with the hay.'

'I'll see her later then,' said Naomi, mentally noting George. Villagers always assumed you knew who everybody was by instinct, but Naomi had become adept at seizing small clues and building up a rapid picture. George evidently belonged to the inn. Alan's brother perhaps, or cousin, or uncle.

She left the children swinging on the yard gate and returned to the crossroads. The four roads ran downhill from here. She glanced back down the road to the south. It was revealed in daylight as a muddy track disappearing between the grove of beeches. The village proper lined the road to the north. Naomi wandered slowly down it. As in all villages, there were several derelict houses in the main street, adorned with the skeletons of rampant nettles, brown and withered now, and dry stalks of rose bay willow herb with drifts of seeds still clinging to their heads. The ruined houses were open to the clouds, the slate roofs having been carefully removed. Elsewhere, erstwhile cottages had become byres and barns and stables, and the square windows overlooking the street had been boarded up with stout planks. Clachanpluck can never have been very big; there were no surrounding areas of hummocks and broken gable ends and slabs of concrete, as were common around most villages. Instead, the trees crowded close around the houses, brooding over the habitations like sleeping sentries.

The street was wide and cobbled on the slope down to the burn. Just before the bridge over the burn there was a workshop with a wide door, and a low chimney with a curl of blackish smoke emerging from it. There was a heavy smell of charcoal and hot metal. So this village had its own smithy. There were people standing at the door. A couple of men, both young, and two young women. They all looked up when they saw Naomi, and watched while she approached.

'Hello,' she said.

There was a general murmur of response, and the man nearest her said, 'You're welcome to Clachanpluck.' He had obviously been working in the smithy, for his working clothes and his face were black with charcoal, and he had stripped down to his shirt in spite of the chill November air.

'Thank you,' said Naomi.

'You're playing at Emily's tonight?' asked one of the women. 'We're looking forward to it.'

'Thank you,' said Naomi, and went on. It looked as if there was to be quite an audience. A moment later she heard the sound of metal on metal ringing out behind her, hard hammer strokes from the smithy. They'd only stopped work because they'd been told she was coming down the street. Now she was out of the wilds privacy would simply not exist. But there would be enough to eat, and nothing to worry about, until spring. Naomi was used to being on her own, but the sacrifice of her solitude didn't particularly bother her.

There was another household on the other side of the burn. Two women were at the barn door, loading hay on to a small pony. They stared at Naomi and wished her welcome, then turned back to their work. The barn behind them was piled high to the ceiling. It had been a good harvest all along the coast, and clearly Clachanpluck was no exception. The houses had been freshly whitewashed too, and there was glass in every window of the dwelling houses. Naomi stood back out of the way of a couple of children on a go-cart who veered across the road in an attempt to avoid her, managed to right themselves, and careered on down the hill, turning to stare at her as they went. They both had boots on. Boots on every child and hay in every barn.

The last household in the village appeared to sprawl over several buildings. There was a long two-storeyed house with byres attached, and a plethora of barns and outhouses behind. The road to the north meandered on past it out of the village, fringed with hedges of hawthorn and wild rose. Naomi stopped. It was the village she had come to survey. There was a track leading off to the right between the scattered farm buildings, very muddy, with deep cart ruts. Naomi followed it tentatively, to see if it went on or merely stopped in the yard. Chickens dodged in front of her, and a posse of three white ducks waddled past her towards the road. A cart stood in the yard, resting on empty shafts. There was nobody in sight, and the track didn't seem to go on. Naomi turned to go back, then jumped when a voice said from about six feet above her head, 'Are you looking for Emily?'

She looked up. There was a hayloft door just above her, with a man standing just inside it, leaning against the doorpost and looking down at her. He was very like Emily, was Naomi's first thought, dark-haired and blue-eyed, but considerably younger.

'No,' said Naomi. 'I was just looking round the village. Is this Emily's household?'

'Yes,' he said. 'You've come to the right place. I'm Davey.'

'Hello.'

'Hello.'

'Well,' said Naomi, after a short pause. 'I'll be getting on. I don't want to keep you from your work.'

'I'm not sure that I was working,' said Davey. 'But tell Emily you're here. She's round the back, in the storeshed by the back door.' He pointed.

'Thank you,' said Naomi, though she hadn't really intended to come visiting. She followed the direction of Davey's pointing finger, and found a green door open. There was no one there. She looked back to the hayloft, but Davey had gone.

There were movements inside the shed, and somebody said quite clearly, 'Shit!'

'Now what?' came Emily's voice, resigned.

19

'Bloody mice,' said a man's voice. 'They've shat everywhere. Who wrapped up these cheeses anyway?'

'We'd better shut the cats in here at night,' said Emily. 'Go on.'

'Goats' cheeses,' said the other voice, rather muffled. 'Twelve.'

'Yes?'

'Cows'. Eight. That's because we kept the extra calf.'

'Butter?'

'Wait a minute. I'm still stuck on top of this bloody shelf.' There was a slithering noise and a heavy thump. 'Butter.'

'Salted,' said Emily.

'Two barrels.'

'Oil,' said the other voice, now muffled again. 'Who's that?'

The shed was suddenly dark as Naomi moved hastily into the doorway. 'Hello. I didn't mean to disturb you.'

'You're not,' said Emily, who was standing by a blackwashed wall with a piece of chalk in her hand. 'We're only stocktaking. This is my brother Andrew.'

'Hello,' said Andrew, looking distracted. 'Welcome to Clachanpluck.'

Naomi saw a dishevelled man with cobwebs in his grey hair. He wasn't looking at her, but at the well-stocked shelves that reached from floor to ceiling behind her. Like Emily, he was dressed in rough working clothes, and like her, he gave the impression of physical strength of one who had done heavy work all his life. He was older than Emily; his face was lined and roughened by the weather, but he was very like her. Looking at Davey, she had seen a male version of Emily, but younger. Looking at Andrew, she saw something else of Emily, which made her realise that Emily herself was not young either. Andrew seemed to have a gentleness to him that his sister lacked, or perhaps it was he that lacked her sharpness. Naomi wondered if the two of them had discussed her.

Emily herself was looking more presentable this morning, in clean jacket and trousers, but still the blue stone hung on its chain of gold round her neck. Naomi took her eyes off it with an effort, and said, 'I'll see you tonight then. With my music.'

'You'll find half the village here,' said Emily. 'The word's got round, you know.'

Naomi grinned. 'I'd noticed.'

'It's the bairns,' said Andrew. 'Alan was straight down here after you came, telling Molly. And then they're all round the village before you can say knife. There's Davey spending half the morning tuning his fiddle. Seems like we're starting our winter festival before November's out. As if there was no jobs left to do.'

'I'll go now,' said Naomi hastily. 'Let you get on.'

'Indeed you shall not,' said Emily. 'Come into the kitchen. It's time we stopped for a cup of tea. It's just what Andrew needs. Isn't it, Andrew?'

He laughed at her, nodded to Naomi, and went out.

'He's gone to put the kettle on,' said Emily. 'He wants to hear your music, you know. They all do. We have our own music here in Clachanpluck, but nothing can live for ever entirely on its own. You'll have noticed that? Come into the kitchen.'

Andrew and Emily were no effort to be with. Partly, thought Naomi, because they were very easy in each other's company. It was clear they were close, these two, and had been used to running this place together for years. Seen side by side, they were obviously brother and sister, not so much because of any similarity of feature, but because they shared the same gestures and manners of speech. Such likeness was often found in village people who grew up together and stayed together, worked together and belonged to the same family all their lives. It was the very thing Naomi had turned her back on years ago. She knew that if she were ever to see her own people again everything would be different, because she would have changed and they would have changed, and all the years between would be lost. She had rejected what seemed to be stultifying closeness before it suffocated her. But these two were not suffocated. They were quite at ease with themselves and their own independence, and they shared each other's company with an unconscious facility which made Naomi aware for the first time in years that solitude implied a sacrifice.

They said nothing to her at all about themselves. They asked her a little about her journeyings, but not intrusively, and they were anxious for news from the world outside the village.

'We hear a bit from Patrick,' said Andrew. 'But he goes no further now than Carlingwark, since he came home. We grow out of touch, in winter.'

Naomi knew nothing about Patrick or Carlingwark, but she agreed readily. She was able to tell him it had been a good harvest everywhere. They had expected that, said Andrew, and went on to question her closely about agricultural matters elsewhere, questions which Naomi found herself quite unable to answer.

'You can't expect her to have talked to everyone about potatoes,' said Emily. 'She's a musician.'

'Even musicians eat potatoes.'

'But they don't grow them.'

'I did when I was little,' said Naomi. 'We had to help pick them every autumn. It's probably why I left home.'

Emily took that as a joke. Andrew didn't.

The best news she was able to give them was that salmon had been observed in two of the rivers flowing into their own sea. Untouchable still, but still salmon.

'That's something to celebrate,' said Emily, bright with enthusiasm again.

'It'll be something when they've spawned again in our own waters,' said Andrew. 'We won't know that yet.'

They asked her then where she came from, but her news of her own land was so old now that she had nothing to tell that they had not already heard. 'I've been on the road ten years and more,' she told them, 'since last I crossed that sea. I've been right through Cumbria and Northumbria, and north beyond Lothian. The travelling's mostly pretty rough up there. Walking all day across empty hill and moorland, and maybe going three nights and more before coming to any village. And when I do they're usually too poor to have me stay for long. But it's worth it because they're usually glad to have music, even for a night. There's not many of us bother with that kind of country, for such poor settlements. But I like exploring.'

'The hills can be wild at night,' said Andrew.

'There's plenty of shelters if you stick to the road, ruined though they are.'

'There are shelters in the forest here,' said Emily. 'But few travellers to use them.'

'I'm not familiar with the forest,' said Naomi.

A silence settled between them, so that the bubbling of the kettle sounded loud on the stove. Andrew reached over and shifted it to the edge.

'The forest won't hurt you,' he said, 'if it's treated with respect.'

Naomi paid for her night at the inn with money. Bridget was doubtful whether she should take it from her; hospitality rebelled against accepting a coin in payment, but a musician was not a pedlar or a merchant, and had nothing else of any substance to offer.

'No,' said Naomi. 'You take it. It's not a lot of use to me. I was given it for playing at a naming, in a village on the coast. They said it was lucky, and they didn't want their bairn to start out in life with a debt over its head. So I took it. You can use it if a pedlar comes in spring. It's worth something to them.'

'Well, thank you,' said Bridget doubtfully, looking at the coin as if it might bite her. 'I won't deny it might be useful, but I know that money is an evil thing, which can bind a person, so one remains in bondage to another. There's a powerful kind of magic to it, and it's done more harm in the past than can be told.'

'Only in the wrong hands,' said Naomi. 'In some places, in the towns, they use it quite a lot. It's useful, you see. It saves carrying things about.'

'But you carry nothing about.'

'That's just it. These people were weavers. They wanted to give me a roll of cloth, but how could I have brought that here?'

'It's a pity,' said Bridget. 'We could have used that. There's a pile of weaving to do this winter.'

'I'll come and help you with it if you like.'

'Instead of the money?' said Bridget brightening, pushing the coin back across the table.

'No, no. As well. But let's say, I'll do some weaving in return for my night's lodging, and you take the coin as a gift from me, as an appreciation. Then you can feel all right about taking it.'

'Ay,' said Bridget thoughtfully. 'That could be right. You mustn't think me uncivil,' she went on, 'but I know too much about the past. They used money to win people away from their land. They took their birthright from them and made them sell themselves for money. What's a person without the land? What stake have they in the world then?'

'I have no land.'

'Ah, but you know that's different. You have a gift.'

'Sometimes a gift is like a burden. I should be glad to stay in one place all winter.'

'Do you find the travelling hard?'

'No. But sometimes lonely.'

'Each of us is alone,' said Bridget.

'But you have a family.'

'Ay, but so do you.'

'In another country.'

'We're both grown up,' said Bridget. 'We have to stand alone. Only little babies think themselves part of someone else. After all, we die alone.'

'We do,' agreed Naomi. 'How many children do you have?' She felt she knew Bridget well enough to ask, and had made it clear enough that she had taken her in as an individual. Otherwise the question would have been unpardonable.

Bridget was not offended. 'Just the one. Alan,' she said. 'I've no sisters either. My son is the only bairn in this house.'

'Alan told me that everything happened in this village.'

'He's proud of the place,' said Bridget. Naomi thought she was perhaps being evasive. 'Like George. My brother. The men of this house are too chauvinist, I tell them. They think Clachanpluck is the only place on earth.'

'But there is something different about it?'

Bridget looked away from her, out of the window. 'Oh well,' her tone was suddenly distant. 'I wouldn't say that.'

Naomi changed the subject. 'Does anyone in your house play music?'

'I do,' said Bridget unexpectedly. 'I have a harp. It's years since I played it though. You play the harp?'

'Yes, I do,' Naomi tried not to sound too eager. A harp as well, that would be riches beyond asking for.

'You must try it sometime. And maybe give me a tune or two. I'd like to hear it again. George plays the penny whistle. He's taught Alan a tune or two, but Alan's like George, won't play in front of anyone. Not like his friend Molly.'

'I met Molly this morning.'

'You were bound to. But she's a good girl. Thick as thieves with Alan. You'll probably have the pair of them pestering you, but be firm with them. Don't let them bother you.'

'I'm used to dealing with that,' said Naomi. 'There's always children, wherever I go.'

'Ay,' said Bridget. 'It's a blessing. Healthy children in every house in the village. It's not always been like that.'

'No.'

'There's been hungry times, even here in Clachanpluck. But the harvests now are good, and the children strong and healthy. And no sickness, except sometimes a cold when the first travellers come through in spring. Last year the children had the chickenpox. But that's a blessing in disguise, it saves them from the smallpox. I can remember that. This is a village of children, but I hope more of us will grow old. We have reason to believe we may.'

'Why?'

Bridget looked away again. 'The land is good,' she said presently, 'and we have good farmers to tend it.'

'You have your own farm?'

'George minds our farm mostly. I look after the inn. George is a good farmer. But the best farm in the village is where you're going tonight, Emily's.'

It was well into the afternoon by the time the stores were checked. The sun was sinking down to the south-west, and the woods were silent under the evening frost. Emily pulled on her jacket and walked briskly away from the houses on the road to the north, until she reached a loch. The water was still, already freezing a little at the edges, and gleamed coldly gold under the long rays of the setting sun. Beyond it a tree-covered hillside stretched upwards to the sky, and at the top the sun caught the last of the autumn leaves and turned them red and gold. It would be a hard winter, but they could afford that now. It had been a good season, so they could thrive like squirrels and hold a midwinter festival that would not be soon forgotten. The musician had come, and there would be music through all the months ahead, and enough for everyone to eat.

What would it be like, thought Emily, to travel the roads alone, to belong nowhere and be always seeing new faces, new land? To be sought after for a gift that brought more than sustenance into the lives of the villages? I don't know. I love this place so much, and I would like to be able to say it. I would like to take the loch and the brown trees and the red sun, and I would like to make it all into something I could give, that I could carry from village to village to share with them all. I know what it is that we hold here in Clachanpluck, as well as ever it can be known. It's too soon to tell, but I think the musician will be part of those things too. I must be cautious. I am not a cautious person, but the secret of Clachanpluck is not my secret. There is so much to express and I cannot express it. But I have made gardens and orchards and children, and this village would be a different place without me.

4

It was always the same, this matter of performing. Naomi stood at the crossroads, her fiddle tucked under her arm, waiting for Alan. The same tension inside, half fear, half anticipation. The same thinking of what she would play, how she would get across to them, knowing all the time that when the time came she would follow no plan, forget the programme she had rehearsed for them, and let the music dictate, and the spell would work for these people as it did with everyone. Naomi was under no false illusions. She knew that she was good. She knew she could give them everything they wanted, and the thought of failure never troubled her. The danger these days was more one of too much success. It was always possible to weave the spell, the magic of it was under her command, but she was afraid of where it would take them. It was only quite recently she had understood that there were limits, and that she had stayed within them. She had once heard a story, in a different village, of a piper who came and played through the streets until all the children of the town were bewitched, and followed him away into the forest, never to be seen by human eyes again. Naomi had no wish to enchant anyone, far less to bring pain or loss to any community. But what she brought was unpredictable, even to she who was mistress of it. Perhaps it was impossible to go too far, but she could not see what lay over the horizons of possibility any more than anyone else. She might only lead them there.

The early mist had quite dissipated now, and there were no clouds overhead. Instead the village was open to the stars. The whole firmament was clear in front of her, the Plough pointing to the North Star in front of her like a familiar friend. It was the same night as everywhere.

There was a paleness in the sky to the north, a faint flicker of light. Then a spiral of bluish brightness that wove its way up the sky and was gone. She'd seen lights like that before, but more often further north than here. Nothing new. Naomi watched and the north sky darkened again, and the stars blazed out. There was a touch of wind on her face. The trees behind her whispered. She turned west to face the forest. Perhaps the image of the northern lights still dazzled her, though it had not been bright, but for a moment she was sure there was light among the trees too, a trickle of blue-green light that slipped away into nothing as she watched, and a rustling among the trees that must only be the wind. Naomi held her fiddle tight to her chest.

'Are you ready?' came a clear treble call behind her. She jumped round.

It was Alan, in a woollen hat and jacket, with a dark lantern.

'Yes,' said Naomi, hoping her voice betrayed nothing. 'Lead on.' The darkness was forgotten. It was her turn to play to them, and she would make them remember it.

Alan led her down the street to Emily's house. There was nobody in sight. Only a few lights showed at scattered windows, but when they reached the last house there was a lantern hanging outside illuminating the whole street, and the outer door stood open. There was a murmur of voices from within, and when they reached the open door they saw that the hallway was piled with boots, while jackets and coats were draped everywhere.

'Everyone's come,' remarked Alan, and there was satisfaction in his voice.

After the dark, the room was dazzlingly bright with lamplight and candlelight. It was a big room, the whole length of the house, with a stove burning at one end and an open fire at the other. It took Naomi a moment to realise she had been in this room only this morning, drinking tea with Andrew and Emily by the stove at one end of a bare and empty room, furnished only with a long table and benches. The whole place now was bright and hot and crammed with people. Some of them greeted her when she entered. Vaguely she recognised the young woman from outside the smithy, and Molly running to greet her and Alan. Then Emily was in front of her, welcoming her formally to her house, and taking her by the hand. A different Emily again this time, in a woven shirt of all colours of blue, and the blue stone round her neck exposed and glinting in the candlelight. She's even brushed her hair, thought Naomi, as she thanked her in the formal words expected on such

27

occasions. Emily took her to sit by the fire, and they brought her a mug of wine, very sweet and strong. The slight hush that had fallen over the room on her arrival was lifted, and people turned away from her, back to their own conversations. But Naomi was well aware that they were watching her covertly. Indeed, she had taken pains to give them something to stare at, for in a country where people wore the blues and greens and browns of hill and forest, it was rare to see anyone dressd in vermilion and yellow with a gold crescent moon embroidered on her back, and silver stars all across her chest. Certainly not a woman with flame-coloured hair who was inches taller than nearly everyone else here. Naomi was quite aware of the effect, and she gave them a little time to let it sink in while she took equal stock of them.

Alan seemed quite at home here. He sat on the rug by the fire with Molly, eating hazelnuts and waiting patiently for something to happen. Molly was clearly over-excited. She kept trying to knock him over, or tickle him. Alan accepted this treatment stolidly, but remained unresponsive. Naomi caught the eye of the young woman from outside the smithy, who smiled at her. Naomi smiled back. There was another girl with her, who presently came over and took the nuts from Molly and Alan, and told them not to be pigs.

'Shut up, Fiona,' said Molly. 'They're not yours.'

'Shut up yourself,' said Fiona, 'or I'll put you out.'

Sisters? thought Naomi. Or sisters' daughters? They must both belong to this household, to be as rude to each other as that. Fiona looked about fourteen. She was brown and skinny, and might have been good-looking if her mouth were not so sullen.

'Are you wondering who they all are?' said a voice in her ear. 'I shouldn't bother. They're only my family, hardly worth knowing.'

It was Davey. He was looking at her with frank appreciation, and Naomi remembered one of them had said he played the fiddle. 'You're the musician, aren't you?' she said tactfully.

'Who told you that?' he asked, trying not to look pleased.

'I can't remember. But maybe we could play together later.'

'We've come to hear you,' said Davey. 'They have to listen to me all the time.'

'Is all the village here? It looks like it.'

'It does, doesn't it? But they wouldn't all fit, not quite. Wait until midwinter. That's when we really start celebrating.'

'If I'm here.'

He looked at her in surprise. 'But you will be. I heard you were staying all winter.'

'That's more than I knew.'

'Well that's often the way,' he said easily. 'Those it concerns are the last to hear about anything.'

'Except it's my decision,' pointed out Naomi.

'That's what they all think,' said Davey. 'But wait until we've had the music. I think my sister decided as soon as she met you, and that's what matters.'

'Your sister?' said Naomi, hoping to confirm what she already knew.

'I've only the one,' said Davey. 'Emily.'

'Ah.' said Naomi. 'Then I met your niece Molly this morning.'

'I know,' said Davey. 'And Fiona. You spoke to her outside the smithy. She's my other niece.' He spoke proudly, which made Naomi look again at the sullen girl who was now sharing the nuts with her friend. Perhaps there was more to her than met the eye. It must be a little overwhelming to have Emily for a mother.

She finished her wine, and began to undo her fiddle case. There was a stirring of interest through the room. People began to shift around so that they could see better, making themselves comfortable on benches and rugs. The table was pushed back against the wall, and a row of children sat on it, their legs dangling.

With her fiddle in her hands, Naomi at once became the focus of the whole scene. She was enjoying herself now, knowing what she could do, and happy in being asked to do it. The fiddle was battered and travel-worn to look at, but its tone was as good as ever. It had been made in the place where she was born, and it had accompanied her on all her travels. She could play other instruments, and usually in the villages people would press these upon her and ask her to play, but her own fiddle had become her talisman. Without it she was lost, without company or a voice of her own, or a way to earn her own living, wherever she was or whatever happened to the world.

She took her time tuning up. The stage was hers; she had their attention, and that helped, but then they slipped away to the edges of her consciousness, and instead she summoned up the music, letting tunes drift into her mind and flow through her, while her fiddle was there waiting for them. There was no music written down for anyone to read in her world, but the music itself had lived on in a chain of memory which remained unbroken when almost everything else out of the previous world had vanished into ruin and forgetfulness. Naomi's country was a dark place; at night no lights shone out but faint pinpricks of lamplight in far-flung hamlets. The roads were black and silent, showing tracks of hoof and paw in the morning, but no human feet passing in the night. No messages passed from village to village, no word or thought traversed the long distances of the night. Each small settlement was locked away into itself, hearing nothing. But when a traveller came at last, bringing music, the tunes were the same, handed down the dark centuries out of another civilisation, and the people in the remotest farms in the hills and in hamlets buried in long forgotten valleys recognised them as familiar friends. Even if a tune was heard for the first time, it was heard with understanding, and remembered. Naomi brought old music and new to Clachanpluck, and the old tunes were welcomed as well-known friends, and the new were taken in and carefully remembered, to enrich the only treasure that these people were able to hoard or to pass on.

When at last she stopped, and accepted another mug of wine, Davey said to her, 'That last reel you played. I know it. I've heard it before but I never remembered all of it. Would you teach it to me?'

'Of course,' said Naomi. 'I learnt it at home when I was quite small. I'd like to pass it on.'

'I'd be grateful for any,' he said. 'We don't often get new tunes. And you played another one . . .'

'Davey's teaching me,' said Molly, her head appearing between them. 'I can play two jigs and a wauking song.'

'And we sing,' said Alan. 'My uncle George is the best singer. He has a song for that other one you played. You know, this one.' He began to hum inaudibly against the chatter of voices.

Emily watched them surrounding the fiddle player, besieging her with questions and requests. Emily could remember no tunes, and had no sensible questions, but Naomi's music had left her moved and excited. And she had what she wanted: they wanted Naomi. Davey would certainly be wanting her to stay the winter now, and Andrew wouldn't object. He might make a little fuss about the food stores. No one in her household was hungrier in spring than could be helped, and even in the worst years Andrew had taken care that they had conserved enough. There had been no famine in her lifetime, but Andrew had other memories, and she could forgive him his caution. Andrew would think food too valuable an exchange for music, but even he would see that this was a good year. Perhaps Naomi would teach Molly to play the fiddle. Even Emily was growing fairly accustomed to Molly's present repertoire. Davey was an encouraging teacher, but Naomi would do it better. Molly had music in her, unlike her mother. More like her uncle, or her father.

'All right,' Naomi was saying to Molly. 'You play to me.'

'On your fiddle?' asked Molly reverently, as she handed it over. 'Me?'

'Go on.'

Naomi watched Molly plough her way through her wauking song. She looks much more like Emily when she concentrates, she thought. Molly's cheeks were hot and red and her tongue stuck out a little with effort. She came to the end of her tune, and Alan applauded. The others seemed to have heard it once too often. Naomi turned to Davey. 'Have you your fiddle?' she asked him. 'We could maybe play a tune.'

He accepted at once. That had been the right move to make. The idea of a winter here was very attractive, and it seemed as if Emily's household were as eager to have her as Emily herself. Naomi wondered about Andrew. He was friendly enough, but less enthusiastic. But Davey wanted her, for certain.

Davey knew what he was doing. She consulted with him briefly, and they picked on a couple of reels they both knew. He tuned his fiddle to hers, and stood ready, eyes fixed on her face. 'One, two, three, four,' she mouthed to him, and he came in at once. There was no awkwardness about him, none of the effort required to match her music to some village player who thought he knew what he was about, no trying not to show anyone up, because that wasn't her function. Davey slipped up a couple of times, but he only made a face and recovered himself. The second reel was very fast. His eyes never left her face, and she held his gaze and played on. There might have been no one else in the world, just her and this man she'd hardly met who could play his fiddle and keep up with her, whose eyes were fixed on hers, matching his beat to hers, while the tune got faster and faster, and wilder and wilder. Naomi was aware of the beat echoing back from the listeners, the clap of hands and the stamp of feet, but it was all nothing, there were only the two fiddles, and her and Davey and nothing else that mattered in the world. Faster and faster she made him play, while the sweat dripped off his nose and ran down his neck into his shirt collar. But he kept up, and they reached the last beat with a flourish. He lowered his bow and bowed to her in mock reverence, wiping his forehead on the back of his hand. Then he collapsed on the settle, and took a swig of wine that would have left her reeling.

'That settles it,' he said to them all. 'She has to stay the winter. We can't let a gift like that slip through our fingers.'

The response was plain enough. Applause echoed back across the room. Naomi grinned and bowed to them, and looked round at Emily.

'If you want to stay the winter,' said Emily, 'we'd be very happy.'

5

Two rowing boats were kept by the loch, lying upside down like turtles. In summer when people went fishing, there were more, but at this time of year there wasn't much need for them. The far shore was deserted, where the forest grew thick and untamed. No foresting was done there, and no one tried to reach the moors through the choked undergrowth that covered the steep western slopes.

There were, however, two people down by the boats today. One was Fiona, Emily's daughter, and the other was the young woman who had spoken to the fiddle player when she passed the smithy. Fiona no longer looked sulky. She was small and freckled, with straight fair hair, quite unlike the rest of her family to look at, but her manner was Emily's now that she was alone with her closest friend. She was saying something very vehemently, leaning across the boat she had been examining, hands clenched into brown fists, gesticulating emphatically. 'I told you, Anna. I saw them. They passed under the headland, and then they went out of sight. It is the place, I tell you.'

'But we know it so well,' objected Anna. 'Everyone goes there. It couldn't be kept secret.'

'But it has to start from the village,' said Fiona impatiently. 'The path can only possibly begin from where we are.' Her body was taut with energy, and she looked quite fierce in her effort to make Anna understand.

Anna stood looking over the loch, thinking. She was a year or two older than Fiona, and where Fiona was skinny and tense as a fiddlestring, Anna was sturdily built and dependable looking. She had a broad pleasant face with high cheekbones, and a wide mouth that smiled deceptively easily. This being coupled with long-lashed blue eyes and dark curly hair, she was given every reason to believe herself attractive. Like Fiona, she wore loose thick trousers and a jacket the brown colour of the forest, but round her neck she wore a bright green scarf, and a string of coloured beads. Fiona wore no embellishments, and looked as though she had hacked off her own hair in a fit of impatience on a dark night, which indeed she had. All she had round her neck was a knife on a string.

'If there is a path,' Anna was saying doubtfully.

'Of course there's a path! I told you, I saw them. I saw where they took the boat.'

'But everyone goes there. We've been there, swimming in the summer.'

'Yes, but we didn't know. Now that we do, we have to look at it in a different way.'

'I don't know what you expect to find,' said Anna.

'If I knew that I wouldn't need to go,' said Fiona impatiently. 'Listen, Anna. We belong here. It's our village. We're not children any more. If there's a secret, we have a right to know it.'

'If there's a secret,' said Anna, 'and I'm not sure that there is, mind you, I think we'll get told.'

'Who by?'

'How should I know?' said Anna. 'I didn't even think there was one. Who took the boat?'

'I told you. I never saw.'

'It was probably Patrick,' said Anna with a touch of resentment. 'He's always going off into the forest, and no one knows what he does.'

'Rubbish. He just goes shooting things.'

'I'm not so sure,' said Anna.

'No,' said Fiona firmly. 'This is something else. There's no mystery about Patrick. He's just in love with you, that's all.'

'No, he's not!' said Anna, stung. 'Anyway,' she added, as if that proved it, 'I don't love him.'

'You used to.'

'Oh shut up, if you want me to come. You don't know anything about it.'

Perceiving that she was about to lose her companion altogether, Fiona said tactfully, 'Which boat shall we take?'

'The blue one,' said Anna at once. 'The other needs bailing all the time.'

They turned the blue boat and launched it. Anna, at the bows, waded in until the water was nearly over her boots and pushed off. The little boat floated, and Anna pulled it back by the painter. 'I'll row. then you can point out the way.'

'All right,' said Fiona, pleased at her cleverness. Anna was always cooperative if you let her take charge.

Anna waited until Fiona had settled herself in the stern, then she climbed in and pushed off. Fiona sat facing the curtain of silent trees opposite. Anna rowed steadily, keeping a straight line. 'Left a bit,' said Fiona, and Anna altered course and rowed on.

The water was quite still, brown below the trees, reflecting back the hillside like a mirror. In the deeper water the loch was almost white, cold as the winter sky that illuminated it. There was no sound but the dip of the oars and the regular creak of the rowlocks. Fiona stared at the forest and frowned. She had always known, or thought she had known, what it was they held here in Clachanpluck, but now she was growing older, and although nothing had changed she realised that things were not exactly as she had thought they were. Memory was confused. As a child she had known the forest in another way, but now she was not a child, and certainties seemed to be dissolving all round her. It was like looking at familiar pathways and noticing for the first time that they formed a maze to which she had no key. And the infuriating thing was that until she had thought of it, she had known the way in without.

Anna, at the oars, looked back at the ripples that radiated outwards behind them, dissolving the slow reflected clouds into shimmering patterns of black and ice. A couple of geese glided silently out of the yellowed rushes at the loch's foot, and the ripples they made seemed no more than a flicker of light across the surface. Anna shipped the oars for a moment, and the boat slid silently on. It was cold out here. Within her layers of socks her feet were chilly as loch water. There was no wind, just a chill in the air that nipped her cheeks with a touch like ice. Fiona had a bee in her bonnet again, thought Anna, but it was beautiful out here just the same. Suppose it was Patrick Fiona had seen? Anna felt a slight thrill of anticipation. She still wasn't indifferent to Patrick, she had to admit that. She didn't like thinking about it, and how close she'd let herself be to him. She was much younger then, and now she knew better. It was all past, how much in the past she didn't like to tell Fiona, because the present concerned Fiona's uncle Davey. At least, she hoped it might.

'I'm freezing,' said Fiona. 'What have we stopped for?'

'I like it.'

'Well, it's pretty cold being the passenger. Keep moving.'

Anna pulled on the oars again, and the boat shot forward, spreading ripples like a fan. 'Fiona?'

'Yes?'

'What's the fiddle player like?'

'You saw her.'

'I mean staying in your house. Is she nice?'

'She sleeps late,' said Fiona. 'And she makes good griddle scones. She's teaching Molly scales, which is fairly unbearable. And she plays the fiddle with Davey. She's all right.'

'Can Davey play well enough for her?'

'I don't know,' said Fiona. 'I like hearing it, anyway. Just as well, seeing as I sleep over the kitchen. Wait, we're nearly there. To the right a bit. Now straight. We're coming in now. That's it.'

They were drifting into the shadow of the trees, and the hillside hung over them. The boat touched stones and stopped with an abrupt cessation of fluidity. Anna shipped the oars and got out, holding the painter. Fiona followed, and they lifted the boat up on to the beach.

'So now what?'

It was a very narrow strip of beach, because the loch was still high from autumn rain. Behind it the bank was crumbled and washed by past floodwater, and broken sticks and rushes marked the level left by the last rainstorm. The forest came right down to the water, colonising every scrap of soil until it reached the place where the stones were washed bare and clean. The land rose up steep banks in a mass of briars and dying bracken. It was much lighter than it had been in the summer, when the interior was protected by a thick curtain of green.

'We'll make our way along.'

There was hardly any space to move along the shore. Once it rained again in the hills there would be none. As it was, the beach soon gave out. They scrambled on over roots and overhanging clumps of matted grass that threatened to slither down into the water under the weight of their feet.

'No one's come this way for sure,' said Anna.

'Because we didn't land in the exact place. I couldn't see any better from the other side. It's along here somewhere.'

Anna made a face which Fiona didn't see, and followed patiently. Fiona pushed her way through a bit further, brushing aside overhanging branches of alder, mixed up with a trail of brambles which caught at her with thorns that had lost none of their summer sharpness.

'Fiona, wait!'

'What?'

'Push that branch back – the one you just passed.'

'Which? Why? That one?'

'Yes, that's it. Look. No, you can't, not holding the branch. Come round here.'

Anna scrambled up a bank of loose soil and stones, exposed under the place where the alder usually hid the ground. Fiona let go, and Anna stood back, holding the scrub back to let her pass. 'See that?'

The ground was quite clear under the trees, scraped clean even of grass, as if by passing feet. It seemed to form itself into a little track that disappeared into a maze of young birch and alder. Anna's interest was aroused at last. Her face was intent and eager, her thoughts forgotten, and she was suddenly as childlike and excited as Fiona. 'You'd never have seen it from where you were, and I wouldn't have seen it if you hadn't pushed the branches back. No one would have found it on their own.'

'If it is.' Fiona was the cautious one now that her belief was apparently confirmed. It wasn't a game to her.

'Well, let's see.'

They had to bend almost double to follow the track under the trees. It was hardly a path at all, but for the fact that there was always a clear space in front which was the only way to turn. They seemed to twist to and fro across the steep face of the hill, now between brambles and dead stems of foxgloves, now between low spruce scrub and birch branches that flicked their faces painfully if they did not stoop low enough.

'We're going uphill.'

'I think so.'

The path led them by roundabout ways, then seemed to peter out altogether, but when they pushed back the sweeping boughs of a fir that loomed in front of them, and crawled into the dry space underneath, they saw the path clearer than ever, stretching away from the other side of the fir tree, apparently with no further

attempt at concealment. They could walk upright now. The path
ceased to wander about, but took a purposeful line upwards. The
ground underfoot was dry and soft with last year's leaves, but here
and there in the hollows rainwater had turned the earth to mud.
Fiona stopped short at one of these. 'Footsteps!'

'Then you were right,' said Anna generously.

Fiona fitted her foot into the print exposed before them. It was
exactly the same size.

'Don't,' said Anna, who was entering into the spirit of this. 'If
you put yours on top it won't tell us anything.'

'There's more anyway.'

Anna looked thoughtfully at the prints. 'They're boots just the
same as ours.'

'What did you expect? It's our own people.'

'I wonder who.'

'Well,' said Fiona, still passionately serious, 'whoever else it is,
it's now also us.'

Anna glanced at her, a little puzzled. 'Come on,' was all she said.

Through the faint rustlings and the soft sounds of slow leaves
falling, another rushing sound was becoming evident, muffled by
trees, but growing more insistent.

'Water.'

'It doesn't give us any clues,' said Fiona. 'There'll be little burns
all over the hill after the rain.'

The path seemed to be going up parallel to the water. They could
see very little through the thick growth·that pressed in all round
them. The forest was untamed here. No human touch had
impressed itself upon it, except where the tiny path wound onwards,
sensitive to every contour, winding its way round rocks and steep
outcrops as the soil grew thinner. Even where the bare rock showed
through, small rowans clung to the ledges where a little soil had
settled. The presence of the trees was overwhelming. Anna and
Fiona scrambled up on to a large rock and surveyed the forest round
them. They were not used to the trees being quite like this. Around
the village there were paths and traces of people, and along the
roads one was aware of a human presence; even the intermittent
passing of travellers made a strong difference. Otherwise, the forest
was impenetrable. But here people had made a way, and yet had
not impinged upon their surroundings. It was like being the first
people who ever sat upon this rock and saw these trees around

them, yet they had followed the footsteps of others like themselves. There was something lacking in the human presence here, or rather there was something gained, a more subtle presence that changed nothing.

For the trees seemed quite unchanged. The air was heavy with their being, as if the forest itself was more alive just here, or more aware of itself. The trees neither watched nor listened; their presence was quite unhuman. Moreover, they were already locked in the semi-lifelessness of winter. Anna and Fiona sat at the foot of a rowan that clung to the summit of the rock, and felt themselves surrounded. A chaffinch hopped in the faint sunshine on the rock beside them, as though their presence was not significant, for in that place they meant nothing.

Neither of them spoke. Words seemed a chattering, momentary thing, which would create foolish ripples in this place of centuries of silence, that might fritter on through nothingness for another thousand years. It did not seem to be a place that would tolerate misuse. Yet it was not frightening either, merely different, like a change of element. The air was unlike the air they breathed at home, as unlike as mountain snow to the kettles of drinking water that bubbled on their own stoves.

Presently Anna touched Fiona on the shoulder, and pointed out the path winding on still further uphill, apparently making for the heart of the forest. Fiona started, as if woken from a dream, and followed Anna down the rock. The forest of Clachanpluck enclosed them, two small dun-coloured figures vanishing into the muted winter thickets. The trees dreamed on, regardless, undisturbed by flitting figures or passing human thoughts. The path threaded through them unbroken, weaving its way further into the depths of the hill. Overhead the tips of the branches were caught by a low sun, like gaunt frosted fingers held before a frail fire. The strangeness of the place enveloped them, yet it was only what they might have expected, or rather, the thing that they had known all the time. Anna and Fiona did not hesitate, but walked quietly on.

The rushing of the burn was suddenly louder, wilder in tone, straight ahead of them. The path twisted once more, then disgorged them into a small clearing before a wall of rock. A waterfall confronted them, white water plunging down into a brown pool adorned with birch and rowan, surrounded by a bare platform of rock. The clearing was quite empty, thinly carpeted by short grass browned by frost. The water drowned out the silence, but they caught an edge of meaning to it, like a whisper at the edge of the water. As if magnetised, they slowly crossed the clearing to the brown pool. At the base of the waterfall the rock was slippery and dark with wet. Ferns hung down over it, withered now, but still with a ghost of green about them. The waterfall had made a little gully for itself, smoothed out between tumbled rocks. The pool caught a faint glimmer of sun from the open sky above the clearing, and small rainbows danced above white water, cold as frost. More frost lay at the edges of the grass where the trees shaded it, a cold finger of winter drawn down the edge of the clearing.

Standing on the rock above the water, they were touched for the first time by a flicker of fear. They seemed very close to the heart of this strangeness. The water flowed on into the pool, and the burn overflowed it and took its endless course downhill. Anna and Fiona watched it while time drifted past them, and the forest waited.

This time it was Fiona who touched Anna's sleeve and pointed. Anna followed the line of her finger and her heart gave an unaccountable lurch, out of all proportion to what she saw. It was only a brown pot, a plain round earthenware pot standing in a niche of rock at the foot of the waterfall. They stared at it, and the water flowed down past it, just lapping the edge of the niche in which it stood with small splashes.

Fiona stepped down across the rock, went up to the niche, and picked up the pot. It was full of clear burn water, and the earthen sides were cold and damp to her touch. She placed the pot gently back, and frowned down at the waterfall.

There was a darkness to the left of it she had not noticed from where she stood before. She registered it with a sense of shock, although there was nothing mysterious to it. Merely a slit in the rock, a crack of darkness splashed by white water, with a small growth of dying ferns at its feet. Fiona crossed over to it carefully, for the rock was very slippery, covered with ancient moss.

The cave, if it was a cave, was quite wide enough for one person to slip in through the crack at the entrance. Anna came up behind her, and they stood looking at it while the waterfall dampened them with fine spray.

Fiona turned and looked at Anna.

The question hung between them. Anna's round face was damp with spray, and her curls were adorned with fine droplets like spiders' gossamer. Fiona could feel her own hair growing damp, plastering itself down on her forehead, so that small water drops ran down into her eyes. She blinked, and drops like rainbows hung on her lashes and turned the sky all colours.

The darkness within the cave was quite opaque, giving away not the vestige of a shape or presence, or of anything substantial within at all. But it was not alien. It was like looking into a mirror, except that mirrors only reflect the light. Perhaps the opposite of a mirror, thought Fiona, whatever that may be. Mirrors make everything back to front, so perhaps the opposite is just the way I have been all the time. I would like to go in.

There was so much light in the forest, thought Anna. The pale sun illuminated the water, and the sky was bright and clear behind the crisp black outlines of the trees. Out here was form and colour and light; everything that made the world knowable. As if everything she didn't know was hidden within there, everything that hovered beyond the edges of thought or vision, all the things not put into words that no one had been able to mention. Anna recognised the place, and thought, I'm not sure that I want to go in.

Fiona took another step forward and brushed back the ferns that grew across the crack of the rock.

Her hand touched something smooth and solid, and she jumped. Then she looked down, and slowly lifted up the thing that she had found so that Anna could see it.

It was a lamp. A twisted wick set floating in a pool of oil in a round earthenware dish with a curved handle. Fiona reached out to the little ledge on which the lamp had stood for the object she should find with it. It was there sure enough: a little pot with a close-fitting lid. Fiona handed the lamp to Anna, and opened the pot. It contained flint and fresh tinder, just as they knew it would.

Their eyes met. It was the prosaic nature of the things that was so disconcerting. A hillside, trees, a burn with a waterfall, a brown pool. Nothing there but what was everywhere. And a plain brown pot, with a lamp and tinder box. And yet the place was charged. It was like standing in the current of an invisible river, or being buffeted by a silent wind that did not stir one twig. The trees seemed to have become conscious and wove their dreams around them in a web of electric motion, like being caught up in a vortex of whirling energy that moved nothing.

Are we going in?

Fiona knelt on the wet rock and put down the tinder box. Anna laid the lamp beside her. Fiona took the flint and struck it. She lit the lamp with a spark of tinder, and handed it to Anna. She put the lid back on the tinder box, and replaced it on the shelf. Then she grasped a point of jutting rock, worn smooth by many handholds, and swung herself up into the cave. She could see nothing. A thin grey light shone on bare rock walls at the entrance, but within the absence of light seemed substantial, dense and black, so she found herself reaching out her hand as if to touch it, and feeling nothing.

There was a movement behind her, and a soft light gleamed, and Anna was standing beside her with the lamp. Now she could see bare dry rock floor, and curved rock walls. If we were upside down it wouldn't make any difference, thought Fiona. It was terrifying. Her hands were suddenly clammy, and she felt cold inside. They were not meant to be here. She could hear her heart beating, or Anna's heart, or a heartbeat too large for either of them that reverberated through them so that their bodies vibrated with the sound.

Beyond the light it was not entirely dark. But there was no daylight, merely a point of brightness, a distillation of colour that confused their senses and forced them to shut their eyes against it. Or perhaps it was not that either, but merely the reflection of the flame that dazzled their eyes and hovered before their sight in a sharp greenness that was more than sunlight. If it were real then it was too bright, and they stood paralysed, helpless and blind as moles. There was a cool breeze on their faces, none of the stuffiness or damp of underground, but more like being under the open sky at night, and the smell that came on the air was like thyme in summer. The wind grew stronger, and the light brighter. They put their hands over their faces to shield themselves against it. The sound was loud as blood pounding in their ears, swamping all other senses, overwhelming them. Their hands met and clasped in terror, and the hill echoed back their fear like a giant image of themselves.

There was a rushing of water, and the light was changing again, losing all its colour and turning dull and grey, like a December sky. The rock was solid again under their feet. Slowly they opened their eyes. The blank face of the hill was in front of them, and the waterfall gushed into the brown pool at their feet.

6

The best place to be alone was in the haybarn. This was something which Naomi had found out before in other villages. They had given her a pleasant room here, adjoining Emily's own, looking out over the street. Space was never lacking in the villages. There were plenty of buildings which only needed a little repair before they could be made habitable, so people were accustomed to having all the room they wanted. Naomi found that important. Living as she did, always among strangers, it was good to have a place to retreat to that was entirely her own. Her room here contained a low wooden bed covered with woven blankets and a striped quilt, and a woven rug on the bare board floor beside it. There was a carved chest, far too large for her own few belongings, but useful for the clothes she had been lent or given. It was assumed that a traveller would need to be provided with all these things. Music weighed nothing, and could be exchanged for everything.

But on days like today, when the first snowflakes were drifting past the windows, and the cold pierced the houses with icy draughts, the room was not much good to her. It would be all right if she could sit on the bed and wrap herself in the quilt, but she couldn't practise like that, and when her hands were too cold she couldn't play properly. The kitchen was warm, and smelt comfortingly of fresh bread and barley soup, but she couldn't be in there because everybody else was.

That left the haybarn. In December it was still piled with hay nearly to the roof, and four months' winter feed insulated her from the cold that crept up through the ground. The acoustics were hopeless, hay being absorbing stuff, but there was a part of the barn that had a separate loft with a wooden floor of its own, where rows of apples and sacks of potatoes were kept, ready to be carried down to the storeroom when necessary. Protected from the hay by the floor, and with a slate roof over her head, Naomi was able to hear herself well enough. She came up every morning, when she had helped out a bit in the kitchen, while the others were busy with the outside work. In the evenings she was there to entertain them, but the music she made here was for herself.

She was happy. Clachanpluck was a good village to be in. The people were prosperous enough to grudge her nothing. They liked her music. She liked Emily better than she usually liked anybody. Naomi was used to being friendly, and to making easy acquaintances, and then passing on. Emily met few strangers, and ignored most of them. She loved her own people passionately, and Naomi had already felt a little of this intensity turned upon her. She was not sure about it. Love from Emily would be worth having, but in the end perhaps there would be pain attached to it. Pain of parting, pain of too much given. Emily had said very little to her after their first meeting, but Naomi had already divined her secret. Emily cared about her music. She listened to it like a hungry child, but like a child she could only take it in. Well, I'm willing enough to give it, thought Naomi, but the pity is she can't keep it. Except through Davey. I'll teach Davey what I can, and so repay my debt to Emily. But I don't know who will owe whom the most, come springtime.

And Davey was in love with her, which made things more complicated. That was another situation to which Naomi was fairly accustomed. Usually she dealt with it by moving on. Here, she was committed to stay till springtime. She didn't need Davey, or anyone else come to that, as a lover. But the man had music in him. More than anyone else in Clachanpluck except, Naomi suspected, Bridget. But Bridget was elusive, as if she were afraid of being woken up again from a long sleep. Naomi had met that before too. She would go and see Bridget, maybe tomorrow, and work the conversation round to looking at the harp.

Naomi thought about these new people perfunctorily as she tuned her fiddle and played a few desultory tunes. Then she became absorbed in her work, and they faded absolutely from her mind.

Davey was perfectly aware that Naomi practised in the hayloft. He had not told her so. Today he loaded up the hay early, and was round the fields and had all the cattle fed by mid-morning. A light snow was falling as he turned the mare loose into the field. It would be cold tonight, very cold for so early in December. He thought of the new fruit trees planted in the orchard, and shrugged. Emily would have put straw round them, and they would have to take their chance. He went back into the stable and cleaned the tack quickly, then quietly opened the barn door wide enough to slip through, and crept inside.

It was half dark inside with the door pulled close. Hay towered up to the ceiling on the one hand; on the other, it was stacked up to the floor of the little loft above. Sure enough, she was playing her fiddle. Davey sat down on a pile of loose hay and tucked his feet up off the cold earth floor.

A lot of what she played he knew already. Some tunes were new, but their form was so familiar that he seemed to recognise them even while trying to memorise them for the first time. He knew what she was doing. It was what he did himself with his smaller repertoire. Memory was tricky, and things left unused rot to dust and fade away. There was no place in his world for anything to lie forgotten and be reclaimed again. Things were kept by constant vigilance and change. Nothing was ever repeated. It could only be renewed again and again.

Davey sat back and listened to reels and jigs and waltzes, new variations on familiar themes, music that he knew the words to sing to, or the steps to dance to. She played better than any fiddler he had heard before. He leaned back against the hay with his eyes closed, and let the music wash over him.

But then it changed. Davey opened his eyes and sat up, frowning. It was quite unlike anything he had heard in Clachanpluck. It was almost not like music any more. It was as if a horse and cart trotting cheerfully along the road to Carlingwark had spread its wings in sudden flight and soared skywards over the village. It was like the salmon coming back upstream after the long years of poison. It was like the trees growing back where no trees had stood for centuries, or the little blades of grass that forced their way through concrete, and through long ages broke it back to dust. It was like water flowing down from the hills as it had done for ever. She could not have made that up herself. People didn't make up things. Sometimes they made variations, sometimes they renewed something which had been thought lost and forgotten. He realised what it must be. It came out of the past, that music. It belonged to the time before the world changed, and when she brought it back again into the world it was as new as the leaves are every spring.

Davey stood up and moved quietly over to the loft ladder. The notes were slower now, more long drawn out, but there was a hint of the earlier melody to it. Slowly he climbed up the ladder, like a man mesmerised.

She was standing with her back to him, by the light of a small rooflight. He stayed at the top of the ladder, leaning his arms across the top of it, and watched her as if it were his eyes that listened and could never hear enough. He began to see the pattern to it, the same tune coming back again, but different, like a burn flowing into a loch, and out again as a river. The same water, but different. It was more satisfying than anything he had encountered in the world before.

She stopped at last, and turned round to him, apparently aware that he had been there all the time. She lowered her fiddle and waited for him to react, and he realised that far from being angry at the interruption, she was above all a performer. He grinned back, thinking ruefully, I forgot, she's a musician. Emily would have been furious.

'What was it?' he asked her. 'I never heard anything like it.'

'No,' said Naomi. 'People usually haven't. They don't usually want it either. It was made by a man called Beethoven. I learned it from a musician across the sea, who had it from a woman who had it from further east, a generation before that.'

'When was it made?'

Naomi shrugged. 'Before the world changed. You can tell that.'

'How?'

She seemed to seek for words. 'It has a kind of innocence to it,' she said eventually.

'I don't understand.'

'I don't mean simple,' she said. 'It was a much more complicated time than ours.'

'How can you know that?'

She shrugged again. 'I don't. After all, what does anyone know? But small things show it, little fragments that we might piece together. He taught me more music of the same kind. I stayed with him two years in order to learn it, though there wasn't much to eat. And afterwards I found that no one wanted to hear. But I try to remember it when I practise.'

'Will you play more like that to me?'

'Perhaps.' She looked at him consideringly. 'It makes me sad,' she said.

'Why?' he asked gently.

'To know that so much is lost.'

'But everything must die, or nothing would be renewed.'

She sighed. 'You speak like a man who grew up in a forest. I didn't.'

'The forest holds everything, in Clachanpluck.'

'I have understood that. Davey, have you ever been away from here?'

'No,' he said, as if her question puzzled him. 'No further than Carlingwark. Why?'

'I can't explain,' said Naomi almost impatiently. 'I would like to have been there when that music was first played. I think it would be quite unlike anything we could imagine.'

'No doubt,' said Davey. 'But surely the point is that you have the music?'

'I think it's only a fragment though. You heard it. Can you imagine what the whole would have been?'

'I don't know,' said Davey slowly. He felt like a man struggling in a new element, fighting to grasp concepts that no one had ever suggested to him before. 'I have heard of the ruins of great cities, and towers and domes that still stand out against the sky. But I think they were places of suffering. You know as well as I do why the world had to change. Nothing else could have happened.'

'But it's still possible to regret.'

'Regret?' asked Davey. 'Like guilt, you mean? I think not, in Clachanpluck.'

'I shall probably teach you to play Beethoven,' said Naomi. 'But I would like you to tell me something in return.'

'If I can,' he agreed readily.

'What is it that you hold here, in Clachanpluck?'

His eyes dropped at once. 'I think you're asking the wrong person,' he said.

'Then who?'

'Naomi,' he said. 'You may not have been born in the forest, but you were born of the earth. You are as we are.'

'Of course.'

'Then you must know who. I'm a man. I would like to be your friend, but I can tell you nothing.'

'I know that's true,' she admitted. 'But you understood my music.'

47

'And I love you,' he said.

She shrugged again, but not unkindly. 'Do you speak as a musician,' she asked, 'or as a lover?'

'Are they so very different?'

'Yes.'

'Then as a lover,' said Davey. 'I would like to start again from the beginning.'

'No,' said Naomi. 'You came up the ladder because you were a musician. If you stay, we'll play music. If you want anything else, you must find a time and place for it.'

'And then?'

'How should I know? Speaking as a musician, I mean.'

'All right,' said Davey, resigned. 'I'll get my fiddle. May I?'

7

Bridget and George had worked together all their lives. They had
learned the same ways from their mother and her sisters, who now
did less of the heavy work, so that the main share of the outdoor
work fell upon the brother and sister. There was more than enough
to do, for the household required nearly all its food to be grown, its
land to be kept hearty, its sheep and cattle to be looked to, its
repairs done, and its fuel to be brought down from the forest. The
indoor work, the baking and the poultry were left to the eldest and
the youngest of a household. At the inn, that left George and
Bridget to do most of the other work throughout the year.

They never moved like people in a hurry. Neither ever seemed
moithered by the necessities of living. They were very seldom seen
idle either. In Emily's household there were times of intense activity
when everyone would lay hands to a job and work all the hours of
the day until it was done. There were also times of feasting,
evenings of music and stories, celebrations of every birthday and
naming day and festival in the year. At the inn they were more
inclined to spend their evenings darning socks. But they never
lacked visitors while they did it. In the daytime they were usually
found out on the land, working as steadily as the vegetables grew
and the sun rose in the mornings, very often together. There was
hardly a year in age between them, and they had always done things
together.

They were not at all alike to look at. Where Bridget was small
and round, George was one of the biggest men in the village, and
certainly the strongest, if the amount of heavy work he was able to
do were anything to judge by. There was no other way to tell, for
George was no fighter. He kept out of other people's quarrels, and
out of other people's business too. At the inn they had a reputation
for keeping to their own household. George was generally

accounted a silent man, but he was friendly with the travellers that passed, and usually picked up any news from them that was to be had. He was well liked both by passers by and by his neighbours, because, although he said little, he knew how to listen. He was a good uncle to his nephew Alan too, often taking him with him when he went to work in the forest, for George was a forester, and was willing to barter timber with anyone who needed it. It was as well for Alan, people reckoned, that his uncle took trouble to teach him his own skills, for Alan had neither sisters nor brothers nor cousins, and seemed unlikely to have any family of his generation, unless Bridget were to have another child. And Alan himself was like enough a changeling for any household, with his black hair and tanned skin and brown eyes. There was no child like him in the village. One would never think that he and George were of one household, for George as a boy had been as fair as any bairn in the village, though since then his hair had turned darker and his eyes greener, he was still fair, and when he stripped off his shirt in summer his skin was very pale and freckled. Various people had owned to finding George attractive, but he was usually considered so unresponsive to any personal overtures that it had been rumoured he was stupid. It was true he couldn't read or play chess, but he could sing and weave cloth, and his defenders said no one who was stupid could do either the way George did. But no one could deny that he was often quite indifferent to matters that were of vital import to everyone else, and it was understandable that people should be annoyed by it. But he was never superior, always friendly, and he never appeared to be out of temper either.

Today George and Bridget were making a muck heap. It rose steadily between them, the same shape as the tumuli up on the moors, and behind them the heaps of dung and ashes, kitchen waste and rotting green stuff grew lower. They did it as they did everything, walking steadily round and round the heap as if performing some ancient ceremony, sometimes passing one another but never in each other's way, wielding their pitchforks as if the tools had grown from their hands, part of their own being. They built up the walls first very methodically, a layer of dung, a layer of kitchen stuff, a sprinkling of ash and a layer of weeds. Then they tossed a mixture of everything into the middle, round the two pipes that rose like chimneys from the growing pile, keeping the airways open. George and Bridget never spoke about the work, because there was nothing the other would not know about it, but occasionally they lapsed into desultory conversation, but only about a few matters of fact that disturbed nothing, and then the friendly silence drifted back between them.

Now and then, after a layer or two, one of them took a bucketful from the big barrel of urine that stood behind the shed, and splashed it over the heap. Then they carried on their constant round, and the heap grew higher between them.

'I was thinking we might fetch the trees,' said Bridget presently. 'As the ground's not freezing yet.'

'I thought it might turn that way when it snowed on Wednesday,' replied George. 'It seems to have passed off for a while.'

'Carsphairn is white,' said Bridget. 'But it's mild enough in the forest.'

'I'd like to get a couple more rowan, as well as the thorn.'

'Ay, it would make a better boundary.'

'Thorn for the hedge, and rowan to keep the land free within it.'

'We could go tomorrow.'

'It'll be wet.'

'Better for the trees, anyway.'

Silence settled again. A blackbird alighted on the post of one of the storage bins, watching the pile of nutritious stuff growing with an attentive eye. Bridget looked round at him and smiled.

'There's that robin too,' remarked George. 'Behind you.'

Nothing more was said for a long time. They sprinkled the last of the wood ash, and went on without it. The day became cloudier, and the haze of mist which hung in the air began to form itself into a slight drizzle. Bridget and George were too warm to feel damp. They had thrown down their jackets, and presently Bridget stopped and rolled them up so only the outsides were exposed to the mizzling rain.

'Patrick's going into town tomorrow,' said George presently. 'I told him to get the chalk for Alan.'

'Oh, that's good,' said Bridget, and then, 'I must look out the slate for him. I know I stored it somewhere.'

'There's slates enough surely, in the yard?'

'This one had a back and a frame. They just fall apart otherwise.'

'Well, you'd know about that.' George paused, and said, 'Did he tell you why he was so set on this, all of a sudden?'

'I suppose it's Molly. Always taking something into her head.

And then there's the books. That'll have got their imaginations going.'

'Oh well,' said George. 'I did without it myself.'

'I can't say I've ever made much use of it. Though I tried to read one of the ones Patrick found. It doesn't seem to be about anything much.'

'Well, why not?' said George, apparently reverting to Alan. 'It won't hurt him. Better than trapping things that don't need eating.'

'It was Patrick started that,' said Bridget. 'Showing the little ones.'

'I'd rather Alan stayed out of it.'

'Should you forbid it?'

'Would it help?'

'I think not,' said Bridget.

George stood back while she climbed up on to the heap and pulled the pipes up a bit to loosen them. She wedged them and jumped off the heap again, as George scooped up another forkful of muck. He walked round the heap testing the walls, pulling them out here and there where they were sloping in too sharply. There was a dip at one end, and he carefully repaired it before he spoke again.

'I saw the fiddle player was at the house again.'

'Ay,' said Bridget. She seemed disinclined to pursue the subject.

'Was it about the harp?'

'Ay.'

George went once round the heap again, before he pressed the point further. 'She wants to borrow it?'

'No.'

'No?'

'She'd like to hear me play. Maybe put some tunes together.'

'Well now,' said George, surveying the almost completed heap, and then scrambling onto it to take the pipes out. 'Would that be a good thing, Bridget?'

'It's been a long time.'

'All the more reason to take her up on it, now the chance is there.'

'You think so?'

'Ay.'

'There's plenty to do this winter.'

'There's all the evenings.'

'And then there's the weaving,' went on Bridget.

'There's enough of us for that. I think you should play your music. It's a good thing to have in a household. Maybe we've let such things slip by too much.'

'That's what Emily said to me.'

'She'd know,' said George.

The piles behind them had shrunk almost to nothing. A slow twilight was creeping in among the mist. The black earthen shape loomed between them, shoulder-high. They raked the bits together that littered the ground, and tossed on the last scrapings until the area was as clean as their own backyard. Then they shook out sacks of dirty straw and threw them up on top. Bridget took a running jump on to the heap and spread the straw out neatly. Then she lay down and stuck her arm down one of the air passages. 'It's warm inside already.'

'And so it should be.'

'Shall we net it over?'

They spread the net over the top and weighted it with stones at the corners.

'That should hold it.'

Bridget sat on the edge of the heap, muddy boots dangling over the edge. George scrambled up beside her. 'Mind the walls.'

Now that they had leisure to look up they saw that the sky had thickened to a soft dark blue. The drizzle had melted away with the dusk, the clouds were clearing and the night growing cooler. The first few stars showed cold as splintered ice. The heap under them was warm, shrouded in straw and already pulsating with life beneath them. It was for the garden. The fields they simply spread with muck, but their garden had the best that they could give it.

They sat side by side for a long time, shoulders touching, and slowly the stars pricked out one by one above their heads. To the east the three jewels of the Hunter's belt dipped towards the horizon, as the dusk rolled in from lands and seas the two of them had never seen, covering over events of which the two of them would never hear, drifting in over this one village where the two of them were born and lived and intended to die. In winter Clachanpluck lay naked under the stars through long frosty nights, and there were no lights or sounds to ward off the emptiness of space above them. It was a small world they lived in, but there were no boundaries to it, no limits to what was offered to them. They sat there until the night breeze grew too cold, and their still bodies cooled down and grew chilled. Then they jumped softly down, picked up their tools and jackets, and made their way quietly back to the house.

A little while after supper George left the house again. 'Remember to ask about the books,' Bridget said as he pulled his boots on. Then she turned back to the fire and went on telling Alan a story.

There was a thin sliver of moon in the sky, and the stars were now abundant. A breath of frost wafted around the still houses. The road was dark, but George knew it well enough, and walked as fast as if it were daylight between the silent houses. He passed by low windows, and was caught for a moment in soft tendrils of lamplight that fastened themselves on the polished buttons of his jacket, and alighted for an instant on his face. He shook them off unnoticing, and strode back into the shadows, so only his footsteps gave the clue to his presence. They were firm and heavy, and his nailed boots sparked on the cobbles.

Down by the burn it was quite dark. The hollow sound of water on pebbles gushing under the arch of the bridge penetrated the darkness and was left behind as George walked on.

Emily's house was unlit, but George went straight up to the door and opened it softly. He slipped into the dim passageway and shut the door behind him. A line of light shone under the inner door and illuminated a patch of rough flagstones, and from within the room came the sound of voices, and the thin strains of a penny whistle. George kicked off his boots and placed them in the corner behind the door. He stood listening for a moment at the inner door, but whoever he expected to hear within was not there. Behind him a narrow stair led upwards, and this he followed, feeling his way along the wall in the darkness until the stair ended and the wall vanished under his touch. He stepped forward confidently until he felt another door with his outstretched hand, and upon this he knocked softly.

'Come in,' called Emily.

George came in and closed the door, blinking a little in the lamplight. There was not only a lamp, there was also a fire burning in the grate, and Emily sat cross-legged on the thick rug beside it, leaning back on a big cushion propped against a chest. There was very little furniture in the room, only Emily's bed, which was raised an inch or two from the floor on rough planks, and covered with a rainbow-coloured quilt. Above the bed there were fragments of pictures painted on the wall, a tree with long roots that twined down until they were lost to sight behind the pillows, and a series of moons drawn in an arc that rose and fell from one side of the wall to the other, turning from dark to new to full, and back again from full to crescent to dark. Below it there was an unfinished picture of a waterfall that flowed into a brown pool, but here the artist had apparently given up, for the remaining patch of wall was given over to shapes of triangles and stars and bits of mazes, some shaded to become three-dimensional, some mere charcoal outlines. There was nothing else in the room at all, although it was quite large. The lamp, sitting low on the chest behind Emily, threw vast shadows over the walls so that the far corners were dim and indistinct where the drawings trailed off into uncertain greyness.

George came and sat on the rug beside Emily, who moved up to make space for him.

'A fire,' he remarked. 'That's a luxury.'

'You only live once,' said Emily. 'I swept the chimney yesterday.'

George leaned back, stretching out his legs to the flames and putting his arm round Emily.

'Your socks are steaming,' she said presently.

'I'll take them off in a minute.'

They sat in companionable silence until a log shifted in the grate and Emily sat up to poke the fire and put on fresh wood.

'I see you've got the books,' said George.

'Yes, didn't Bridget tell you? I've been trying to read them. It isn't very easy.'

'Is it worth it?'

'Oh I think so.' Emily turned round, the poker still in her hand, and looked at him enthusiastically. 'Don't you ever think, George, there was once so much that was different in the world, so many things written across it like writing on a slate, and suddenly it was all wiped out – but carelessly, so there are just little bits of words left here and there, which would have a meaning if one was able to make a context to them.'

'There is no context now,' said George. 'We're in a different world.'

'But we're still people. You know, look at this.' Emily laid down the poker and picked up one of the books, handling it very gently as if it might fall apart at any moment. 'Such an ancient thing it is, look, but when you open it, if you can make out the words, there's a person speaking to you, just as you sit next to me in the same room and speak to me now. It's extraordinary, isn't it, that so much can happen, so much has been destroyed for ever, and across all that one human being can reach out and touch another, with nothing more substantial than a voice?'

'No,' said George. 'They died long ago. There's nothing they can give you now.'

'But that's not true. Listen, can I read it to you?'

'A little bit,' said George. 'But not all night.'

Emily chuckled. 'Are you afraid I might?'

'I never knew anyone harder to stop, whatever she did.'

'I promise not to,' said Emily. 'But listen to me for a moment now.'

George settled back against her shoulder and closed his eyes. 'All right, for a moment.'

Emily picked up one of the books. 'This is the difficult one,' she said. 'The other is easy, quite clear and plain and about everyday things that anyone could comprehend. But this is very complicated. Sometimes I think it's an account of a sickness, and other times it seems to be about possession. Or perhaps it's just a fantasy, a kind of nightmare.'

'It doesn't sound very encouraging. What happens in it?' asked George sleepily.

'It's hard to say. The first pages are missing, and that doesn't help.' Emily opened the battered volume very carefully. The pages were dry and crackly, discoloured with age and dust. The writing was very close together, an archaic small print that was so stained and blotched in places it was difficult to make out the unfamiliar shapes of the letters at all. Some of the pages were torn, and a few clung to the binding by a thread. 'And it's not in modern English either,' said Emily. 'I can't read all of the words, and of course they pronounced everything differently. I'm not even sure if I'm reading what I think I'm reading.'

'What do you think you're reading?' asked George without opening his eyes.

'Well, it seems to be about a woman.' Emily paused, apparently seeking for words. 'A woman who seems to be living in some kind of bad dream. She's an orphan.'

'How do you mean?'

'It says her mother is dead, and another word I can't read –

someone else is dead too. But she seems to have no aunts or uncles or cousins or grandparents or brothers or sisters or any relations at all. She begins quite alone in the world.'

'No,' said George. 'That must be nonsense. Why do the people of her village not adopt her then? Is she lost?'

'I think she must be. Perhaps a great natural catastrophe.'

'A forest fire,' suggested George, allowing his imagination to stir in its sleep a little.

'She has to go out to look after children.'

'What's wrong with the children?'

'It doesn't say. They don't seem to be badly hurt. But a man takes her to look after them. The word is here. It begins with a g. I think it is a g. They live in a large house.'

'Whose household is it?'

'That it doesn't say. She's not there. Only the man is there. He's called Max. Or sometimes, my lord.'

'He has two names?'

'Oh, several. But then the nightmare begins. She becomes possessed.'

'By whom?'

'I don't know. She can't stop thinking about the man. Even when he kisses her.'

'Don't you think about a man when he kisses you?' asked George, opening his eyes for a moment.

'Don't be silly. She doesn't kiss him back. She goes away and has a lot of strange feelings about it.'

'It sounds very unusual.'

'And the man is definitely very sick. But I can't work out what's supposed to be the matter with him.'

'What symptoms does he have? That's the first thing to ask.'

'Well, none exactly. It's not like us. For example, George, what symptoms do you have when you're sick?'

'Stomach ache,' said George promptly.

'Exactly. This person is much more complicated. She says about him somewhere, something about him being "cruel and . . ." what's the word? – "overbearing, and yet at heart he is still only a lonely little boy". How does that sound to you?'

'Morbid,' said George. 'I shouldn't read this book if I were you. You'll have nightmares.'

'But, George, it's important to me. We know so very little, and I think this book must have so much to say, if only I could understand.'

'Why must it?'

'Well,' said Emily doubtfully, 'because it's so difficult. I feel it must be holding a secret.'

'That world can keep its secrets,' said George. 'We know what they did to the land. Isn't that enough?'

'No,' said Emily unhappily.

George took her hand in his and squeezed it comfortingly. 'How about the other book? The easy one?'

Emily smiled at him, and kissed him briefly, then she picked up the second book. 'I like this one,' she said. 'It might have been written by one of us, if only we had found the words for it.'

'Then it's about trees?'

'No, just about what everybody knows, but the words are put together very differently, like music. I want you to listen to this.' She began to read slowly, stumbling over the archaic words in their outlandish script.

'*Time past and time future*
Allow but a little consciousness.
To be conscious is not to be in time
But only in time can the moment in the . . .'

'In the what?' asked George, when the silence had grown too long.

'The next bit is all messed up. I think the book got wet at some time. But there are bits in it, George, just bits of lines here and there, that are like that. As if someone had just said them here in Clachanpluck. And then when you see how old the book is, it makes you think there is nothing new in the world at all.'

'Of course there isn't. Where would it come from?'

'Look at the book,' commanded Emily.

George sat up and rubbed his eyes, and took the book carefully from her.

It was a faded grey, perhaps it had once been blue, quite a thin book, with a loose binding. There had once been gold letters written on the back of it, but they were rubbed away now, and only a few specks of glitter remained. George opened it gingerly, as if it might crumble to dust in his large hands. The pages were faded and discoloured, but the book seemed to be intact. The strange script sprawled across the pages, not very much on each, and not tightly-packed like the other book which he had squinted at briefly over Emily's shoulder. There were divisions here and there, and strange signs. He could make nothing of it. There were no living words lying there for him. No voice echoed through the centuries to speak like a familiar friend in his ear. Only Emily was given such a gift. He handed the book back to her.

'Read more,' said George.

Emily opened the book at the beginning. The words at the top of the page were impossible, not even in writing. She skipped them, and began:

'*Time present and time past*
Are both perhaps present in time future,
And time future contained in time past.
If all time is eternally present . . .'

'What?' said George.

'*All time is unredeemable.*'

George sighed, and let the words wash over him. He did not stop listening entirely. It turned out the story was about the forest after all. He recognised the bird, and the trees with the empty pool in the centre. But the words went on, and George sat up and stared at Emily over the top of the book, as if waiting to seize the meaning of every word she spoke. She read hesitatingly, stopping at difficult words and struggling for a meaning, and George waited like a blind man waiting to be told what it is that he senses, what meaning can be given to the strange sounds that assail his ears, and what the scent in the air may be that he seems already half to recognise.

Eventually she stopped, and looked up at him.

'How does she know?' asked George, and his voice was awed. 'How does this dead person know what it is that we hold here in Clachanpluck?'

8

Long ago, a monster was brought into the world. It was not a bear or wolf or serpent, it was no creature of moor or forest or water, nor was it a ghost or a straying spirit, for it belonged on no other world. It was a thing born in the dreams of people, a creature made by the dread of children who are left alone in the night and have no one come to them. The monster slunk into the world through a chink left in someone's thoughts, perhaps through the gap left in the mind of a child who had lost its own people. But once born on this earth, the monster found plenty to nourish it, and it grew strong in the imagination of all people. It grew so substantial that it became visible to all eyes, and the deeds that grew from the thoughts it nurtured began to change the world, until the creature had devoured more living things than were even born. Much of the sea and land which had been filled with life became deserts, and nothing could live there any more. Some species vanished from the earth, never to return again. Some changed, fleeing to isolated corners where the breath of the monster could not breathe upon them, and from their hiding places they returned again in a new shape when the danger was over. And some stood their ground and said, 'We refuse to believe in this any longer. This is a creature of nightmare, insubstantial as mist, which the people have brought on to this earth, and which they now believe is their ruler. But we will not believe it. If you would all do likewise, the monster will shrink and grow transparent. It will become a small shadow of the thing that it now seems to be, and when the last living thing has decided that they no longer believe it, it will slip away into nothingness like the thing of imagination that it is.'

There was no difficulty with the plants and animals, or with the birds or the creatures that live in the sea. There was only one species out of all that exist which could not bear to part with the monster, and that was the species which had dreamed of it in the first place. The people thought about ceasing to believe. They thought about what it would be like if the monster withered away and vanished, and they thought, 'But that would not be any kind of a world at all.' They had forgotten, you see, that things were ever different. They thought that if they let the nightmare go, everything real would drift away with it, the earth, the planets and even the stars would vanish as if there had only ever been the dream. 'We have to believe in the monster,' they said. 'Look, this is real, and there is nothing else that can be real if we do not accept this.' And because of their fear, they began to prove in every way they could that the monster was real. The monster being in their minds a thing of destruction, they proved that destruction was real. In the world nothing is lost, only changed, but in the dream things died and were not reborn. The people imposed their dream upon the world, until much of the world indeed ceased to exist. They made images of destruction, engines which were designed to kill, machines that could destroy the earth many times over, and the more they did so, the more secure they were that the world of nightmare was the real world. 'Look,' they said, 'you can see now this is real. Here are the machines to prove it, and so much has been killed already, which proves it even more.'

They grew vehement with one another. Threats and protestations rang across the planet, and the machines of destruction circled the outermost reaches of the world. But the plants and the animals and all the other beings still circled through the years as they had always done, and though they could say nothing, in their being they stated, 'This is not to do with us. We live in a world that never dies, and we have never dreamed of such a thing as this . . .'

'There's someone at the door,' said Alan.

'Come in!' called Bridget.

Naomi came into the kitchen and, finding the two of them on the big chair by the fire, hesitated on the threshold. 'Am I interrupting you?' she asked, 'Because I could come back another time.'

'Alan was just going to bed,' said Bridget. 'If you don't mind waiting while I finish the story.'

'No,' said Alan, regarding Naomi with some disfavour. 'We'll have the rest tomorrow.'

'Would you like me to go away and come back later?'

'It doesn't matter,' said Alan, but he seemed glad to be asked. He got up, wrapping the blanket which draped him closer about him, and trailed away, the ends of blanket sweeping the floor as he went. The women waited while he went through the door, tried to close it, pulled his blanket out from under it, and shut it behind him. 'I'll come up soon,' called Bridget after him.

'Well, I'll tell you right away,' said Bridget. 'I've done nothing about it. I was working with George all day, and I thought of it last night, but then Patrick called because it was market day tomorrow, today that is, and I gave him my messages, and that was the evening half gone. I don't even know if it's still got all its strings.'

'Maybe we could have a look?'

'Well, sit down first and I'll make some tea. How are you getting on at Emily's?'

'Fine,' said Naomi, leaning back in the chair where Alan had just been sitting, and staring into the fire. 'I'm just beginning to sort them all out. Who's Patrick?'

'Patrick? Oh, he's from the smithy. Mind you, they take most of the work into Carlingwark, except the shoeing and the bits of mending, and that. That's why he gets all the messages to do. But he's a good-natured lad really, whatever they say.'

'What do they say?'

'Nothing of account,' said Bridget, filling the kettle again. Naomi realised she'd been too curious. No one was going to tell tales, not while she was still a stranger. It always took a while to find out what was going on in a place. But there was always something. No such thing as a sleepy village, not in this country. She looked thoughtfully at Bridget, and wondered where George was. But that was the sort of thing no one ever asked about anybody. It made it difficult if one didn't belong, and wanted to be clear about things.

'I was playing a few tunes with Davey,' said Naomi diffidently, as Bridget poured the tea.

'Ay? He's the musical one in that household. He plays in the band.'

'So there is a band?'

'Oh yes. For the ceilidhs, in winter. You've not met them yet?'

'I don't think so. Who are they?'

'Well, there's Davey of course, and Patrick and his brother, and Anna, from across the road there. She's young, but she plays as well as anyone. And sings too. You've maybe met her. She goes down to see Fiona. And Davey, of course.'

That could be a warning, thought Naomi. Unnecessary. I have no intention of getting involved like that with anybody. I just like to be clear about things. Aloud she said, 'It'll be good to have a ceilidh. You're not so quiet in winter, then?'

'Well, of course the travellers pretty well stop coming. We more or less shut the inn up in winter, though it's there if someone like yourself comes by. The village uses it if there's anything to celebrate. But evenings like this it's empty, mostly. People like to stay at home on winter nights.'

'Yes,' said Naomi, almost brusquely. Bridget glanced at her. She hadn't thought of this tough, well-travelled woman being homesick. She certainly hadn't meant to hurt her. She'd only been thinking about the village, and being careful, and not betraying anybody. It hadn't occurred to her that Naomi must always feel like an outsider. Now that she saw it, she was immediately sorry. 'Do you want to come up?' she said. 'And we can try the harp?'

Bridget's room was directly above the inn parlour, looking out over the crossroads. It was small and warm, even on a raw December evening, lined with wooden boards that had mellowed with the years to a rich brown. The roof was directly above, so that the walls sloped to within a few feet of the floor, but the window was set in a gable overlooking the road. There were hangings on both the straight walls, strange woven patterns in blues and greens and greys, like an insubstantial forest under what might be hills, or only clouds seeming to be hills. There were rugs and sheepskins scattered on the wooden floor, and the bed against the back wall was comfortable with embroidered cushions and a thick patterned quilt. There were two large carved chests, one under the window, so that one could sit and look out on the road below. It was a welcoming room, thought Naomi. I would like to be invited into a room like this. I wonder if anybody is?

'Through here,' said Bridget.

There was another door tucked out of sight on the far side of the bed, hard to see because it was of the same burnished wood as the walls. The room beyond was very bare and plain. It contained a loom which stood right in front of the window so as to catch the light, and one wall was lined with shelves stacked with cones of wool in varying shades. The only other furniture was a high wooden bench in front of the loom. The harp was in the far corner, standing behind stacked boxes of cloth and wool, with a cover draped over it.

'I'll just move these,' said Bridget. 'Oh thanks. Just put them down over there, will you?'

Naomi glanced down at the box in her hands. 'What's that?' she asked, before she could stop herself.

'What?' Bridget didn't seem offended by her curiosity. 'Oh, that's books.'

'Books?' repeated Naomi, laying the box down with awe. 'A box of books?'

'Oh no, it's scraps of wool underneath. Patrick bought it at the auction as a lot. He knew I'd want the wool, and when we opened the box the books were at the bottom.'

'But that's incredible!' said Naomi. 'How can that have happened?'

'I don't know. There were quite a few. Some were too torn or stained to be readable.'

'But you could read some?' Naomi stared down at the books, wondering if she dare pick one up without being asked.

'I lent a couple to Emily. She can read. So can I, just a bit, but I couldn't make much sense out of that old stuff. But Emily was fascinated by it. I don't know how she's got on with it. I'll ask George in the morning.'

Ah, thought Naomi, so that explains that. 'I can read,' she said.

'Can you? You're very talented.'

'Reading's not a talent. It's just a thing you can learn. Or not learn. Being a poet would be a talent. Or a storyteller. Do you tell stories?'

'Only the ones everyone knows. I tell them to the bairn.'

'I interrupted you tonight.'

Bridget gave her another sideways glance, and uncovered the harp. It was hard to fathom Naomi. In a way she made Bridget nervous. She wore her flamboyant ragged clothes with an air, almost a swagger, as if she liked herself and wanted nothing and needed nobody. And then I made her feel excluded, thought Bridget, and for a moment she looked lonely as a child that has no village to go home to. I wonder if she ever had a child? Well, if we get to know one another she may tell me. Do I want that? Plenty of strangers came to the inn, and Bridget felt no need to cultivate them more than hospitality required. But Naomi was staying all winter, and Bridget found her intriguing, attractive even, as if Naomi represented some part of herself that she might have been but had not quite become.

'We can go on tomorrow,' said Bridget. 'It doesn't matter at all.'

But Naomi was no longer listening. She was looking at the harp. 'Can we bring it out a bit? And hold the lamp up higher?'

Bridget held the lamp up obediently, and waited. Naomi seemed to spend a long time, testing the strings gently, so that faint notes stirred in the stillness, gradually growing more true as Naomi tuned the dusty strings. Bridget was astonished to find herself angry, impatient at holding the lamp so long, so bored at this long procedure she felt like screaming. There was no need to touch the harp. It had lain long enough. Why had she allowed this woman with her clever fingers to come in here, into her private space, and stir up old notes and thoughts that had lain forgotten so many contented years? I don't want this, thought Bridget resentfully. I haven't time for this. It's winter, and I have my family and a man to love when I want, and I have the stock to see to, and the land to tend, and weaving enough to last me till ploughing time. I'm not a traveller, I'm not a musician. Trust Emily to bring this into our lives. Bridget loved Emily as much as she loved anyone outside her family, and shared more with her than most people knew, but she was wary of her too. Emily was sudden and eager, and Bridget was not. Emily had brought a stranger in, knowing that thereby they must all be changed, and Bridget would have to take account of it. Emily had done this to her. It would be Emily. The soft notes sounded through the room, running together now, merging into small tunes and scraps of melody. A scale. Bridget watched Naomi's hands running up and down the strings, and her mouth set sullenly.

'It only needed tuning. Do you want to try?'

'No.'

Naomi nodded, unperturbed. She pulled a box over and sat down on it, and went on playing, ignoring Bridget completely. Bridget put the lamp down, and from the floor it threw up huge shadows against the dim walls; the shadow of a small straight woman standing rigid, her head turned away, and the shadow of a grotesquely long figure, her limbs made spider-like by the trick of the flame on the wall, crouching over an instrument whose strings were not even shadowed, weaving a web of nothingness around the flickering lamplight. Bridget stared out of the window into the blind darkness, twisting her hands together and crying out silently for Naomi to stop, to stop before the whole fabric of life was rewoven, before she took Bridget's ordered years and unravelled them, setting them up in a new pattern, a new weaving of threads which would wind her away from everything that was sure and familiar. She had forgotten that the harp sounded like that. This was the only one in the village, and it had belonged to her great-grandmother and her grandmother, and now it belonged to her. Leave it alone! screamed Bridget, but the thought was given no voice, and Naomi played on.

The shadows on the wall flickered with a flame that needed trimming. The fantastic weaving shadow played on, long shadow hands with long unhuman fingers flicking up and down over invisible strings, and the small straight shadow beside it never turned its head. But then the picture on the wall changed. The straight shadow crumpled, its head dropped down on its hands, and it cast itself down among the square shadows of the boxes, and the room was filled with the sounds of low sobbing, and the notes of the harp echoed on around them.

Naomi came to an end, and let the harp drift back into silence. She looked round and waited quietly until Bridget raised her head.

'I don't know what's the matter with me,' said Bridget. 'It's that long since I played. I suppose it reminded me.'

'It would,' said Naomi gently.

'Of what didn't happen,' finished Bridget. She sniffed and wiped her nose on her hand, and looked at Naomi almost belligerently. 'So have you come here to change us all?'

'No,' said Naomi. 'That would be far too conceited.'

'Then what?'

Naomi shrugged. 'Chance, I suppose. I was heading this way. Does it matter?'

'There's no such thing as chance.'

'Fate then,' said Naomi lightly. 'Call it what you like.'

'No,' said Bridget. 'We have names for it here, but they are our own.'

It was like a slap in the face, and Naomi flinched. 'As you wish. Do you want me to go away?'

There was a long silence.

'No,' said Bridget.

'Then what?'

'Listen,' said Bridget. 'You have played me out of my life, I think. But we have music here in Clachanpluck. If you listen, perhaps I shall play something to you.'

She stood up stiffly, like an old woman, and stepped over the boxes. Naomi moved away from the harp to give her room.

'I am listening.'

9

'Bridget suggested that I came to see you,' said Naomi. 'She told me you played in the band.'

She was relieved to see that Anna looked pleased to see her. It had taken her a few days to get round to calling. The overgrown cobbled yard and firmly closed front door of the house next to the smithy did not seem to invite visitors, but today she'd seen Anna in the garden at the side and seized the chance to speak to her over the wall. Anna hadn't noticed her at first; she was pruning raspberry canes with a sharp knife, very deftly. Naomi watched her for a while before she spoke. There was something about the way Anna moved, her total absorption in her task, that reminded her of Emily. The same familiarity with her land, the same easy efficiency of one who knew exactly what she was doing without having to give the matter any conscious thought. If I'd had to guess, thought Naomi, I'd have thought Anna was the one from Emily's household, not Fiona. She looked tough and sturdy, though not very big, in patched navy trousers rolled up over her boots and a navy jacket with a swallow embroidered on the back. At least someone in the village made her clothes slightly more interesting than potato sacks. And Anna played the flute.

'I wanted to see *you*,' replied Anna. 'Yes, I play. Come in. Not round the front, it's sealed up for winter. Can you get over the wall?'

Naomi vaulted over. She might just about be old enough to be Anna's mother, but she wasn't that decrepit. She stumbled, and Anna grabbed her arm.

'Come round the back. I'll put the kettle on.'

The garden stretched a long way back behind the house. It was very neat, the fruit trees bare and pruned, the empty beds spread with dung for winter. A few rows of kale and cabbage still stood at the end, their outer leaves yellow and battered after the autumn gales.

'You've got a good garden here.'

'Yes. It's always been a good one. My mother made it mostly. And now me. Do you want to see round it?'

Naomi didn't particularly. She never knew what to say about muck and cabbages, but she did want to get to know Anna, so she assented. She followed Anna down the path, trying not to appear totally ignorant.

'This is the herb garden. It looks a bit straggly, I know. I don't usually cut everything back till spring. I used to. It was neater, but not so good against the frosts.'

'You've got a lot of herbs.'

'We always had the most, and I've been collecting more. There's a merchant in Carlingwark looks out for them for me, and the pedlar comes in autumn. He's brought seeds sometimes. It's something every village needs, and we've been lacking.'

'You don't seem to be lacking now.'

'Oh, there're gaps. It's so hard to find out. I've talked to folk in Carlingwark, but no one in Clachanpluck knows more than I do now. How do people find out new things? I was thinking about that after the other night when you played tunes we hadn't heard before. I wanted to ask you about travelling.'

'Do you want to travel?'

'Not for a living. I belong to Clachanpluck. But there are things I need to learn, and I can't do it here. There are plants I have names for, and I don't know what they look like. There are plants I have, and I don't know what they do. Sometimes I know what to give to people, and just as often I don't know at all. There must be more plants in the world than I've ever heard of. The only way is to go and look, then remember, and bring home seeds, if I can get them.'

'Or find a book.'

'A book?' asked Anna, puzzled. 'What would I do with a book?'

'There used to be books that told people things like that.'

'I can't read. And how would it know what questions I wanted to ask?'

'It wouldn't, but you'd make it tell you the answers anyway.'

'Oh,' said Anna. 'Like that. But if you really become wise enough to make answers give themselves to you, you don't need toys and tools. That's only for children's stories. That's what Bridget says.'

'That's not exactly what I meant.'

'Do you know much about plants?'

'Almost nothing,' confessed Naomi. 'But I'm sure you'd find out what you wanted if you took to the road. When would you do it?'

'In the spring. My mother died last year. I don't have anyone to look after here now.'

Anna turned and led Naomi back towards the house along a narrow path bordered with clipped bare lavender bushes. There was a paved yard sheltered by the house, with a washing line strung across it, hung with nappies. Anna pushed them aside and ducked under. 'We could sit out here,' she said, 'if you'd be warm enough.'

There was a rough bench by the door, in a sheltered corner where the sun was trapped into shedding a little meagre warmth. Two empty flowerpots stood beside it and a few stacked up seed trays, weighted down with a stone.

'That would be nice,' said Naomi politely, sensing that Anna didn't want her to come inside.

'Sit down then. I'll get some tea.'

Anna left the door ajar behind her. It was dark within after the light outside, and Naomi could see nothing but a passageway of scrubbed flags covered with threadbare matting. There was a murmur of voices. 'Do you want some too?' she heard Anna say.

'Not now. Is that Fiona? Why doesn't she come in?'

'It's not Fiona.'

'Who then?'

Anna's reply was inaudible, but Naomi heard more than one voice exclaim at it. 'So why keep her all to yourself? Aren't you going to bring her in?'

'What's she come to see you for?'

'Hear that, Susan? Anna's got the fiddle player out the back.'

'She's come to talk about the band,' said Anna firmly. 'I'll maybe bring her in before she goes.'

'Well, let me sweep the floor first.'

'Ask her to play us a tune.'

'I might,' said Anna, and Naomi heard a door shut, and the voices were cut off. Anna reappeared with a tray. 'There's scones,' she said, 'if you'd like one.'

'Did you make them?'

'No, my cousin did. There's a lot of us,' said Anna, setting the tray down carefully. 'Do you like jam? That's why I thought we'd sit out here. They're all right, my family, but one thing I won't do, and that's have six children myself.'

'You've a lot of cousins then?'

'Nine,' said Anna. 'We've talked about making another household. There's not a lot of room.'

'Would you like to hold household?'

'Me? I'm one of the youngest. They wouldn't want it to be me. My sister has children too. Enough for one family. And I need to think about going away, if I'm to do the plants right.'

'You could do both, in time.'

'I'm not sure,' said Anna. 'I'll go away first. I've got family I can trust, but if I had a child, I'd want to be with it too.'

'Yes. Once you have a child, it's very hard to leave again.'

A question hovered in Anna's mind, but she knew it was impossible to ask. It was easy to tell Naomi things, but Naomi asked nothing impertinent, and Anna knew she should be even more careful because Naomi was her guest. 'Where did you come from?' she asked eventually, spreading jam neatly on half a scone.

'Across the sea. Donegal.'

'Is that very different from here?'

Anna was the first person in Clachanpluck who had dreamed of asking her such a question. Naomi was quite aware of the other, unspoken question which had led her to it, but the thought was genuine for all that. Perhaps it's because she's young, thought Naomi. She still has curiosity about the world outside. She felt a sudden unexpected warmth for the young woman beside her. She's not yet swallowed up in their forest, she hasn't grown roots, she's still ready to take off. Like me. She has a swallow embroidered on her back, and too many cousins, and she plays the flute. Naomi felt an ache in her chest, a shadow of cold loneliness suddenly given substance and clinging round her heart.

'I don't think about it a lot,' she said. 'I'm a musician, a kind of actor, I suppose. A spectacle for people who don't know me. It's easy to forget that I have any substance at all. But the past doesn't change. I had a village the same as you. Most days I never give it a thought.'

'But when you do?' Anna was wary, afraid of losing by her clumsiness such surprising confidences from a woman who appeared to have everything that was missing in Clachanpluck.

'I don't belong to a forest,' answered Naomi. 'I never saw

anything like this until I left. There were no trees. My village was by the sea. There were cliffs, and the birds used to come back every spring to nest, and in winter the waves used to break against the cliffs until the whole sea was white, and you could hear the sound of it even when you slept. Sometimes I hear the wind in the trees and I think for a moment that it's the sea. Then I remember.'

'No trees?' repeated Anna, uncomprehending.

'Heather,' said Naomi succinctly. 'Bracken, and grass. Peat, which we used for firing. So there were trees once.'

'The sea is only ten miles from here,' said Anna. 'Bridget and Emily have seen it. They went there together, when they were as old as Fiona and I are now. It was dead.'

'Our sea's not dead,' replied Naomi. 'There were more fish again, every year. It wasn't a rich village, except in music. I was lucky that way.'

'So you learned to play the fiddle?' Anna's voice was deliberately neutral, and she stared out over the brown garden. It was a breath of life, to hear this, but she had to be careful. One could show interest in the world outside, and ask without seeming to ask.

'We had a fiddler in our village who was the best musician in all that country. I've never met anyone who played quite like him. Though I must know much more than he did now,' added Naomi after a pause.

'You were lucky then.'

'I might have been. I was very young.'

There was a silence. Please, thought Anna, go on. 'Would you like some more tea?' she asked.

'No thank you.' Naomi looked at her companion. Anna was sitting cross-legged on the paving, blue eyes regarding her thoughtfully. She wore a scarf round her neck that was exactly the colour of her eyes. She was round-faced and sunburnt, and full of attention, like a dog at an unfamiliar scent. Most people in Clachanpluck succeeded in being incurious. Not this one, though she did her best to hide it.

'So no one else in this village wants to go away, except you?' asked Naomi.

'Patrick went away,' said Anna reluctantly, not wanting to change the subject. 'But I don't think he noticed much. He was too full of one idea.'

'I haven't met Patrick.'

'He plays in the band.' Anna didn't want to talk about Patrick. It might be uncivil, but she desperately wanted to understand. 'Please,' she said, 'I don't mean to be rude but . . . why did you leave?'

There was another pause, and Anna waited to be snubbed. 'You're not,' said Naomi. 'Sometimes it's important to ask things, or how else can you understand? If you are speaking to a stranger, that is. It's so easy to make mistakes, if you're not allowed to be curious. I know that, because I'm as much a stranger to you as you are to me.'

'Sometimes I feel like a stranger here myself.'

Naomi thought about that. 'Perhaps they all do, inside.'

'No,' Anna shook her head very decidedly. 'I know they don't. Fiona would never dream of such a thing. I asked her, you know,' – Anna seemed to be searching for an example – 'I said, should we go to the sea, like Bridget and Emily did? Do you know what she said?'

'What did she say?'

'She said, "What for?"'

Naomi grinned. 'She must be more like her mother than I thought.'

'But Emily went.'

'No, I didn't mean that. I mean they're both unshakable. They see things as they see them, and have no difficulty in not asking questions.' Naomi glanced up again. 'But you asked me a question.'

'Yes,' said Anna in a level voice.

'I left because I made a mistake. I told you there was a man in my village who played the fiddle. He gave me a great deal. But it was the music I wanted most, and I thought it was the man.'

'I can understand that,' said Anna. 'Sometimes I think I'd like to stay here, where I have someone to love. Perhaps even have a child, in spite of all that lot.' She jerked her thumb towards the house behind her. 'Other times I know I want most to go away and find out more about the plants.'

'There's no reason why you shouldn't have everything. You just have to be clear about which is which.'

'There is something that we hold here in Clachanpluck,' said Anna, apparently inconsequentially. 'I don't know if you knew.'

'I haven't asked,' said Naomi with a touch of a smile.

'I have no secrets to tell,' said Anna. 'Only, I know who goes into the forest, and I think I have a right to know. I asked if I could go with him, but I think I might be wrong. I try to be clear about which is which. Fiona says it's nothing to do with him, but I want to find out. It would be much easier if it were somebody else. Patrick confuses me.'

'I don't know anything about your forest, but I know confusion can hurt.'

'I think I can keep it clear,' said Anna. 'Thank you for telling me all that.'

'You were interested, so you deserved it. Thank you for showing me your plants.' And now I've given away enough, thought Naomi. She's young, and this place is still new to me. 'Can I ask you now about the band?' she said.

10

'Watch carefully,' said Patrick. 'That's the only way to learn properly. That's the powder, see, and here's the shot. So when you load it, you put the shot into the slot there, look. And the powder – like this. And once it's loaded you take care. Carry it half-cocked, like that. Don't ever carry a loaded gun ready to fire. You'll end up shooting yourself as like as not.'

'Can I try it?' asked Anna.

'Just watch today,' said Patrick. 'I've never lent it yet, and the only other person I've ever let try is Davey. I'll have to see.'

'I might not even want to,' said Anna. 'But I do want to find out.'

Patrick had his back to her, measuring powder into a small leather pouch. 'Why?' he asked abruptly.

'Why what?' countered Anna defensively.

'You've been avoiding me for weeks,' said Patrick, standing up straight and picking up his gun. 'And then you say you want to come with me into the forest. Why?'

'I told you. No one else hunts. You keep bringing us meat. I want to know how to get it.'

'Shoot it,' said Patrick offhandedly. 'What else?'

Anna stood her ground. 'I haven't seen what it's like,' she said stubbornly. 'I don't know what it means.'

Patrick abandoned the argument by walking out of the smithy, apparently expecting her to follow. 'I'm off now,' he said over his shoulder. 'If you're coming.'

It was all she could do to keep up with him. Not a word passed between them until they stood on the ridge of hills right above the forest. There was no mist up there today, for the wind tore the clouds into grey shreds as fast as they gathered to the north-west. It was colder up here, and wilder. Patrick offered her no better company than his back, clad in an ancient jacket, the gun slung across it by a worn leather strap. He seemed to be making for the very top of the ridge, where a cairn stood out among the wind-whipped winter grass.

'Patrick?' The words were whipped away by the wind, and he never turned. 'Patrick!' shouted Anna, louder.

He turned to face her. 'What?'

'Why are we going up there?'

He looked impatient. 'The wind,' he said. 'We have to come into the forest south of them. And I like to start this way anyway.'

He was off again, and Anna panted behind him, hot with effort and resentment at herself. She was tough enough, but it was galling to have to admit that he was stronger.

They reached the cairn, and to her relief he stopped and surveyed the forest. It was freezing up here. The wind seemed to have come straight out of the heart of winter with the keen bite of snow in its teeth. No place to linger, but Patrick seemed quite unhurried. Anna had been hot and sweating under her jacket, but in a few seconds she was chilled through. She stood with her back to the wind while the cold pierced her. She followed his gaze southward, over the backs of wind-tossed trees to a ridge of hills, beyond which lay the sea. Grey clouds raced one another towards it, cleansed and broken by the northern air. Patrick stared out over the trees, then jerked his head eastward, indicating their line of descent. They were off down again, and he didn't slacken the pace until they reached the fringes of the forest.

'What can you tell from up there?'

'Ask, not tell,' said Patrick.

'Ask?'

'The deer aren't mine,' said Patrick. 'One has to take account of the forest. You can look down and see it from up there.'

'I don't understand.'

He didn't bother to answer, but began to thread a path through the scattered trees. It was only the beginnings of woodland, consisting of scrub and birch and young spruce seedlings.

'Someone ought to thin these,' said Anna. 'In a few years you won't be able to pass.'

'There's always ways,' said Patrick.

The ground was less rough just here, and the trees were still not very dense. It was possible to walk side by side, and to her surprise he waited for her to catch up and fell into step beside her. 'Well, you can keep up, anyway,' he said.

'Of course I can,' retorted Anna, stung. 'I've got legs, same as you.'

'Not as long,' said Patrick, grinning.

At least he'd stopped being surly. Anna decided not to take it as an insult. 'Tell me how you got the gun,' she said pacifically.

'You know that,' said Patrick. 'The whole village knows that.'

'I know you were gone for months,' said Anna. 'And I know you went beyond Cumbria, and that you bought it from a smith down there. But that's all.'

'That's it,' said Patrick. 'It's not so easy to find a good gun,' he went on, encouragingly talkative. 'They've not made any like this for centuries. I thought it might take years, and I nearly gave up hope as it was. But then a man in a market south of the Wirral told me of a smith who lived at a crossroads on the road to the south, and said he might have what I wanted. It was midwinter then, too, and there was snow on the ground. The place was way up in the hills, a road hardly used at that time of year. But I got through and found him. And this,' he jerked his head back to indicate the gun. 'I paid for it dearly enough. I'd brought money with me, for that's a thing we do come by in the metal trade, but it wasn't enough for him. He took all I had and gave me the gun, but made me promise to be back again, within the year and a day, with as much again. I didn't know where I'd find it at that time, but I knew there'd never be a chance again, so I took the gun, and promised him.'

'And you paid him?'

'You know I did,' said Patrick. 'Last year. I went back. I borrowed money in Carlingwark, and I got it back to him, exactly thirteen moons later to the day. I don't know what he'd have done if I hadn't, seeing how far it is, but I'd not dare to have crossed that one.'

'But you got what you wanted.'

'Ay, and debts to last a lifetime.'

Anna considered. 'Why?' she asked presently. 'Why's it worth so much?'

'Were you hungry this winter?'

'No.'

'Have you ever been hungry in winter?'

'Yes,' said Anna. 'Yes, I know. I know it was a gift to all of us. It's made this village a better place to be.'

'The forest is there for us. It's foolish not to use it.'

'I know,' said Anna. 'But is that all?'

'How do you mean?'

'I don't know. I just don't think it's all.'

'Hush,' he said, putting out a hand to restrain her. 'We need to go quietly now.'

She followed him along the line of the forest's edge. He was gradually descending until gaunt winter trees surrounded them. At least he had lowered his defences a little and was being more like he used to be. They used to come up to the moor in summer, when the younger people brought the cattle up to the summer pastures. He'd been one of the oldest and she'd been one of the youngest. He'd been quite tolerant about being tagged after then. He hadn't stopped liking her, thought Anna. It was more that she'd stopped thinking he was wonderful. But she still wanted to know about him, and about the hunting.

Patrick stopped and touched her arm so that she jumped, her thread of thought broken. 'Look.'

She followed his pointing hand and saw a straggling shape across the sky, a wide V driving down on the wind from the north, sailing the open sky in fleeting formation. There was a guttural honking that blew down to them on the wind, and the sound of heavy wingbeats in tumultuous air. Anna and Patrick watched, feeling suddenly earthbound, rooted ground-dwellers presented with a vision of another way of being, the unconfined drift from one season to another.

The geese flew over them and disappeared again into the grey light of the south, towards where the sun lurked behind fitful cloud. Anna realised his hand was still resting on her arm. She thought of moving, but it seemed more sensible to ignore it.

'Where they've come from,' said Patrick, still staring after them, 'it never grows light in winter. It's dark from harvest to springtime, with never a glimmer of light.'

'Oh, come on.'

'It's true. You don't hear much in the village.'

'There's stranger things than that in our village,' retorted Anna, and waited for a reaction. But what he said was quite unexpected.

'Anna?'

She froze. This was the other Patrick. She had told him quite clearly that she wanted no more of it, and she had trusted him to

78

keep his word. 'Yes?' she said warily.

'I love you,' said Patrick, without preamble. 'I still love you.' There was a pause. 'That's it,' he added.

In her anger she forgot what it could possibly be like for him. 'You promised not to come back to that! You said you'd agree that it was over. You promised!'

His hand dropped. 'I promised what?'

'After we were playing in the band. When the others had gone home. You said all that, and I told you I wanted to be your friend, and to play music, and you said that's how it would be. You promised.'

'About the music, yes,' said Patrick slowly. 'But not for ever. We're not playing music now.'

'It's the same thing. It's not what we came for.'

'You chose to come out with me. After what I said, you asked me. So what was I supposed to think?'

'That I trusted you,' said Anna at once. 'That I trusted you to keep your word. I don't want to be your lover, Patrick. I've changed.'

'And I haven't. You'll have to face up to that.'

'I accept it,' said Anna more quietly. 'I have to, don't I? I don't want to hurt you either, but there's nothing I can do Please, can't we go on now? Forget it, for the moment?'

'Forget it? You must be daft. All right, we'll go on.'

He turned his back again, and Anna followed him as quietly as she could. She'd made a mistake, she saw that now. Fiona had been right, and whatever the forest might be to Patrick, it had nothing to do with what they sought. The past was not so easily left behind, after all. Patrick had been gone nearly two years since the summer they'd been together, and when he came home she was different, and she found him different too. Only Patrick seemed unable to believe in change. He seems to think he owns me, thought Anna resentfully. He seems to think everything I say or do relates to that. Well, I won't have it, she thought fiercely, pushing past a larch tree, prickly branches scratching her jacket.

'Quiet,' hissed Patrick, not looking round.

Anna scowled at Patrick's back, and trod as silently as she could.

Further downhill the view opened out a little over a rough clearing. A small burn flowed not far off so that they could hear the gurgle of water over rock. Patrick began to skirt the top of the clearing, watching the ground below intently. He stopped at the head of the burn, waiting until Anna was standing right by him, then pointed silently across the clearing. There was only a tangle of hazel beyond a strip of browning bracken and another cluster of larches beyond. A bare branch of hazel moved a yard or more behind the bracken. Anna almost jumped. She could see the stag quite plainly now, two hinds behind him, not hidden at all.

How far did a gun shoot? Anna's heart was thumping. I don't want to be here, she thought. I made a mistake.

She didn't move. The stag's head went down again, grazing. Then she nearly did cry out; Patrick's mouth was right against her ear. 'We have to get nearer,' he whispered. She swallowed, and nodded. 'Keep down. Follow me.'

He dropped down into the bracken and crawled on silently. Kids' games. Anna felt suddenly lightheaded. A bubble of laughter rose in her throat but she quenched it. Hysterical, she thought, and nearly giggled again. She dropped to her knees and began to crawl after him. This is silly, she decided, after what seemed like several miles, and was just ready to rebel when he stopped. She nearly bumped into his heels. She couldn't see a thing. There was dead bracken all round her, and her knees were wet and numb. The same larches rose like a pale brown curtain ahead of them, and the same fir tree blocked out the light behind. Patrick very slowly unslung his gun and cocked it. Then to her annoyance he began to crawl again, more slowly than ever.

This time he knelt on his heels with maddening caution. Then he raised the gun slowly to his shoulder. She still couldn't see. Patrick's finger was on the trigger. Laughter and annoyance evaporated. The whole thing was real. He knew how to kill. Anna put her hands over her ears and shut her eyes.

Nothing happened. She opened her eyes again slowly. Patrick was still kneeling in the bracken, the gun still aimed. Still as a tree, or as the rock itself. Anna relaxed a little, took a deep breath.

The shot was so sudden that she cried out, an explosion like a crack in the world, the air torn apart. Another shot, like a reflex. Birds rising in the trees, a squawking and shrieking out of the roof of the forest. The slow silence settling, like a pulse beginning to beat again. Anna took her fingers from her ears and stood up.

Patrick was away again, striding across the bracken. The deer were gone. Relief swept over her. He'd missed. There had been no death, no cry of pain out of the heart of the forest. Anna slowly followed him, the shot still ringing in her head, but the burden lifted.

'There!' said Patrick, satisfied.

'You mean you got him?'

'Of course,' he said, startled. 'Whatever did you think?'

The stag was lying among last year's hazel leaves, big and inert, eyes already glazing over. The brown coat was rough and thick for winter, the antlers brown like polished wood. Anna looked, and said nothing.

Patrick knelt by the carcase, examining it. 'See the shot?' He was quite loquacious now, cheerful and animated after the long silence. 'In the chest. I must have killed him at once.'

'Good,' said Anna. 'What was the second shot?'

'What second shot? Oh, you must have heard the echo. I can't afford to waste shot. I knew I hadn't missed.'

'Now what?'

Patrick unsheathed a long knife. 'This is where the work starts,' he said cheerfully. 'I'll show you.'

She wasn't sure if he was genuinely unaware, or merely testing her. Either way, she wasn't going to fail. Anna looked down unemotionally at the dead stag at her feet.

'All right,' she said coolly. 'I'll help you if you like.'

11

Naomi didn't find it easy to get up in the mornings. She tried to wake when the others did and appear in the kitchen at dawn, showing herself willing to join in the work. She knew that staying up late meant using their wood and lamp oil, but it was hard to sleep when she felt awake, and wanted to talk or play music. It was all the more tempting because Davey was always prepared to sit up and accompany her. It was his household too, so presumably it was up to him to say if they should be less prodigal with light and fire. He never did. He would willingly play the fiddle with her until far into the night, and then when she suggested they stop in case other people were lying awake and angry, he would talk to her into the small hours, about music and travelling, about the world that she had seen and he had not, and he told her many things about Clachanpluck which he knew and she did not. It was all the harder to resist him because it was only during these times with Davey that she ceased to feel like an outsider, and relaxed with one of her own people. Naomi had no village or family, but she had other musicians, and in Clachanpluck that meant Davey. It was far more important than the fact that he found her attractive, which might have created some constraint between them. He had never attempted to speak to her about that again, anyway, since the first time they had practised together in the hayloft. But Naomi was too honest with herself to let herself believe that his feeling for her was not there all the time, like a strong undercurrent in a smooth river. In the end she did speak to him about it, late one evening when everyone else was in bed.

'Of course I think about it,' he said. 'I agreed not to speak, and those were the terms you said you'd teach me on. So I haven't spoken. But love isn't a little thing that melts away if you pretend not to be looking at it any more. I'll agree not to say anything, but don't kid yourself.'

'I haven't,' said Naomi. 'I'm not entirely stupid either. Or insensitive. But I've been alone a long time. It's tough, but it works, and the reward is I am who I am and I do what I do. I want to play music with you. I like talking to you. But I don't want to want a lover.'

'You mean you find it hard not to?'

'I mean I don't think about it,' said Naomi firmly. 'It's possible not to.'

'You're suggesting that I pretend it means nothing to me?'

'If you like.'

'I don't like,' said Davey. 'I'll do what you say to have what I can, that's all. But it's like asking me to pretend that we're sitting here in dead silence, while there's a full band playing right in my ears the whole time. It makes it difficult to hear you very clearly sometimes.'

Naomi wondered if she dared ask him what she wanted to know, and found that the words had slipped out while she was still debating about it. 'Don't you have a lover here in Clachanpluck?'

Davey looked at her in shock. Naomi knew very well that such a question was inadmissible, especially if Davey did love her, and he had already said as much. It was not a thing one asked anyone outside one's family. Naomi and Davey were not kin, and could be lovers; moreover, they did not know each other very well, as people of the same village knew one another, for example.

'You have no idea,' Naomi tried to explain, 'how difficult it is to live among strangers. The things that everyone thinks are so obvious that they're not even worth mentioning, are quite incomprehensible to me. It's the reason I decided to stay always on my own. I never knew enough of the implications of what I chose to do with a person. And no one in any village could ever understand that. It hurt. It hurt me and it hurt them. I stopped getting involved before I made a conscious decision, and then when I found it was perfectly easy to live without sex, and I didn't fall apart, and in fact it was far easier and friendlier and less complicated, I decided to keep it that way. But you're asking me to reconsider it, and not giving me any light to do it in. How am I supposed to know what's going on?'

Davey listened to this very attentively, as if he were trying to follow words spoken in a foreign language. 'I suppose I understand,' he said. 'But aren't you asking me to tell you about other people? I don't mind talking to you about myself, though I can't think that it would be particularly interesting. But how can I tell you about anyone else I love? The world wouldn't be safe for anyone if people went around doing that.'

'But you must talk about it. Everyone needs to talk.'

'I talk to my family, don't I?' said Davey, totally bemused. 'Who else?'

'Then who am I supposed to talk to?'

'I don't know,' said Davey. He thought a bit, and said, 'Other women.'

'And suppose all my lovers were women?'

'Well, that certainly wouldn't be my business,' said Davey. 'Besides, you said you were celibate.'

'If I did decide to be your lover,' said Naomi, 'it would be worse. I don't belong here, and I don't know anything about your life.'

'Why does it matter?'

'Because everything has implications. You see,' she tried to explain to him in another way, 'customs are made by people in villages for themselves. I was taught, just like you, that the important thing is to respect people, and asking questions is not respectful. But it doesn't work for the people who don't belong. Surely you can see that?'

'No,' said Davey, 'I don't. A village needs strangers. We treat our strangers with respect and we don't make unfair demands on them. But we need new blood. Like the herb pedlar. It's necessary. But no one would expect him to ask questions about us. Why should he do that? If everyone has what they need, what difference does it make?'

'Who's the herb pedlar?'

'Oh,' said Davey. 'I thought you'd know that. But I can hardly tell you, being as we are, you and I. It's too much of the same thing.'

Naomi seized hold of her own hair and pulled it hard. 'I give up,' she exclaimed, and jumped to her feet. Davey watched her apprehensively as she strode up and down the room, shaking her fists and swearing under her breath. She stamped her foot and he winced. 'I won't wake anyone!' she whispered furiously. 'Don't you worry about that. I won't disturb anyone, ever. I won't ask any questions. I'll expect nothing and take nothing and never have what

84

I deserve for the rest of my life. Or I will take it in spite of you, and then you'll wish you'd been a bit braver, Davey of Clachanpluck. You'll wish you'd been a bit more honest with me then.'

She almost hissed the last words at him, right into his face. He opened his mouth to speak, but she had turned on her heel, and strode from the room. He thought she was going to slam the door, and held his breath, but at the last moment she jerked it still, and closed it quietly behind her, and he heard her quiet tread on the stairs, going up into the sleeping house.

The next morning Naomi woke up later than she ever had before, and when she finally came into the kitchen there was nobody there but Fiona, who was making bread at the table. The room was very hot, with the fire roaring in the chimney, and a row of bread tins warming on top of the stove. Fiona was kneading dough vigorously, a too large pinafore tied round her which sat oddly on her skinny form, over a patched shirt and grubby trousers with a large hole in the seat. She gets her taste in clothes from Emily, thought Naomi, shutting the door quickly before she let the cold in. She was a little unsure of Fiona, who very seldom addressed a whole sentence to her, and always appeared slightly scornful. Fiona this morning looked as sullen as ever, and her shorn head and the enveloping pinafore made her appear alarmingly stern. She probably thinks I'm decadent, thought Naomi. 'Good morning,' she said aloud.

Fiona nodded to her and banged the dough down on the table.

'I'm sorry I slept in,' said Naomi. 'Do you want any help?'

'No,' said Fiona. She relented a little, and added, 'There's still porridge on the stove if you want breakfast.'

'Thank you,' said Naomi meekly, and helped herself. 'Is Emily anywhere about?'

'No.' Another silence, then Fiona said with the air of one offering a gratuitous piece of information. 'Ellen's baby was born in the night. So she went.'

Who's Ellen? wondered Naomi, but she was too dispirited to ask. 'You didn't go then?'

'No way,' said Fiona.

There was another silence. It was odd to think that this shrimp of a girl with her disdainful manner was Emily's daughter. They could hardly be more unlike. Naomi had at first thought Fiona to be about twelve, and had been surprised to learn that she was all of fifteen.

Looking covertly at her now, she saw that Fiona did have a woman's body under the ridiculous apron, so probably she'd stopped growing. She seemed to do her best to make herself unattractive. Davey thought the world of her. That was odd too, because Fiona appeared to be as unmusical as her mother, but without her touching dependence on the musicians around her. Fiona was very sure of being dependent on nobody. She was a woman of Clachanpluck, and she did an adult's work around the place. The only person Naomi had seen her smile at was Davey. Oh yes, and Anna, whom Naomi found a far easier proposition. But it was Fiona who lived in this household, not Anna.

'Did Bridget go to the birth?' she asked, more by way of making conversation than out of interest.

'Of course.'

Now why on earth should she have known that? Naomi was ready to be infuriated again, and a sudden impulse led her to tempt fate with another question. 'And who's the herb pedlar?'

Fiona stopped kneading and glanced at her, a quick appraising look. Then she bent over her work again, and said, 'What you said. He comes in the autumn usually. He brings herbs. And spices. He stays at the inn and sells them there. You know, nutmeg, cinnamon, pepper, stuff like that.'

'I've met a few herb pedlars,' said Naomi, 'so I wondered if I might know him. What's he like?'

Fiona thought about that, and seemed suddenly much less formidable. She rubbed her nose reflectively, and left a smear of flour across her cheek. 'Not like us,' she said eventually. 'It's a good thing, to bring in new blood, in a small village.' She sounded as though she was repeating something someone else had said. 'He's called Michael. Alan's very like him,' she added.

'Oh,' said Naomi, rapidly digesting this. 'And he comes every year, does he?'

'You must have known that when you asked about Bridget, surely.'

'When I asked what about Bridget?'

'Being pregnant,' said Fiona.

Naomi bit off the next question. She had her answer anyway. Her silence was rewarded because Fiona, quite animated now, went on talking.

'I wouldn't bother with it,' she said. 'Having bairns. My sister can do that one day if she likes. But I could hold household. The herb seller would be better than a man from the village. People get too involved in a little place. Aren't you glad to have nothing to do with it?'

'I never heard anything like it,' said Patrick.

Davey lowered his fiddle. 'Of course you didn't. That's what I'm saying. I want to know what you think about it. I can't play it to you the way it should be played, and there was more, much more. It's so much harder to remember than our music. But I have to, don't you see? If we are to keep this beyond the springtime, I'll have to learn it all I can. No one else can do it.'

'It confuses me,' said Patrick. 'Play it again.'

Davey picked up his fiddle again very willingly, and played the piece again. He went on further this time, and the music changed, still the same theme, but altered, becoming stranger and more sombre, until Davey hestitated, so that the last note hovered uncertainly, and faded into silence.

'It frustrates me,' burst out Davey. 'She has the wealth of years to offer, and who am I to take it in just a few short months? She has genius, and I'm no more than competent. It's like learning to swim in the burn, and then being shown the sea. The more I try, the more I can hold in Clachanpluck. But I don't like working that hard in winter,' added Davey gloomily.

'I don't know,' said Patrick. He squatted in front of the smithy fire, and piled in more logs. It was beginning to get hot in here, not hot enough to start work, but pleasant after the damp chill outside. Davey sat down on a barrel, and began to retune his fiddle. 'It would take some getting used to,' went on Patrick presently. 'It's a bit tragic, isn't it?'

'What does that mean?'

'I'm not sure.' Patrick closed the door of the stove again. 'It was all right at the beginning, the fast bit, but there was something underneath it, even then. And that last bit you played – I'd say it was depressing.'

'Oh,' said Davey, a little hurt. 'I thought it was magical.'

'Oh, quite probably. I'm not a magician or a musician. I wouldn't know.'

'You can play music. You opinion is more use to me than anyone else's.'

'Ask George. I'm only a drummer.'

'It's easier to talk to you. Patrick, I want you to think about it. What I played just now – that was only with one fiddle. When we both played, it goes in parts. Naomi said there were supposed to be four of them, to do it the way it was meant to be done.'

'You'd be lucky to get four fiddlers at once.' Patrick tied a leather apron round himself, and began to work the bellows.

'You never heard music like that when you were on the road south?'

Patrick shook his head. 'But then I wasn't looking for music. Also,' he added, 'it wouldn't be the sort of thing you'd hear. Every village must have its own things hidden from passers by. To be honest, I'm surprised she hands it on so freely.'

'It's not like that. She sees it as a gift.'

'And you'd make any woman feel generous,' said Patrick grinning. 'But a gift can be a danger too. If there's magic in it, as you say, and a sorrowful kind of magic too, from what you played to me, there could be a need for protection.'

'It seems harmless enough to me,' said Davey doubtfully. 'Who could it hurt?'

Patrick stopped pumping, and there was only the sound of the fire roaring in the chimney. 'I'll have to start work in a minute. No, don't go, Davey. I'd be glad of company. The others are bringing wood down today. Sit down.' Patrick began to lay his tools out methodically, and went on. 'I'm no good at explaining. Only, it's like that,' he nodded towards the gun which he kept on a rack on the wall. 'Like bringing that back. It's brought good to all of us, sure enough, but I wouldn't go lending it to your Molly. Or anyone else, for that matter.' Patrick picked up a pan with a hole in it, and examined it thoughtfully. 'Except perhaps you,' he added abruptly.

'No, you wouldn't,' said Davey comfortably, leaning back against the wall and testing the fiddlestrings. 'You know I wouldn't know what to do with it. But about the music, Patrick. Is that all you think about the music?'

'I'd be interested to know what you thought about the musician.'

'What's that got to do with it?' demanded Davey defensively.

'A good deal, I imagine. Oh, I'm not asking you. But I'd be interested to know where she got it from, and what path led her to it. I think you'd do well to be clear about that, for it could change things here in Clachanpluck.'

'It's beautiful.'

'What did you say?'

'The music. When I first heard it, all I thought was that it was beautiful.'

'Well, you would,' said Patrick, but not unkindly. 'All right, play it again if you like, before I have to start making a noise.'

'I was hoping you'd say that,' said Davey, getting up.

'So your bairn will be the next,' said Emily to Bridget. 'Come June.'

'I hope it's as easy as Alan was,' said Bridget, 'but I'm not as young. Sometimes I've wondered what I was about.'

'To decide on another, you mean? Well,' said Emily prosaically, 'you don't expect Alan to hold household on his own.'

'That wasn't why,' said Bridget. 'If Alan had no household of his own he'd not find it hard to join another. Those things don't bother me as much as they do you. I just wanted another, that was all.'

'But not Andrew's?'

Bridget shrugged. 'I love Andrew well enough,' she said. 'But bringing a child into this village, it's a better thing to bring in new blood. There's few enough of us as it is.'

'And Michael comes every year,' said Emily. 'Bringing spices and brown eyes to Clachanpluck. Does he know?'

'He knew what I wanted,' said Bridget. 'I was hoping it might be so last year. I don't doubt he'll be back in the autumn, but it's not important.'

'No,' said Emily thoughtfully. The two women sat by Bridget's fire sipping tea. They were both tired, for they had been up most of the night. A birth in Clachanpluck was not such a common event that it didn't hold significance for the whole village, and Ellen had given birth to a healthy daughter. There would be a fine feast at her naming. Boys were never spurned or neglected, but there was no denying that a daughter was an occasion for rejoicing, for it was upon daughters that the future depended. No woman would have a child she did not desire, because that would be cruel, but the fact was that the village needed people, and each one was welcome.

'I know you're right,' said Emily. 'We grow too close. I've brought no new blood into this village. You wouldn't choose Andrew to father your child, but I chose your brother for both of mine. After all, we're of different households, so it's not forbidden. How much do you think it matters?'

89

'It doesn't,' said Bridget, 'so long as there is some change. It's a pity your fiddle player can't give us a bairn to remember her by, but that could hardly be.'

'I don't know if she ever had one,' said Emily. 'She's very determined about having no family. Davey would like to be a lover to her, I think, but I don't suppose she encourages him.'

'And you shouldn't either,' said Bridget. 'She's too strong for him.'

'Does it matter? She'll be gone in spring.'

'Long enough to swallow a man,' said Bridget and chuckled. 'Half an hour would do, I think, if she chose to bewitch him.'

'I wouldn't know,' said Emily, cutting herself a large slice of fruit cake. 'I don't think I ever bewitched anybody.'

'I wouldn't be so sure,' muttered Bridget.

'What?' asked Emily, who was slightly deaf.

'You were right to choose George,' said Bridget to her, 'because you don't bewitch him. You don't realise how strong you are. What do you think about the fiddle player?'

'Me? How?'

'You're strong enough for her,' said Bridget. 'What does she offer to you?'

'Music,' said Emily promptly. 'Being able to express something that I want expressed. She heals me of frustration.'

'Emmy', said Bridget, 'I think it's you who should take care.'

'Why?'

'You're not used to asking for anything. It means you have no defences.'

'But no one wants to hurt me.'

'No one ever wanted to hurt anybody. But it happens.'

'Music never hurt anybody.'

'The musician is not the music.'

'That can't be true,' cried Emily, sitting up suddenly and sending a shower of crumbs into the hearth. 'It's all one. It all has to be one. It's like saying the people are different from the earth. What are we, if we're not what we create?'

'Calm down,' said Bridget, stolidly cutting cake. 'We are what we are, but only in the present. You know that. Her music is honest, while she plays it. But when the music is not there, there is still Naomi. You know that too. You're not static either. You're responding to something all the time. How else could you see in the dark and in the daylight? You expect that people should behave like rocks. Well, they don't, and certainly not the ones who play music. When you brought that woman here, you brought in fire, and I thought then it would mean a burning. But you chose to ignore it because she could seduce you with tunes. She did the same to me, and I never asked for it. Surely you know, Emily, that by doing this you've made everything different? Don't you know your own power?'

Emily flushed a little, but then she turned to her friend and smiled. 'And you told me to calm down?' she said ruefully. 'But haven't you done the same? To bring in Michael's child. Doesn't that change everything?'

'Michael is a different thing. He imposes nothing. He asks for nothing. He is willing to love and be loved. He's not afraid of our forest.'

'Is Naomi afraid of our forest?'

Bridget stared at her as blankly as if Emily had just asked whether the sun rose in the morning. 'Sometimes,' she said hollowly, 'I just wonder if you're all right.'

'Thanks,' said Emily, grinning, and helped herself to more cake. 'I take it I should have noticed?'

'With regard to what we hold here in Clachanpluck?' said Bridget slowly. 'I'm quite certain that you should.'

12

Two people climbed up the hill into the forest, along a track that forked off from the road to the west. Up here, only a mile from the village, a thin sprinkling of snow was lying, so that the walkers left clear tracks behind them; two pairs of boots with identical soles, one pair large, one small, and between them the parallel ridges of an empty sledge that left only the faintest grooves behind it. Presently the prints left the track and followed a winding path up through the grey trunks of beeches where the ground was clear of scrub. The hill began to slope steeply, and the going was rough in places, so that they left broken snow and skid marks in their wake, exposing grey streaks of rock.

They did not travel quietly; the smaller person was talking all the time, rather breathlessly in difficult places, but never subdued for a moment. Her companion's replies were much briefer, and less penetrating, but always to the point. Emily was a good listener on the whole.

Molly stopped on a rock and scraped up a handful of snow, which she nibbled delicately, chattering the while. 'If you wanted to stay in the forest in winter,' she remarked, 'you could always live on snow. Could you live on snow, Emily?'

'No. It's not food, only water.'

'But you can crunch it. It's more food than water.'

'There's nothing in it but water. If you had a fire you could melt it, and you'd never be short of drink. But it doesn't taste very nice.'

'Have you drunk it?'

'Yes.'

'But if you did need something to eat, you could put it on a plate and eat it with a spoon and then it would be food, wouldn't it? Except it isn't the right colour. It would stop you being hungry more if it was a different colour.'

'Yes,' said Emily absently, scanning the hillside. 'We need to be over that way.'

'Things would taste different if they weren't the same colour,' went on Molly. Perhaps they would, thought Emily. Or feel different. But red hair would hardly feel different from brown, though it might look as though it would. It would feel different because it was curly. Molly's hair was thick and straight and mouse-coloured, very soft to the touch. Emily turned and lifted the dragging sledge over a tangle of tree roots. Molly needs a haircut anyway, she thought, her fringe is almost in her eyes. And Fiona has chopped all of hers off, although, or probably because, it was so fair and beautiful, like George's when he was the age that she is now. A small hot hand grabbed hers, and tugged it for attention.

'I said, can food ever be blue?' demanded Molly.

Emily gave the matter her attention. 'Bilberries?' she suggested.

'Bilberries are purple.'

'No, then, I can't think of any.'

I've brought no new blood into this village, thought Emily. It was George and I that stayed out in the forest in winter, and when the burn froze we melted snow to drink, and kept each other warm. It seems a very uncomfortable thing to do now. Is that what twenty years have done for me? I haven't thought much about anyone who wasn't there already, not for a long time. I've been doing other things than bothering about new people, for more years than seem possible, when I think about it. Emily became aware that the chatter beside her had taken on a questioning note, increasingly insistent.

'Yes,' said Emily, at a guess.

'I said,' said Molly patiently, 'have you ever eaten a worm?'

'Have I what?'

'Eaten a worm?'

'No, I can't say I have. Why?'

'I was wondering what it would taste like.'

'Gritty, I should think. And chewy on the outside.'

'Why gritty?'

'Because the earth goes through them.'

'I don't think I'd like that.'

'Nor me. See that green? That'll be the special holly.'

'Then we're nearly there,' said Molly, pleased. 'Have you ever eaten a caterpillar?'

'Not on purpose.'

'How could you eat one not on purpose?'

'They're fairly easy to miss. You probably have too.'

'Ugh!' shrieked Molly, doubling up. 'Ugh! That's horrible. I haven't! I'm going to be sick!'

'It hardly seems necessary. There couldn't have been one in your porridge this morning.'

'Are you sure?'

'Positive. Look, we're here.'

They were standing in front of a tall holly. It was worth coming all this way for, being quite unlike any that grew near the village. Its leaves were bright and polished-looking, but different, being of two colours, familiar dark green in the middle and bright yellow round the edges. There was no tree like it anywhere near Clachanpluck, and among the stripped trunks of the dormant beeches it seemed quite magical. There were berries now among the patterned leaves, like beads of blood.

Emily pulled up the sledge at the foot of the tree, and stood before it. Molly took a serviceable knife from her belt.

'Wait,' called Emily. 'Look at it.' Molly looked obediently. 'It's a gift. I don't know if it was given by the forest, or made like that by an art which existed in the past. I don't know much about that. But it's like this in midwinter, bearing all the colours of summer, and that's important to us. We have to acknowledge that before we take what we came for.'

'I want to climb up. There's much more berries at the top.'

'You can. Remember it's alive, that's all.'

'Will you give me a leg up?'

Emily hoisted her up into the tree, and Molly scrabbled for a branch, caught it and swung herself up. She hugged the trunk and pulled herself upright, then began to climb fast, close to the trunk, hampered a little by the boots she had to wear in winter, but still very quick and neat. Emily sat cross-legged at the foot of the tree, and leaned back against the trunk, staring up into the bright branches.

'Aren't you going to cut any?'

'Give me a minute.' Emily stood up slowly, and called up, 'Remember to cut at a join, so's not to hurt the tree. And only one from each place.'

'I know!'

A couple of prickly stems, laden with berries, landed at the foot of the tree. Emily laid them on the sledge, took out her own knife and began to reach down branches, selecting carefully, laying the cut pieces on the ground as she circled the tree.

'It's really hard from the middle,' called the voice above her. 'I've done the top. I've got to get out sideways a bit.'

Emily glanced up. Molly was nearly at the top of the tree. She could see a pair of scuffed boots and lichen-stained trousers, then a small body in a brown jacket, edging its way along a skinny branch towards thin air. Emily felt a slight lurch in her stomach, but refrained from saying anything pointless. 'Just bear in mind it could be slippery in this weather,' she remarked casually.

'I know that!'

Emily stopped watching, and continued to work her way methodically round the foot of the tree. More twigs descended from above, landing almost on top of her. She laid them with the others, and went on cutting. 'What would happen if we didn't have midwinter?' asked Molly chattily.

'How do you mean?'

'We would have to live on snow for ever,' said Molly. 'And flour and potatoes because they never run out. Do they?'

'At least there wouldn't be any caterpillars.'

'I can't get any more from here.' There was a rustle in the branches above, and a pause. 'I'm stuck,' said Molly.

'No, you're not,' said Emily with conviction. 'Think about something else for a minute, then decide which hand or foot to move next.'

There was a very short pause. 'I can't.'

'Yes you can. Do you feel safe where you are?'

'Yes, but I can't move.'

'That's all right. Keep still. Think about each hand, then each foot. You'll find a place for one of them, then you'll be all right.'

'I can't!' said Molly on a higher note.

'Are you quite sure?'

'Yes!'

Emily put down her knife and pulled herself up into the tree. She had none of Molly's lightness or agility, but she climbed with a steady efficiency that came from long experience.

'Are you coming?' called Molly anxiously.

'Yes. Slowly, that's all. I'm a bit out of practice.' Emily eased her

95

way up until her head was level with Molly's feet. The branches grew close together up here, and there wasn't much space for her. 'All right. I'm here. There's a place for your foot. Hold tight, and I'll guide it down.'

'I can't reach!'

'It's only a couple of inches. If you let go I'll catch you. That's it. Now the other one. All right? Now let go.' Molly slithered down in front of her. 'I'll go down a bit further, then you can follow. All right?'

When they reached the bottom Emily jumped down with a thud, and turned to catch her daughter. Molly's face was smeared with bark and lichen, but she was no longer shaky. As soon as her feet touched the ground she began to talk again.

'Yes,' said Emily. 'Now let's pick up what we've got.'

It was an impressive sledgeful. They tied it up with twine and surveyed it together.

'No one else has holly as good as this,' said Molly with satisfaction.

'No, but they will if you start telling them all which way we came.'

'Oh, I won't do that,' said Molly confidently, and went on talking.

13

There was once a child who was alone in the world. Days followed nights, and summer followed winter, and the child was delighted by it all, for it knew that whatever happened on earth it was all one. The child lived on its own, and wandered through the forest, and swam in the water. It climbed to the hilltops, and slept in the shelter of the trees below, and there was no place in all the world to which it did not belong.

But at last some people came that way and found the child, and said to it, 'You cannot live like this. You have to make a choice. Either you can be a creature of the day, fearing the dark, and sleeping away your time through the long nights of winter. Or you can belong to the night, where nothing is made plain, where there are no horizons, only the sound of unknown creatures moving through the dark.'

So the child struggled with this choice and thought, 'Which am I to be? Which can I bear to lose? For the pain of giving up either seems to be too great. Never to know the daylight, never to feel the warmth of the sun on my skin, never to see the ridges of the hills, or the place where distant mountains merge into the sky? Or never to walk in the dark with my ears open, and the smells of the night reaching me on the wind, never to watch the moon change, or other worlds circling in a silent sky? How can I make such a choice? How can I give up so much of what I am?'

The choice hung over the child like a huge burden, the weight of generations of grief from which there seemed to be no escape. So when the child went to give the people their answer, it fought against the fate that was offered it, and said, 'No! I cannot give up half my life. I will not make this choice. I cannot live without the day. I cannot live without the night. I will not choose!'

But then they told the child the bitter truth. 'But you have no choice. You never had a choice. You must belong either to the day or to the night, and you are already branded. You bear the signs in your body, and have done from the moment that you were conceived. You see before you the people of the day, and the other people who belong to the night. You see your own body, which you cannot deny. You are already what you are.'

The child cried out in its last moment of power, 'But I am everything. I am the day and the night. I am the moon and stars and sun. I am dark earth and translucent air. I flow for ever from the hills to the unending sea, and I am the land that lies naked under the summer sky. Everything that is is within me, and I belong to everything which is this world.'

So the child stood before the people, unaware that it was small and helpless, not knowing that it could not do anything alone, still believing that the world was new and waiting to receive it. It stood there in its last moment of innocence, before it was struck down.

We have to remember, we who have inherited what was made to happen then, that not one of the people had accepted it. Not one of them had given in without a struggle. Not one had made that choice, but each was forced to it. Nobody ever denied the day, or renounced the night. We hate what they did, we mourn what they destroyed, we bleed for the wounds inflicted upon our world, but we have to understand.

At midwinter everyone in Clachanpluck went into the forest and brought down evergreens for their houses. They came home laden with young spruce trees, cuttings of ivy and holly, and yew bright with berries. They used the branches to decorate their houses, and on the shortest day of the year they set lamps in their windows to burn throughout the festival as a token of the light that never goes out. Huge fires were built in the hearths and fed with logs of beech and holly and apple wood, so that sweet-smelling smoke hung over the village like wreaths of incense. December had been dark and wet, beset by gales blowing unceasing rain in from the west, but at the solstice the sky cleared to reveal a waxing moon that dimmed the cold stars around it. The stars had shifted since last they were visible, and the Hunter lay further to the south than when Naomi arrived in Clachanpluck, the three jewels of his belt shining palely through the light of the rising moon.

With the stars came the frost, and suddenly the thick mud in the yards and the sodden puddles on the tracks were frozen hard in jagged ruts of wheels and hooves and footprints. The fields were white with frost and the cattle gathered at the gates, standing patiently huddled in the frozen air, waiting for their winter feed. Beyond the fields the forest was silent and motionless, open to the stars.

When the sun went down in the afternoon the celebrations began. On the longest night the fires could not be allowed to die down nor the lamps be dimmed until the sun was reborn in the eastern sky. This was the night of watching, for the sun must be brought back again into the world, and the circle completed.

Fiona stood on the little hill that overlooked the fields of their own farm to the north-east of the village. From here the houses appeared as a huddle of white rooftops, crowded together in their sheltered fold among the wooded hills. Dusk was falling fast, and already the sun had vanished behind the ridge to the west. There was a wind coming down from the north, bringing the smell of snow. Fiona turned her face to it so that her eyes watered, and saw a patch of loch, the hills beyond it white under the darkening sky. The North Star was out, and the Plough pointing it out was slowly becoming visible. A strain of music drifted up from the village, carried over the fields in the icy air. Down below in the houses the first circles would be forming.

The light was almost gone, a faint tired light it was now, a mere ghost of the year past, dimming away into nothing. The hills were still white with moonlight. There was a warmer light down in the village, a soft haze of lamplight and firelight, with no power to carry out over the night air. Fiona took one last look over the forest, and began to climb down carefully over the slippery ground. It would be a long night, and a cold birth. She was glad she had come out, but it was too cold to stay.

Davey was very hot. He had stripped off his thick jacket, and was playing dressed only in his best shirt and trousers. The firelight gleamed on his shining face, and his cheeks were red as flames. Between sets he stopped only for a drink of sweet wine, and to wipe his hands on his hair so that it stood up over his forehead, before he saw Naomi reach for her fiddle again and he had to follow suit. She never seemed to tire, this woman, never made a mistake, never flagged for a moment. It didn't disconcert her to have forty people dancing to her tune, any more than to play to the silent stacked-up hay that absorbed her notes like a sponge, and gave nothing back. The people gave back plenty. They danced like dervishes, and when she stopped they paused only to applaud her and themselves, and when she picked up her bow again they were there waiting for her, to do whatever she called them to do.

Davey watched her all the time. He watched her while they played, never taking his eyes off her, for to lose contact for a moment would be to break the spell, to step out of the circle and find himself alone in the dark, the music lost for ever. Tonight she looked like the flames themselves, dressed all in red and gold and yellow, her clothes bound together with silver thread that glinted in the lamplight. There was something in her red hair that glittered too, and her eyes were bright as stars. She held his gaze, and went on playing, daring him to keep up with her, laughing at him, or with him, or through him. She never seemed to get too hot, while the sweat dripped off him and he could feel his shirt sticking to his back. She didn't drink much either. Davey had a good head for drink, but tonight he felt unreal. The rest of the company seemed to have swum out of focus, blurred shapes outside the ring of light, that responded to the swirling tunes but were not part of their creation. The spell of the night was being woven by Naomi, and by him, and there was no one else at all.

Fiona slipped in through the door from the yard, and the heat hit her like a wave. She blinked in the lamplight, kicking her boots off.

'Hello,' said Anna in her ear, before she could gather her usual reserve. The sharp wind and the brightness of the night still held her; Fiona turned and smiled at her friend, awake and aroused and happy. Anna was quite taken aback, as if, intending to speak to her familiar unemotional friend, she had found herself confronted by a very different person. She's getting like Emily, thought Anna, but was far too tactful to say so.

'Hello,' said Fiona. 'How's the party?'

Anna shrugged. 'Same as usual, I suppose.'

'What's the matter? I thought you'd be dancing till dawn and all that.'

'I don't know,' said Anna. 'I'm not bothered.'

Fiona looked round to try to account for this extraordinary statement. There was a short break in the music. The dancers had collapsed on the benches or withdrawn into small knots. The floor was momentarily empty, so she could see right across to the fireplace and the musicians beside it. She saw Naomi at once, standing right in front of the fire, dressed more fantastically than ever. Fiona recognised the shiny gold material that Emily had once bought from a pedlar and had pinned on her bedroom wall for a while to remind her, she said, that such colours existed. Naomi had certainly made good use of it. Fiona hadn't realised that Emily had given it away. She frowned a little. Then she saw Davey. He was wearing his best green shirt and looked hot and excited. He didn't take his eyes off Naomi for a moment. Fiona watched him reach for his mug, fumbling like a blind man, and drink from it almost without noticing, all the time watching the fiddle player. Fiona frowned again. Then she marched across to the fireplace and tweaked her uncle's sleeve.

'Davey. I want to dance with you.'

'What?' he said, looking round blankly. 'Oh well, I'm playing. Can't you dance with Anna?'

'I may only be family,' said Fiona, 'but that won't do. I'm a person. I count.'

'I'm sorry,' said Davey, blinking. 'All right. Yes. Just let me tell her.'

She waited while he spoke to Naomi, who nodded carelessly and turned to pick up her fiddle. Davey stepped away from the hearth. There was an immediate surge of aspiring musicians and a hurried consultation.

'You're not even indispensable,' remarked Fiona. 'Do you mind?'

He smiled and shook his head at her. Away from the fire he looked a little cooler, and was quite prepared to be sociable. Someone called a reel, and she led him into a forming circle.

Fiona and Davey danced very easily together. After all, he had taught her how to do it almost as soon as she could walk. Anna had refused to dance, and sat watching them thoughtfully. She had never seen Fiona so animated. Naturally she hadn't bothered to dress up, but her trousers were patched and clean, and halfway through the dance she pulled off her jersey in one swift movement and revealed a very tight black shirt she must have grown out of years ago. Anna was quite sure that Fiona had never given the matter a thought, but she actually looked very good in it. She danced very well, and her face was flushed and eager. And the only man she asks is her uncle, thought Anna. I don't understand her at all.

When the reel was done the ring broke, and Anna suddenly found both Fiona and Davey beside her. 'I'm hot,' said Fiona. 'Give me some of your drink, Anna. I need a rest. You can go next.'

'I'm not sure I feel like it,' said Anna, not looking at Davey.

'Tough,' said Fiona. 'He needs the exercise. I'll be back in a minute.' She grabbed her jersey and disappeared through the yard door.

It was very dark after the bright light indoors, and piercingly cold. Fiona turned her jersey right side out and put it on slowly. In the small squares of light from the windows snowflakes were dancing, caught and held for a moment in the patch of light, then drifting on silently into the dark. The sky was still clear, but the wind was blowing harder. There was a scrunch of footsteps on snow, and Fiona looked round. A tall figure was revealed in the light from the first window, whom Fiona recognised at once.

'Hello, George,' she said softly.

He started. 'Fiona?'

'Yes.'

He came and stood beside her. 'What are you doing out here? It's freezing.'

'I like it.'

'I can understand that. I just came in from the hill. How's the party?'

'I was only there for a reel.'

There was a companionable silence between them. The dance of the snow in the light grew wilder and thicker as a flurry of wind drove across the yard. The two of them huddled back in the shelter of the doorway, and the music within filtered through to them like a call from another country. Across the yard, where the gate opened on to the fields, there was a copse of beech trees. They stood facing it, while the wind rustled the branches and whispered among still-clinging brown leaves. Pale moonlight illuminated ground carpeted in white. The beech trees moaned in the wind, or perhaps it was not merely the wind. There was a strange darkness in their shadow, as if they cast the shade not of bare branches but of a full canopy of summer leaves, dense enough to block out moonlight. George and Fiona watched silently. The rustling of the leaves was louder now, not thin and skeletal, but full-bodied and vigorous, and the scent of leaves was in the air. The light among the leaves was green and vibrant, bright as mosses on the forest floor in summer. The breeze stirred the leaves and shifted them; there was a point of blueness clear as the sky in maytime, so that their eyes, attuned to moonlight, were dazzled and they turned away, blinking. When they looked up again there was only the moonlight on the snow, and a red blur in front of their eyes like an image of vanished light.

It was Fiona who finally broke the silence. 'George?'

'Ay?'

'Do you know a place where there's a brown pool, and a waterfall with a rowan, and a crack in the rock beside it?'

'It's not the place that matters,' said George. 'You should know that.'

'Perhaps I do. But it's the way other people have taken.'

'You take your way,' said George.

'But you understand?'

'Not everything.' There was a pause, then he said, 'Did Emily show you her book?'

'Which one? The one about Clachanpluck?'

'Ah, then she told you.'

'I can't read,' said Fiona. 'I never saw any point.'

'Nor can I. But I remember the last bit she read me:

'And what you do not know is the only thing you know
And what you own is what you do not own
And where you are is where you are not.'

'I don't think I understand,' said Fiona.

'That seems a good place to begin,' said George.

Emily sat on the table among the mugs and wine jugs, letting the gold chain round her neck run through her fingers, the sapphire twisting and winking in the lamplight with sparks of brilliant blue. The band was playing now. Anna and Davey weren't there, but they were hardly missed because there was the fiddle player instead. There had been music all evening and there had been dancing. Emily loved to dance. She wasn't graceful, not like her daughter, but she was wild and enthusiastic, and given a partner whom she didn't have to be careful of she would use all the energy she had and let the music take her. She was out of breath now, and they were playing slower music with more complicated dance steps that she was no good at. It was better when the beat was obvious, best of all when Patrick spelt it out with his drum, creating an undercurrent like a heartbeat that her feet could move to without effort. Emily avoided dancing with her brother. 'Can't you hear the time?' Davey would demand. 'You can't not hear it. Listen. Listen to the beat.' She would say, 'But I don't hear anything at all.' 'But you can't not. It just is.' Better not to dance with Davey, he made her nervous. Andrew was more patient, and he could balance her weight.

It was a good feast. There would be celebrations at every house in the village over the next twelve days, but Emily's was always the first. The end of one year and the beginning of another. Emily sat back and watched her daughters. Molly was looking wild and dishevelled, her straight mousy hair all standing up on end and her freckled face unusually pink. She had danced all evening, demanding to be partnered by every friend in turn. Molly secretly admired the fiddle player, and had accordingly decked herself out in unusual finery. Over her shirt and trousers she had adorned herself with lace and ribbons which she had found somewhere, maybe begged off Bridget who kept such odds and ends. Alan, not to be outdone, had tied red ribbons in his hair, and looked more like a changeling than ever. He was barefoot by this time, and shirtless. His skin was very brown. Emily had a sudden image of the herb pedlar, and a pang of realisation that Bridget had been receptive to something that she had missed, a breath of outside air, a knowledge of something outwith the forest. Emily glanced at Naomi, and understood at last that there was something here that she had failed to face. I have not been courageous, thought Emily, and condemned herself instantly. I love her, and I dare not say so. I love her brightness, the light she sheds on things I have never been able to illuminate. She draws me to her, and I would like to stretch out my hand and touch that hair which would feel so different from my own. She has what we do not have here in Clachanpluck. But I know what this place is, and she is as afraid of me as I am afraid of her. She is afraid that Clachanpluck will drown her, bury her, extinguish her, swallow up the music as if it were nothing but a dream. I can't let her go on believing that. When the dance is over I will tell her how it can be different.

Fiona was different. Emily let her gaze follow her elder daughter. Fiona was drifting among the dancers, self-sufficient and self-contained. She was aware of nobody's eyes upon her, and she demanded nothing of any of them. She was dancing to a pattern of her own, moving through a dream as if there were nothing in the room but herself and the music and her own thoughts. People watched her, and it was not surprising, because she was beautiful to look at when she forgot that any eyes were upon her. She hears the beat, or the time, or whatever it is, thought Emily. I wonder if she knows she hears it?

No wonder Davey was proud of her. But Davey was nowhere to be seen. He had been dancing with Anna for a long time, with relish, Emily suspected. Davey seldom got a break from playing music, so maybe he was glad of a chance to be one of the dancers himself. It drew him back into the circle, and he must miss that sometimes. Emily had thought him fascinated by the fiddle player and, remembering Bridget's warning, had been glad that he had eyes for someone else. She wondered vaguely about Anna until her thoughts were interrupted. 'Emily?'

She turned and saw George, and smiled warmly at him. 'Where have you been?'

'Out,' he said. 'The forest is very near tonight.'

'It would be,' she replied. 'But I was waiting for the moon.'

'Five days,' said George. 'This is a good feast, Emmy.'

'I feel detached. A good feast, but not so much my own any more.'

'Your daughter is a beautiful dancer,' said George. 'And she knows how to be alone. You couldn't have passed on anything better than that.'

'I didn't pass on the dancing.'

'I meant the other. Do you want me to stay tonight?'

'I don't know. There's something complicated I need to think about. Bridget gave me a warning.'

'About the fiddle player?'

'And about myself, I think. Maybe tomorrow.'

'There's nothing wrong with you except too much curiosity,' said George. 'Don't get burnt.'

'Am I likely to?'

'Not with me. I'll come tomorrow.'

Davey's room was quite unexpected. As far as furnishings went it was very bare and ordinary, without even a rug on the floor, and a couple of wooden boxes taking the place of carved chests. It was extremely cold; although there was a homemade woodstove in the fireplace with logs piled beside it, there was no fire lit. The bed was pushed up close to the fire, close enough to put wood in the stove without getting up, and an oil lamp and a tinder box lay on the floor beside it.

What was unusual were the wall paintings.

They were very carefully drawn, and coloured in delicate shades of red, pink, flame, white and crimson. They covered three sides of the room, the three bare walls away from the gable that had the stove set in it, interrupted only by two low windows that overlooked the yard. The paintings were all of flowers. Anna walked closer to inspect. Davey hesitated, then followed her, holding the candle he had brought upstairs higher so that she could see better.

They were all of roses, but no two were the same. There were trailing tendrils of ordinary briar roses, the sort that grew along the hedgerows. There were dark red roses thickset on bushes, the sort that made garden hedges or grew outside people's doors. There were small white roses on climbing stems, and fat flame-coloured roses on sharply pruned bushes. Anna remembered that there was a flower garden attached to this house, and that roses grew there in summer, but not half as many as these. She looked round at the three walls that surrounded her like a thorn hedge, and then her eyes turned to Davey in bewilderment. 'I like them,' she said, 'but why? Why roses?'

He hesitated again, then evidently made a decision. 'I'll show you.' He went over to one of the boxes, taking the candle with him so that she was left in semi-darkness with the shadows of roses all round her. Davey rummaged in the box for a moment, and drew out something very carefully. 'See here,' he said. 'I have a book of my own too.'

Anna looked at him with respect. 'Can you read?'

'Not much,' admitted Davey. 'But this isn't words. Look.'

It was a very heavy book, heavier than the ones Emily had which Fiona had shown her. It had been wrapped in a dark cloth, and the binding was still good. The cover had faded to a dull beige. Anna sat beside Davey on the bed, and took the book gingerly. 'Open it,' he said.

The book had pictures in it. Anna gave an involuntary gasp for she recognised the pictures. They were roses. More different kinds of roses than she had ever imagined existing in the world. Each page was very big, about twice the size of Emily's books, and instead of being covered with black squiggles they were laid out with pictures in delicate faded colours. There were bits of writing in between, but these were unobtrusive and not necessary. The point of the book was quite clearly the roses. Very carefully Anna turned the pages. The paper was old and soft. Sometimes the edges stuck together so she had to blow them gently apart. There were so many sorts of roses. They grew on bushes, on climbing stems, on little trees, on angular bare bushes. They came in every possible colour that a rose could be, but all muted, for the pictures had mellowed with time and the colours were softened with so many passing years.

'But surely,' said Anna eventually, 'surely there aren't as many roses in the world as this?'

'I don't think so,' said Davey. 'Not now.'

'But were there ever?'

He shrugged.

'I never knew you had a book,' said Anna.

'I bought it,' said Davey. 'Five years ago, in Carlingwark.'

'Wasn't it very expensive?'

'Yes.'

'But worth it to you.'

'I've not done paying yet,' said Davey. 'It'll take me five more years.'

'How do you manage that?'

'In the spring I take what goods I have gathered to Carlingwark, so much a year. It's made me a poorer man, but I don't regret it.'

'But why? You can't grow them yourself. Not if they don't exist any more.'

Davey shrugged.

'And then you painted the walls?'

'Yes.'

'I do understand, I think,' said Anna. 'It's an image of a garden that might have been if you had lived in the same time as the plants.'

'I don't know,' said Davey. 'I was never much of a gardener.'

'I like gardening,' said Anna. 'When I've been to Carlingwark I've looked for flower seeds. There aren't often different ones from what we have. I never thought of wanting a book.'

'No. I shouldn't think you're such a fool.'

'But you're not a fool!'

'Chasing rainbows,' said Davey. 'What do you grow in your garden?'

'You mean flowers? Oh, all sorts. I'll show you in the spring. Why?'

'I don't know,' said Davey. 'Why weren't you playing in the band tonight?'

It was Anna's turn to shrug. 'Didn't feel like it.'

'Did you bring your flute?'

'No.'

There was a silence. Anna sat perched on the edge of Davey's bed, hugging her knees to her chest. Her nose was pink-tipped with cold, and she was shivering a little. Davey leaned back on his elbow and watched her. He looked puzzled, and indeed confusion raged inside him. He couldn't expect her to deal with that. She was very young, not much older than Fiona. Her cheeks were still rounded like a child's, but her profile was determined enough. He studied her thoughtfully. It was difficult after knowing her for so long as a child, the friend of Fiona, to take in that she was a woman. Not a stupid or insensitive woman either. She was very unlike Naomi. Anna was not very tall, and her body had a roundness to it quite unlike Naomi's angular figure. There was nothing dramatic about Anna. Her hair was thick and curly, but of a soft brown, and her eyes were round and blue. Just now she looked unhappy. Davey cleared his throat.

'What are you thinking about?' he asked, thinking at the same time that it was a singularly stupid question.

A thought rose to the forefront of Anna's mind and she dismissed it instantly. Davey saw a faint flush rise to her cheeks. 'Fiona,' said Anna instead.

'What about her?'

'Not needing anybody,' said Anna. 'But you're different.'

'You mean I need people?'

'Most people do,' said Anna, and shivered.

'I don't know,' said Davey. 'Sometimes I think I want most in the world to be a musician. But I never want to lose Clachanpluck. This is where I belong.'

'I don't think that answers the question.'

'Was there a question?'

'I don't know,' said Anna, and was silent again, as if he had struck her.

Tentatively Davey reached out and touched her hand. 'I'm sorry,' he said. 'I'm confused. What do you want of me?'

A long silence. 'I want to know what you feel about me,' said Anna, and didn't meet his eyes.

Davey thought about that, and the clouds of confusion parted a little in his mind, and something at least appeared to be clear. 'You're not the only person I love,' he said. 'But I love you.'

Anna turned scarlet. She wouldn't look at him, but he watched her averted cheek burning red, then he sat up beside her. 'It's not really that complicated,' he said, 'if you tell me what you want.'

A very long silence. 'I want to be loved,' said Anna.

The beat of the drum echoed through the house, penetrating far beyond the tunes that accompanied it, echoing between the buildings, vibrating through stone walls and wooden floors, and drifting out into the night in persistent rhythm. Only when a pale light showed again in the east did the drum cease to beat, and the last revellers departed. Patrick stood up and looked about him at the emptying room, staggering a little, although being absorbed in the drumming he had had little to drink.

The party was over. The dancers had gone, and the long room was littered with dirty mugs and jars, the disordered furniture pushed back against the walls. The rest of the band were packing away their instruments. The fire had died down to a heap of glowing ashes, and beside it the fiddle player stood with her back to him, staring down into the last red embers.

Patrick looked round, and gradually people and place swam back into focus, and his mind concentrated again upon the present. Most people had already gone. He regarded the departing visitors closely, but did not see what he was looking for. He turned to the fiddle player.

'Where's Davey?' he asked her. 'I thought he was coming back.'

Naomi looked up vaguely. 'Davey?' she repeated. 'I don't know. He was dancing earlier.'

'I noticed,' said Patrick grimly, and said no more. Naomi picked up her fiddle. 'Good night,' she said.

'Good night,' said Patrick, then turned swiftly back to her. 'Could you give him a message?' he asked.

'Davey?' said Naomi again. 'I doubt if I'll see him. I'll sleep late, and he usually goes out early. But I will if I can.'

Patrick shook his head. 'Doesn't matter,' he muttered, turning his back.

Naomi left, but just as Patrick was leaving Fiona appeared, draped in a blanket, apparently on her way to bed. Patrick barred her way and demanded, 'Fiona, where's Anna? Did she go home?'

'I suppose so,' said Fiona. 'Why?'

'She was supposed to play tonight. I saw her dancing, then she left. And she promised.'

'I don't know,' said Fiona. 'She's not staying with me. I suppose she went home.'

Patrick still barred her way. 'You don't suppose she stayed here with anyone else?'

'It's her business if she did. I'm going to bed. Can I pass, please?'

'Are you not telling me something?'

'I'm not lying to you,' said Fiona impatiently. 'I don't know what I don't know. And I don't want to know either. Excuse me.'

'She's your friend.'

'Of course. And she's not with me. I think you should go home.'

'I need to know where she is.'

'Why?'

'Because she made a promise.'

'I don't know anything about that either. So please stop asking me and let me go.'

Patrick stood back, but as she was passing him he grabbed her sleeve and said, 'Fiona, I've a right to feel hurt. I was promised. Please, tell me, did you see Davey?'

'Not for hours,' said Fiona more patiently. 'Patrick, don't ask me. I know nothing about this sort of thing, and I'm not sure I want to. Look for her in the morning. If Anna owes you an explanation, she'll give it. She's not mean, you know that. There's nothing to be done tonight.'

'Would you not just look in and see if Davey's there?'

'No,' said Fiona firmly. 'I would not. Good night, Patrick. Sort it out tomorrow. There's nothing else you can do.'

He let go her sleeve then. She slipped past him like a shadow, and went upstairs to her own bed.

14

'It's only us,' called Emily, as someone came into the kitchen and obviously hesitated. 'Come round by the fire.'

Naomi walked round the clothes horse which was draped with a blanket to keep the draught out. The stove door was wide open, and flames roared inside. Molly sat in a tub of water in front of it, her skin glowing pink in the reflected colour of the fire. Her eyes were screwed up tightly and she was holding her nose. Emily had a jug of water in her hand, and was trying to rinse the soap out of Molly's hair.

'Ow, that's hot!'

'I'll put more cold in.' Emily nodded to Naomi. 'Sit down. This won't take a minute.'

'Now it's too cold!'

'Tough. It's nearly done, anyway. Lean back.'

'It's in my eyes!'

'It's done. Stand up.'

Molly stood up, and Emily rubbed her head with a towel so hard that Naomi felt her own eyes water in sympathy, but Molly seemed undaunted. 'That was horrible,' she said cheerfully. 'Can I get out now?'

She took a warm towel from above the stove, and draped it round herself. Emily scooped a bucketful of water out of the bath. 'I'll just empty this out, then I'll comb your hair.'

'No! I'll do it.'

'You never do.'

'I will! You'll hurt.'

Emily disappeared with the bucket of water. Molly dried the end of her nose, and she and Naomi looked at each other.

'I'll do it if you like. I can try not to hurt,' offered Naomi diffidently. Molly had already struck her as one of the most self-possessed people in Clachanpluck, and while it was easy to know how to teach anyone to play the fiddle, it was not so easy to know if helping them to brush their hair would be an insult.

'Will you?' said Molly at once. 'Emily pulls.'

She dragged over a stool and sat at Naomi's feet, curling herself up comfortably against her knees. She seemed very small and solid. Naomi took the brush tentatively, and applied her mind to the mass of wet tangles. She felt ridiculously shy, but Molly had no such inhibitions.

'I have to have it cut too,' she remarked. 'Who cuts your hair, Naomi?'

'I do,' said Naomi, untangling a knot.

'How do you do the back?'

'With difficulty.'

'Ow!'

'Sorry.'

'You're better than Emily,' said Molly kindly. 'Perhaps you've had more practice.'

'No.'

Emily reappeared with an empty bucket. 'It's snowing again,' she said. 'Oh. Thank you.' She picked up the bath, and staggered out into the yard again. She was gone for some time. For once Molly was silent, gazing into the fire. Naomi concentrated on her task, and gradually relaxed. 'There you are,' she said presently.

'Will you cut my fringe?'

'Maybe Emily wants to do it.'

'It's my fringe.'

'True. Where're the scissors, then?'

When Emily came back Molly was dressed in a clean and tattered nightshirt, looking very scrubbed and clean, with trim damp hair. 'I'm done,' she announced. 'So you don't have to come near me now.'

'What a relief. Sit by the fire while your hair dries.' Emily mopped the floor perfunctorily, then sank down in the chair on the other side of the fire. 'Thanks,' she said to Naomi. 'Were you looking for me?'

'Not particularly. I just came back from a walk. To the edge of the forest,' said Naomi, and there was a hint of a question in her words.

'Yes,' said Emily. 'I remember you mentioned the forest when you first came.'

'Did I? I don't remember. I said something to Alan.'

Molly looked up at the mention of her friend's name, but they seemed absorbed in other matters. She draped a blanket round herself, and went to sit on Emily's knee. Emily settled herself more comfortably, and Molly lay back, watching the fire with sleepy eyes.

'You said that you wanted to understand.'

Naomi looked at them both, then she too averted her gaze to the fire, and brought herself back to the subject with an effort. 'Naturally I would like to understand.' There was a gust of wind, and the fire roared in the chimney. Unbidden memories receded, to be replaced by a sharp image of the forest as she had first encountered it. Emily was quite right. She had not ceased from the moment she had come here to wish to understand.

'I would like to be able to explain it all to you,' Emily was saying. 'But I have no words, and in any case the secret, if it is a secret, isn't mine. Can you understand that?'

'I understand that words only go so far,' said Naomi. 'The rest, no. But I never thought you owed me an explanation.'

'I don't think I owe you anything,' said Emily. 'Only we affect one another.'

'But your life is untouched by mine,' said Naomi. 'I bring you the music, certainly, but when the spring comes I shall be gone, and you'll sow your seeds without me, as you have always done. It's not easy to be here. I feel as if I don't exist, just a sound or a trick of the light that casts no shadow. You're all very civil to me, but you hold whatever matters inside yourselves, and you don't reflect anything back.'

'I'm trying to tell you something that matters now. But perhaps you don't see it. We're too much opposites, I think.'

'Opposites attract,' remarked Naomi.

'Meaning?'

'Beyond all opposites there is something which is the same.'

'And we are the same,' agreed Emily. 'I knew that the first time I saw you. Did you?'

'I was confused.'

'By what?'

'You'd just come off the fields, I think. You were in your working clothes, and you smelled of earth and muck.' Emily grinned. 'And then I saw what you wore round your neck.'

Emily reached her hand down the neck of her jersey and pulled the gold chain over her head. The blue stone swung gently from its chain. If I opened the stove again a little, thought Naomi, it would sparkle bright azure in the firelight. She remained where she was and took the stone from Emily's hand outstretched across the hearth. The jewel was surprisingly heavy, or perhaps it was only the gold clasp which held it. Naomi cradled it in her palm. It lay inert, lifeless without light, a dull blue like the colour of the loch under heavy cloud.

'Tell me,' said Naomi, 'what has happened in this village?'

'Only people,' said Emily, shifting her arm under Molly's head. 'And the forest has retreated and returned. Houses have been built and have fallen into ruin, and their stones used for new households. Wood has been cut and burned and the ashes given back to the earth. There have been times of building, and times of living and generation. And other times when the wind has blown through broken windows and the rain has rotted away the dwellings of the people. It's only a village, like any village.'

'But it is different,' insisted Naomi. 'Can I tell you the truth now?'

'What else is there to tell?'

'Only this. The night I came I saw something on the road. Felt it. And I have seen it since.

'I know.' Emily saw that Molly was asleep, and pulled the blanket more tightly round her.

'I know that you know. I don't know what to ask. It's like asking, where is the summer when the forest is locked in winter? Where are the lights that I see in the shadow? Is it a memory out of the past or a foretelling of the future? What is it that you hold here? Am I allowed to ask?'

'Or I to answer?' said Emily. 'I have no answers. At least, no different from the ones that have always been known. There was an answer written down by a person who is dead.'

'What person?'

'I don't even know that,' said Emily, 'But I do know this:

'*What is the late November doing*
With the disturbance of the spring?'

114

'I can't remember the next bit. But it goes on:

> '*Scorpion fights against the sun*
> *Until the Sun and Moon go down*
> *Comets weep and leonids fly*
> *Hunt the heavens and the plains*
> *Whirled in a vortex that shall bring*
> *The world to that destructive fire*
> *Which burns before the ice-cap reigns.*

'Does that give you anything?' asked Emily.

'Only music.'

'I never thought you needed anything else.'

'Nor did I,' said Naomi. 'But in you I see what I don't have.'

'And I in you. Perhaps that makes us very dangerous to one another.'

'Or necessary.'

'That's precisely the danger. No human being can be necessary to another. We have to die alone.'

'But the music is passed on.'

'I have no music,' said Emily.

'That's not true. You just never saw it in yourself.'

'How could I do that?'

'By seeing yourself reflected.'

'Like in a mirror?'

'Mirrors show you what you expect to see. They turn everything back to front. No, you have to see yourself reflected in a different light.'

'Which would do what?'

'Make all the colours different,' said Naomi, and laughed. Emily smiled slowly back at her, and impulsively Naomi knelt by the fire and reached out her hand to Emily. It was taken at once in a firm grip. Her hand is much bigger than mine, thought Naomi, and hard, hard with using tools. I don't know what this means.

'I don't know what this means,' said Emily.

'I am a woman,' said Naomi. 'And you are a woman. We are the same. There doesn't have to be a mystery.' She looked down at the blue stone again, still snug in the palm of her left hand. 'What is it for?' she asked.

'How can you ask?' said Emily. 'What is the music for?'

'I've been teaching your brother a different kind of music,' said Naomi. 'A kind not heard for many centuries in Clachanpluck. When I'm gone he can play it to you. I wish I was able to teach it to you.'

'I wish you might come with me into the forest. But I would be afraid for you, and I dare not.'

'Are you going into the forest?'

'In four days.'

'What for?'

'Because there must always be change,' said Emily. 'I don't know any other way of dealing with it.'

'What does the forest give you for dealing with change?'

'Stillness.'

'I know about that,' said Naomi. 'But I don't know your forest. I'm afraid of it, a little.'

'I know.'

'How do you know?'

I was told, thought Emily, but only said, 'I'm not very clever at knowing things, but I have found that out.'

'Are you afraid of me?' asked Naomi.

'Perhaps. Perhaps I'm only afraid of myself.'

'Whatever I do,' said Naomi, 'I do it out of love. I want you to understand that.'

'I think I love you,' said Emily. 'But I know that I'm afraid.'

Naomi held out her free hand with the blue stone lying on the flat of her palm. 'You'd better take it back. Thank you.'

Emily let go of Naomi's hand and looped the chain round her neck again. 'I'm not afraid of you, you understand,' said Emily. 'But there is a change happening, and although the new may be very good, I shall be sorry to lose what we had before.'

'I've not come to take anything away from you.'

'But you must. You couldn't stay among us and be given nothing. I don't know what I did when I began this,' said Emily, looking at Naomi with anxious eyes, 'but I do know that it will make everything different, for me and you and all of Clachanpluck. That's the thing that I'm afraid of. I'm not usually afraid of love.'

'I'm glad about that,' said Naomi. 'My love for you is the same as yours for me.'

Emily sighed. 'I knew it could be no different,' she said, as if the fact were a burden to her. 'There is too much the same.' She looked

116

down at Molly, and saw that she was sound asleep. 'When I come back from the forest I'd like you to play me the different kind of music. I don't suppose I'll understand it, but I'd like to hear it from you anyway.'

'I'd like to do that,' said Naomi readily. 'More than anything.'

The clearing in the forest was bright with snow and moonlight, and the full moon itself was visible above the treetops. The pool was frozen over at the edges, but the waterfall flowed down, white against white. Only the centre of the pool was dark, where the water flowed and would not freeze. The rocks surrounding the pool were splittery with ice that glinted in the moonlight, and on each side of the waterfall icicles hung down like frozen swords. The ferns were gone, and only the gaunt outline of the rowan tree was silhouetted black against the moon-rinsed sky. It was burningly cold out here, even the light was white and cold and held no comfort in it. The whole forest seemed immobilised by cold. The trees slept like dead beings, branches motionless in the bright air, like the roots that probed far down again into the dark. There was no sound of life, only the small noises of cracking ice, and the waterfall gushing endlessly into the black unfrozen pool.

Too cold in the light, too cold in the shadow of the trees, no refuge but the dark. The trees reached down into the dark, rooted in life through the long months of dormancy. The water flowed out of the dark, freed from the ice by the motion of the turning world. Below the frozen ground the soil lived, and waited. Nowhere to go but into the dark. The watcher by the pool slipped out of the shadow of the rocks and stood for a moment in the moonlit clearing, casting a clear shadow behind her as she looked up at the round blank face of the moon. Then she disappeared again into a deeper shade, and there were only a few shallow footprints left behind in the transient snow. The shadow enveloped her and she stepped down, feeling her way with her hands, into the darkness of the earth.

So many shelters in the forest for those who dare to find them. So many places of refuge, so much safety offered to those who are not afraid to walk into the dark. To go down into the dark, back to the beginning, foreshadowing the end. There is a great comfort in this for those who are not afraid of their own death.

Enshrouded by the earth itself, she felt the welcome warmth of a place never touched by cold, where winter could not reach with long white fingers. A place of retreat, of waiting. A way which led down where soil grew rough and gritty and became part of the living rock, where roots twined and slowly pierced the earth with reaching tips, searching for nourishment and water. For there was water. No longer flowing, no sound of rushing falls, but merely a dampness in the earthy air, and a slow drip, and the touch of wetness on the rock. The way went on, down into the dark, the dark which created the forest itself, that dwelt beneath the hills and gave birth to the burns that brought water down into the valley and made a loch, and then a river, and finally the unseen sea.

No moon, no sun, no stars, no flame or lamplight. No movement or colour or shape or image. Only the earth, and the water which flowed through the earth, and the very genesis of the forest itself. Nothing here but the seed, and the possibility.

In the heart of the darkness there was only stillness. A place of silence, of sightlessness, where nothing could be sensed but the rock and the water over the rock. A place of returning, for this was the beginning of life and of all things. A place of comfort, for her first and last home was the dark. A place of knowledge, for the place where consciousness is brought to birth is in the dark. The woman who had come so far in order to understand curled herself up like a small animal in the shelter of the rounded rock, her arms folded across her chest, and her left hand clutching the stone which she wore on a chain round her neck. She closed her eyes, and opened her mind to such dreams as the earth might offer her.

There exists a time, in time, which threatens all things. We are, or we have been, faced with the possibility of an end, an end of our own making. This is the terror, this is the nightmare that is locked away in memory or in anticipation. This is the thing we know will happen, or has already happened, for it is possible we are merely living in a dream. There is war in heaven. The scorpion fights against the sun, and the sun would extinguish the moon, and the moon reflects back nothing but the blank face of craters conquered by the last exponents of a dream.

All opposites are the same. What we are not is merely the reflection of the thing that we are. Love is possible because there is unity in everything. But if a time exists, were to exist, in which a choice must be made? If I am to be the one and you are to be the other? What

118

then? The choice is not a choice, it is only a question. Your death or mine? Which of us now will go down into the dark? You who I loved as the image of myself have become my enemy.

I was denounced by a woman like myself, a woman who feared the dark and rejected me. She condemned me to the fire and I was consumed. I was denounced by a human being like myself who said that I was different, and my bones were burned to ashes so that I should be extinguished for ever from this earth. I was silenced; I was tortured and drugged and battened down behind locked doors. I was driven out of the world because I knew that everything was only the same, and I was destroyed. I have been betrayed by you, my sister, again and again and again. And you and I have both been betrayed, and told that ours was not the image in which this world was made, and that it were better not to exist than be born a woman.

Come away out of this, my sister. Come out, and leave the world of nightmare to the men who would create a nightmare for us all. What then? Then they will destroy the earth, or perhaps they have already destroyed it, and everything that we loved is doomed. The world is turning under our hands, yours and mine, and between us we can make it turn for ever. There will be no annihilation and no destruction, only the everlasting change which is the unending end of everything. You and I know that, for we see the reflection of ourselves in each others' eyes, and we are not afraid.

There is a possibility, if the world I remember is not the real world, that you have created for me another time. Perhaps I do not exist, never can or will exist. Perhaps the forest has been burned to ashes, and the earth been poisoned so that no seed will germinate again, nor any sapling grow. Perhaps the soil has dried out and dislodged itself from the rock beneath it, and has been washed down from the hills with bitter rain that brings no goodness with it, but only burns the earth like fire. Perhaps there is no Clachanpluck, but only the burnt-out shell of a forgotten habitation where the last generation died, leaving none behind it to build a human world again. Perhaps time conquered eternity, and in the last moments of defeat a woman out of another time created me and mine like a cry for help which was never heard in any world. My inception was merely a dream, and the dream itself was lost in a blinding light and a smoke that smothered the earth, bringing a winter without end.

Where now is the light that never failed to dwell in the heart of the darkness? Where is the life that lies hidden in the forest, bringing the promise of summer? Where is the hope and the certainty that have never failed me while the forest was mine? Whose nightmare is this that I never agreed to acknowledge? Whose world is this, for it was never mine?

I have never before found fear in the heart of the forest. Is it something she radiated on to me, this sister of mine? Has she forced me into separation? I have been thrown out of my world into a nightmare of another time, I have been burned, consumed and destroyed. Only the forest can take me back. Take me back, or I shall die. Perhaps I am dead already, or was always dead. I can bear no more of this reality. Take me back! Take me back to my own village, and never let me see what they would make of it again. Take me back to my own place, or I shall surely die.

15

The village street was treacherous with trodden snow that had turned to ice where wheels had crushed it. Ice gleamed in the cart tracks in the colourless light of the full moon. Bare fields of snow reflected back white light; everything was bright and exposed, except in the shadows of the houses where the dark crouched in the shelter of the buildings. There was only one person out in the street tonight, and as she walked carefully up between the ice tracks towards the crossroads, the dark seized her form and elongated it, stretching it out behind her like a weird night creature, with grotesque long limbs and a halo of shadowed curls around her head. Naomi had her face to the moon and never saw her shadow. Although the night was still, the forest frozen out of time under the weight of ice, the windless cold still nipped her face so that her cheeks felt raw and her lips dry and painful. She reached the crossroads and stood at the top of the little hill. Four white roads reached away into the night. The east lay lit and open to the moon; the south held a brightness dissected by the gaunt shadows of the beeches. The west vanished almost at once into the forest which no moonlight could penetrate, and the north, behind her, was the familiar village street of Clachanpluck.

Four ways out of the village, dangerously cold and lit only by the fitful moon, which could be extinguished by a cloud, and pierced no shadow. Emily had gone into the forest, but not, Naomi supposed, by any road that she could see. Naomi stared up at the midwinter moon, and strained her ears for any sound of life. There was only the faint rushing of the burn under the bridge at the bottom of the hill. Not so much as an owl. The other people must be shut in their warm houses, turned to their own firelight. It must be very late. Naomi knew she could not sleep. The moon and the forest had stirred her. She felt a wild impulse to try to follow, to step off the road and disappear into the trees, and trust the wood itself to show her the way Emily had taken. But the trees were motionless and silent, quite unaware of the stranger. There was no help that way.

Naomi stuck her cold hands in her pockets and waited at the crossroads. There were no lights under the trees now, only shadow all the blacker in contrast to the moon and snow. Whatever was hidden here was shrouded in ice, unrevealed. There was no hint of life in the air, no glint of green or summer. Nothing. Whatever it was had retreated into the dark. Sometimes the forest had felt so close that Naomi had withdrawn from it into the house and to her music. Now, when she would have reached out to it if she could, if offered nothing. I should have gone with her, thought Naomi, but I think it would have been impossible.

It was a long time since she had been so aware of her own solitude. Something had been stirred in her, the touch of another hand, clasping her own, other eyes, blue eyes, that looked into her own. An image of herself who was not herself. If I had dared to reach out to her then, thought Naomi, would that have healed anything? She thought of the weight of the sapphire in her hand, an opaque blue stone with no light to bring out the fire in its heart. I am all on fire, thought Naomi, and there is no fire to answer me. Only the cold, and the lifeless forest. I could give so much, if anyone would dare to take it.

She shifted restlessly from one foot to another. The cold of the earth was stealing up through her boots, and her feet felt chilled and painful. I can bear myself no longer, thought Naomi. I have held back so long. I have needed no one and I have loved only the music, and the music and I have made our way through the world and hurt nobody. But there is something in me that has lain dormant through the long years, and is being dragged back to life in this place. She rubbed her frozen nose and looked up at the moon ruefully. A cold night for it, she thought, a cold night for a birth. I would like to find something a good deal warmer than this.

There is one thing that I could do.

At the thought she stood still suddenly, staring westward into the forest with a sudden frown. I have been responded to, I have been offered the warmth I have been without through all these years. Emily has gone into the forest and has left me nothing but restlessness. I cannot sleep in this light. My body is awake, painfully awake when everything is sleeping under the cold. But I want to wake up, and I cannot do it on my own.

Naomi turned her back on the moon, and went back down the village street, her long shadow preceding her.

She never hesitated until she stood at the top of the stairs on a dark landing, and the closed door of a room faced her in faint light. She stopped then, listening, like a person asking a question, and waiting for some kind of answer.

It was a stout wooden door, but it could not keep in the thin strains of sound that filtered out into the darkness of the stairhead. Naomi stood with her hands pressed flat against the door, holding her breath and listening.

It was only somebody playing the fiddle. If she had thought, it was merely what she should have expected. It was like an echo of herself filtering back to her, a response to the gift she had brought into this village, and had already passed on so that it was solely hers no longer. Naomi closed her eyes and saw herself reflected in a mirror, and heard her own music, but not quite as she played it. There was an uncertainty to it, a tentativeness in which she had no part, a hesitation and a straining after a proficiency which she had attained long ago. But there was something new to it as well. It was not played exactly the way she would have played it, more the way a person of Clachanpluck would interpret it. But it was Beethoven quite unmistakably.

The tune wove to its end, and quiet settled itself again on the pale landing. Naomi took her hands from the door, and stood facing it. There was nothing to be seen, no faint chink of light round it, nothing at all. Naomi made a decision, swallowed, and raised her hand and knocked firmly on the panels.

There was a short pause, and a surprised, 'Come in!' Naomi opened the door and entered.

It was hot inside. Heat greeted her like a forgotten element, and she breathed warm air into her cold lungs in gratitude, and found her eyes were watering. 'Shut the door,' said Davey. He spoke as if he were seeing a ghost, but heat was still worth hoarding. Naomi shut the door.

She had never been in Davey's room before. It was welcoming, like a homecoming. The woodstove was lit and open, and the split logs glowed inside it, until the metal sides were almost red-hot. There were logs piled by the stove, and on a wooden box an oil lamp glowed, so that the room was illuminated with soft yellow light. The walls were all flame-coloured, but when Naomi looked closer she saw they were not flames, but flowers. Davey had never mentioned flowers. She looked at him, and found him staring at her, his mouth a little open, his fiddle across his knees. He was sitting on a wooden box very close to the stove, and he was still fully dressed, though it must be well past midnight.

'Come in,' said Davey again.

Naomi came slowly over to the fire, and stood looking down at him. The heat by the stove brought the warm blood to her cheeks, and penetrated her thick jacket like a benediction. 'You were playing the other music,' she said.

'Ay,' said Davey, never taking his eyes off her. 'I have to make sure I never forget, for when you are gone.'

Naomi undid her buttoned jacket very slowly, because her hands were still numb with frost. 'I came to stay the night with you,' she said.

Davey laid the fiddle carefully down on his bed, and stood up. 'I don't think I can bear that,' he said, still as if he were talking to an apparition who might disappear in a cloud of smoke at any moment, 'without being lovers.' He looked at her almost pleadingly. 'I want you too much, you see,' he said simply.

'I want you,' said Naomi.

He didn't seem to be able to take it in at first. He went on standing there, with a question still in his eyes. Naomi threw her jacket down by the pile of logs, and unwound her scarf. 'I can stay?' she asked, but the way she said it there could only be one answer.

'Of course,' said Davey.

He swallowed again, and managed to say, 'Sit down.' He realised he was trembling a little. This was the last thing on earth he had expected. She was looking more beautiful than he had ever seen her, though she was wearing her everyday clothes of red jersey and trousers, and her hair was still flattened a little after wearing her woollen hat. He had never thought much about what anybody wore until he had seen Naomi. She was flushed with the cold, or with the heat, or with this extraordinary decision she had arrived at. She seemed perfectly clear about it, as cool as he had ever seen her. Davey wasn't feeling cool at all. He was hot with excitement, and cold with anticipation, or fear perhaps, and shaking with confusion. 'Can I ask why?' he said.

'I was out,' said Naomi. 'It's full moon.'

'I know.'

'There comes a point,' she said, ignoring the interruption, 'when denying life becomes meaningless. I can't remain detached from you or yours, being here. Whatever I do will make a difference. That being so, I choose this.'

'And what difference do you think it will make?' asked Davey. His voice came out hoarsely, almost whispering. He cleared his throat.

'I don't know,' said Naomi. 'I hate to be cold. I'm too passionate. But a part of me has been cold for a long time. I don't want to carry that with me any more.'

'You're not cold.'

'I don't think you know me very well.'

'Is that important?' he asked humbly.

'Do you think it's important?'

Davey considered. 'How well do you think that you know me?'

Naomi sat down and crossed her legs under her on the bed, and scratched her head so that the red curls were all sticking up again. 'I don't know,' she said eventually. 'I recognise your music. It's the same as my own but also different. But I haven't known any man well for a long time.'

'I love you,' Davey said.

'I think that's reason enough,' said Naomi. She looked at him reflectively. He had sat down on his box again, a couple of feet away from her, and he was looking back at her with a dawning realisation in his eyes of what she was offering. His eyes were very blue, just like his sister's, and there was an expression in them now that Naomi hadn't seen in anyone's eyes for many years. I've aroused him, she thought. It wasn't very difficult. I've never even touched him. And me? I think I've forgotten what I'm supposed to feel. I used to be very sexual with men, and it used to be very easy. Maybe I've forgotten everything, and it's too late. Naomi took her eyes off Davey and stared into the fire. In the respite she gave him he threw a couple more logs on. Naomi watched the flames begin to softly lick the new wood, and it was her turn to feel afraid.

Davey picked up his fiddle, and wrapped it carefully in its cover, and laid it in its place on the other box. Then he sat down on the bed where it had lain, next to her. 'Naomi?'

She didn't look at him, but she held out her hand, and he took it. Her hand was still cold as ice, and his was very warm. He laid his

125

other hand over hers. 'You're frozen,' he said gently. 'You must have been out a long time.'

'I think I was.' Naomi gave him her other cold hand, and raised her eyes to his. 'I've forgotten all about this,' she said directly. 'I've not made love to anyone for a long time. I told you why I decided that. As time went by it became easier and easier to be alone. I sometimes thought that I would never ask for anyone like this again. I don't suppose you've ever felt what it is to be alone like that.'

'No,' said Davey, chafing her hands, 'I haven't.'

'Do you ever make up your own music?' asked Naomi abruptly.

He blinked at the sudden change of subject. 'My own tunes, you mean? No, I never thought of doing that.'

'No,' said Naomi. 'Davey, I find you very reassuring. Do you always keep as good a fire as this?'

'No,' said Davey, 'But I split nearly all the wood in this household. I make it like this when I choose.'

'Couldn't you sleep tonight?'

'Too bright,' said Davey. 'Are you feeling any warmer?'

'I don't know. I'm beginning to be confused. I want to make love with you, and I've forgotten what the feelings are.'

'I haven't,' said Davey. 'Come here.'

He put his arm round her and rolled over so that they were lying on the bed, with the warmth of the fire on her back as she lay facing him. He could still see her face in the lamplight. Her eyes were dark and unfathomable, but her body was warm now against his. He laid his cheek against hers. It was astonishing to touch her like this, after watching her so long. Her skin was cool against his face, her body was real and substantial in his arms, and her feet were cold. He let her warm them against his, and held her tighter. He turned his head so his face was in red curls that felt silken against his cheek. Her body was much stronger in his arms than the last person he had held like this. There was a toughness to her as well as a softness, that was a match for his own. In a way she was already familiar to him, for he had looked at her so much, and thought so much of what this might be like, that reality was like the confirmation of a dream. And she was turning to him. Whatever she said, she was as ready for this as he was. Her arms were round him, and her face against his. She kissed him, and Davey felt his whole being respond to her, and be drawn into her fire.

It was not difficult after all, thought Naomi. The passionate part of herself was not so very far from the surface. And Davey was an easy man to love. There was a surprising latent strength in him, and a confidence she had not known he possessed. He was very warm. Naomi was grateful for the warmth and the last shreds of coldness dissolved in her under his touch. Sexuality stirred in her like a forgotten friend, and she found his mouth and kissed him. It was easy, it was delightful, and she felt his whole body stir in response. She had forgotten it was possible to be like this. It was like stepping into a river, into flowing water freed by the heat of summer, and being released from the cold at last.

His face was flushed by flamelight, his dark hair had fallen over his forehead, and his eyes were soft in the reflected light of the fire. She wanted to know his body which she had seen every day but never seen, because he was always wrapped up against the winter's cold in thick layers of woollen clothing. Naomi gently pulled his shirt out of his trousers and felt smooth skin under her hand. Davey shuddered at the coldness of her hand, and she felt his sudden indrawn breath. His skin was warm and soft. She felt him relax again, and then his hands were on her too, gentle and comfortable. He lifted his head and said to her softly, 'Can we get into the bed? It would be much warmer.'

It was warmer, and it was a relief to take off the enveloping layers of winter clothes. It was usually so cold in Clachanpluck; Naomi hadn't even seen her own body properly for such a long time she had forgotten what it was like. And another person's body, a man's body, was like remembering something out of another world. His skin glowed faintly pink in the firelight. The colour of skin seemed magical, after endless hues of forest and winter. To feel someone so alive under her touch, after the feel of stone and wood and snow, and rough boots and jackets on every human form. The body of a man was something much more than she had remembered it, not the pale image of her own memory and imagination, but actual, substantial, the self-contained body of another human being who was not herself.

To be as close to her as this seemed incredible. He felt suffused with love for her, and the fulfilment of so much desire brought tears to his eyes, so that her image was blurred in the firelight, all colours of white and pink and flame. He wanted to cry, but he wanted to make love to her more. It was not like anything else he had known.

There was an endlessness to it, a blurring, as if her being began where his ended, and there were no boundaries, no form or time that must be held to, merely a fluidity and an understanding.

It was possible to trust him, Naomi realised. What she wanted was what he wanted, and there was no need to hold out on him at all. He was a man, but he was not only a man, there was something between them that was not different, and beyond all separation they were the same. I have not been complete without this, thought Naomi, and never before have I been so much myself.

For a moment he reached away from her, leaning over her to put more wood on the fire. She saw him separately again, another body tinged with firelight, and her heart went out to him. He seemed very vulnerable like that, naked and aroused and wanting her. She pulled him down on to her, and without quite meaning to took him inside her, so that he gave a sound almost like a sob and clung to her, his face buried in her hair.

'We're falling off the bed,' whispered Naomi.

'Oh,' he said, and raised his head. His eyes met hers, and she saw tears which glinted when they caught the light. 'Hold on,' said Davey and shifted back on the mattress. 'I love you,' he said. 'Naomi, I love you.'

What am I doing to him? she thought. He's like a man drowned in passion, consumed. He has no defences at all. He is as open with me as if he had never known anything to be afraid of, had never been afraid. It was her turn to feel tears pricking under her eyelids. 'You give me too much,' she said. 'I am only the fiddle player. I never asked for this.'

He shook his head at her, perhaps not hearing or understanding. His eyes never left hers. He was moving inside her, quick and passionate, but not at all demanding, as though he were willing to be there for ever.

Too much, she thought. You give me too much. She closed her eyes against his steady gaze, but his body was irresistible. It was not possible to forget, or to remember. The river had caught at her now, untamed and intractable, moving in never-ending flow. In front of her closed eyes there was only the dark, and dark within her body. Beyond all ice and light, beneath the ground where the roots delve downward, there is only the dark. The seeds of life are hidden in the dark, to be revealed in no daylight world, but this was a place of flame and fire, and the darkness had been within her all the time.

The life that had lain forgotten was stirring and wakening. She was no longer merely Naomi, no longer contained within herself, but was whirled into the vortex, the place where darkness becomes light, and the brightness is the dark. Like dying, or waking, no longer herself, but Davey and herself, or neither of them, an explosion into another world, with him still with her. She heard him cry out, and felt his body against hers, hot and heavy and wet with sweat. Naomi opened her eyes, and found him still gazing into hers. He had been watching her all the time, as if by sight he could hold her, and never let go again.

She was so beautiful. Davey felt his face quiver, and at last the sobs rose in his throat and would not be checked. He turned away his eyes at last, and without moving away from her wept into her hair, until his whole body was shaking. Naomi held him tightly. 'You're falling out,' she remarked presently, and although the words were prosaic enough, her voice was as shaken as he felt. Davey raised his head and smiled at her mistily. 'Sorry,' he said. 'I don't usually burst into tears. I hope you don't mind.'

Naomi shook her head. After all, she thought, they were musicians, not poets, and there was nothing that needed to be put into words anyway. Davey wiped his eyes and his nose, and smiled down at her again. Then he leant across to put another log on the fire, and slithered off her. 'Sorry,' he said again, 'I'm not doing very well here.'

'That doesn't deserve an answer,' replied Naomi. 'I think we've lost some blankets.'

'Here,' said Davey. He got up and quickly made the bed again. The shadow of his naked body flickered across the wall over the roses, and then he hastily climbed in beside her. 'It feels cold out there now. Shall I blow the light out?'

'Yes,' she said contentedly. Davey closed the door of the stove and blew out the lamp. Then he curled himself round the curve of her body and put his arms round her. Naomi took his hands and opened her eyes against the dark. Only it was not dark. Moonlight filtered through the blinds and made square patterns on the opposite wall. In the colourless light the flowers had faded to indistinct shapes. The stove was closed and black, the lamp out. Naomi shivered a little and pressed herself up against Davey. He stirred sleepily, and cuddled her to him. But he doesn't see, she thought, and separateness flooded back over her. I am Naomi, she said, almost out loud. I am the fiddle player, and in the spring I shall be gone from Clachanpluck. She glanced round to see if Davey had sensed her, or heard her. But his eyes were closed, dark lashes etched faintly on his cheeks in the moonlight, and he was away from her, asleep.

16

The morning was bitter. The outlines of trees and buildings were etched sharply against a still sky. The cold was painful to the touch, every object brittle with a coating of ice. Anna stood on the doorstep buttoning her jacket, her breath turning to mist in the freezing air. She stepped gingerly on to the snow-covered brigstones, which sparkled treacherously in the early light. She picked up a bucket and shovel, and began to walk slowly along the path to the gate, sprinkling ash around her as she went. It fell gently round her feet in pale clouds, soft and brown, still warm from the fire, like the pale ghost of departed trees.

Anna came to the gate, and tipped up the bucket. The last cinders were still glowing, and hissed softly as they blackened and died away into the snow.

'Anna!'

Anna jumped. Her thoughts had been far away, and the last thing she had been thinking of was this.

'Anna, wait. I have to talk to you,' said Patrick urgently.

Her heart sank. He sounded distraught, still trapped in a whirlwind of feelings in which she wanted no part. It was like looking back at somebody from very far away, seeing them still bogged down in the same place. Anna was somewhere different now, if only he would recognise it.

'What is it?' she asked patiently.

'Don't talk to me like that!' He kept his voice low so near her house, but he was still furious. 'As if I were nothing to do with you! You came after me, you followed me, then you just push me out of your life like a cast-off jacket. I deserve something better than that!'

'I'm sorry,' said Anna. It was difficult even to respond. He seemed out of focus, presenting her with old images that no longer had any relevance. 'It's not that I don't care about you, Patrick. But other things have been happening.'

'You didn't say that two years ago,' he replied accusingly. 'You owe me an explanation, at the very least.'

'I was younger,' said Anna with an effort. 'I told you, I've changed. But I still care about you. You can't expect a person to stay the same for ever.'

'I can't expect anything from you! That's clear enough. You've treated me like dirt, and I gave you everything I could. You think you know what you're about. You've no idea how to love anybody! You just trample over people. But I'm a person too. I have feelings.'

'Of course you do. But I haven't hurt you.'

'How can you possibly say that? You've hurt me more than I was ever hurt in my life. You just walked out and left me without a word of explanation. Where were you midwinter night? You never thought of me, did you? Not once!'

'No,' said Anna, honestly surprised. 'I didn't.'

'And you can just stand there and admit it?'

'Why should I have been thinking of you?'

'Because of what's between us!' He was shouting now, so she glanced back at the house, but no one seemed to be stirring. 'You said you loved me! Doesn't that mean anything to you now?'

'Of course it does. But it doesn't mean I have to be thinking about you all the time. Not when I'm with someone else.'

She thought he was going to jump the gate and fly at her, and for a moment she quailed. Patrick restrained himself, grasping the top of the gate so that his knuckles turned white. It was unbelievable that she could stand there so coolly and treat him like this. 'I know you were! I know who you were with! And you can just stand there and admit it!'

'And why not?' She was angry herself now that he should dare to think her so despicable. 'It's my life! What does it have to do with you?'

'I want you,' said Patrick desperately.

'You have me!' returned Anna with sudden rage. 'You have me now. Here I am, listening to you, though I never chose to. You don't hesitate to take what you want, do you? And now you want my attention all the time, even when you're not there. What do you want of me? Do you want me to sit at home and think about you all the time?'

'I want you to be with me!'

'Don't be ridiculous. I can't be with you always. How can I? You just want more than anyone can give, and I'm not giving in to it.'

'I gave you everything I could! It was *you* that wanted me before. I never thought of being your lover, but you never left me alone. It was *you* that made all this happen. And then you chose to come into the forest with me. What did you do that for if you didn't still want me? What was that supposed to be about?'

'I made a mistake,' admitted Anna. 'I was searching for something, and I thought you knew what it was.'

'What's that supposed to mean? You're allowed to want something from me, and I have no right to want you? You act like a baby, Anna. You still think we're all here just to look after you.'

'No,' said Anna, making a huge effort to be calm. 'There's no point in this, Patrick. No one can be part of anyone else. You ask far too much of me. I would go on loving you, if only you would let me.'

'Have me when you feel like it, you mean? On your terms?'

'I'm not prepared to live on any other terms, for sure,' said Anna firmly.

'And what about me? You haven't thought much about me, have you?'

'I think about you. I think you have to look after yourself.'

'You made me feel like this.'

'No!' Anna realised she was sounding defensive. 'Your feelings aren't what I make them. I have to live my own life. Please, Patrick,' she said, suddenly exhausted by him. 'Please, Patrick, leave me alone.'

'I see. If that's what you want. I'll leave you alone. You'll never see me again, if that's the way you want it. But you'll know why I did what I did. And I hope you can live with it. That's all.'

'What?' said Anna, and her voice was frightened. 'Do what? Patrick, wait!'

'I thought you told me to go?'

'Not like that! I don't know what you mean. Where are you going?'

'Into the forest. Where else?'

'But you can't stay in the forest!'

'I can die in it,' said Patrick savagely. He turned and strode back towards the smithy. Anna watched him uncertainly for a moment. Then, without quite knowing why she did it, she was through the gate and after him, grabbing him by the sleeve of his jacket. He tried to shake her off, but she held him firmly, and forced him round to face her.

'Patrick, you didn't mean that. You're just trying to frighten me. Take it back!'

He flung her off, so that she reeled back against the garden wall, but she was up and after him again. 'Patrick, stop!'

He turned and spat at her, and ran back to the smithy. Anna hesitated, and followed. She found the door swinging open, the smithy chill and empty. The back door was open to the fields and forest. The rack where he kept his gun was against the wall next to the water barrel. Anna swung round. The rack was empty.

17

'There's scraps in the bucket,' Bridget told Alan, 'so you won't need much grain this morning. But look right inside for the eggs – not just in the nest boxes. There were two there yesterday.'

'I know,' said Alan.

'We got six at our house yesterday,' remarked Molly.

'Golden ones, I suppose. Now go on, both of you.' Bridget watched them disappear round the corner of the house, and picked up her axe again. There was a pile of split wood behind her, raw and yellow, lying on some bits of sacking to keep it off the melting snow. She took another sawn log off the barrow and placed it carefully on a much hacked tree stump. The thump of metal on wood rang out from the yard, followed by a noise of cracking wood and logs being tossed on to the pile. Bridget swung her axe, and did not hear anyone come round the house to stand behind her, well out of the way, until a voice said, 'Bridget?'

It was Anna, looking pale and unhappy, with dark shadows under her eyes. Not like herself at all, thought Bridget. Has she come to tell me she's ill? 'Hello,' she said, 'I'm glad you've come. I was just going to take a break. Do you want to come in?'

Anna nodded. 'I wanted to talk to you.'

Bridget leaned her axe against the pile of logs, carefully keeping the blade off the wet ground. She couldn't be pregnant, could she? thought Bridget. They're a houseful of feckless women, but surely they must have told her how to avoid that. 'It's thawing nicely,' she said aloud. 'I can't stand the snow myself. It makes the ground seem dead, with nothing growing.'

'I like it,' said Anna miserably.

'Come in,' said Bridget, and led the way into the house.

The kitchen was warm and empty, the windows misted over from the damp that rose off wet clothes draped on the rack above the stove. Bridget shifted a full clothes horse from in front of the fire and put the kettle on. 'Sit down,' she said to Anna.

Anna slowly unbuttoned her jacket. 'I came to ask you if you'd seen Patrick,' she said, avoiding Bridget's eyes.

'Patrick? No. I usually do, it's his Carlingwark day, but not with the holiday. Why?'

'I've not seen him. Not since yesterday.'

'Well, that's not so long ago.'

'He said he was going into the forest. He said he could die in it.'

'Nonsense,' said Bridget robustly.

'I wasn't very clear with him,' said Anna unhappily. 'I never meant to hurt anybody. I thought you might know what I should do about it.'

'He won't have gone far,' said Bridget with conviction. 'If he wasn't in the village last night he must have gone up to the pastures. He may have had a cold night, but there's firing in the bothy. It won't kill him.'

'How do you know he'd go up there?' Anna's voice was sharp and urgent.

'He's done it before. Though not for years.'

'Done what? Threatened to shoot himself?'

'He never said that to you?'

Anna looked down and was silent.

'That's unscrupulous,' said Bridget. 'Why did he do it?'

'I wasn't with him midwinter night.'

'That doesn't seem such a hard thing.'

'When did he go to the bothy before?'

'Oh, when he was a lad. There was no holding him, with no one in that household fit to look after him. It does a bairn no good. He was lost for days the first time, in February, I think it was, and everyone searching the forest. Then George thought of the high pasture, and sure enough, he was there. Hungry, but not cold. There's enough firing, as I say.'

'I'd follow him, if I knew. I'm scared of what he'll do if I don't.'

'If he went to be alone you should leave him. It's hard to find a place alone in winter.'

'But he threatened to kill himself. He took his gun.'

'And are you responsible for that?'

Anna didn't answer. 'No,' she said eventually. 'And yes, because one thing follows from another.'

'So you think you hold his fate in your hands?'

'I don't know. I think he really meant to do it.'

'Or meant you to believe it.'

'I didn't believe him, I didn't think. But he never came back to the village. I watched, and he never came.' Anna controlled her voice with an effort.

Bridget poured out the tea. He had no right to threaten Anna with that gun. Bridget liked him and had often been sorry for him, but there was no trusting him. Better before he came home with that, she thought. It was hard on Anna.

'Why should you have been with him midwinter night?'

A long silence. 'I said I'd play in the band. But then I was talking to Davey.'

To Davey? Davey was an easy man to love, thought Bridget. Too easy. She wondered how he'd responded to Anna. Emily said Davey had eyes for no one but the fiddle player, but then Emily was obsessed with the fiddle player herself, and was not the most discerning of witnesses. Bridget absent-mindedly folded a dry shirt, and waited for Anna to say more.

'It's so hard to know what to do,' Anna burst out passionately. 'None of my family act like him. I haven't much experience. But I'm a woman too. Why are so many secrets kept from us?'

Bridget turned round, the shirt still in her hands. 'Us?' she asked. 'And what secrets?'

'Emily has gone into the forest,' went on Anna. 'Fiona said so. Fiona's scared. She says it's a peculiar moon. She took a boat across the loch this morning. I would have gone with her, but I was afraid for Patrick. I know what I want, and I don't know how to get it. I want to know where you get your power from.'

She spoke the last words like a challenge, and quailed when she had said them. But Bridget didn't seem angry. 'It's a matter of knowing who you are,' she said at last. 'No man can ever show you that. Fiona will come to no harm in the forest. Why do you want a man at all, Anna?'

'You love men!' Anna flung the words out like an accusation. 'You love Emily's brother Andrew, and your son is the child of the herb pedlar who comes every autumn. So why shouldn't I love Davey, and what claim can Patrick have over me?'

'He has none,' said Bridget quietly. 'Except if you lied to him, he can fairly claim your honesty. And you can love anyone you like, but you don't have to make love to them to prove it.'

'I hate this village!' cried Anna furiously, and brushed angry tears off her cheek with her glove. 'I hate these people who are all intertwined with one another. And I hate the fiddle player who has bewitched Davey away!'

'Away from what?'

'From Clachanpluck! He's playing a different kind of music now.'

'Is that wrong?'

'He won't share it,' said Anna. 'He says not yet. Even though he loves me, he's not trusting me with that.'

'He loves very easily,' said Bridget. 'You have to take it as a quality in him.'

'It's all right for Fiona,' stormed Anna illogically. 'She's Emily's daughter. Who am I supposed to become?'

'Fiona is not Emily. The forest is as open to you as it is to her.'

'I stayed with Davey on midwinter night,' Anna flung at her. 'And now I wish I hadn't. He's no idea what it's like to be me.'

'How could he have? You're different people. What were you expecting?'

'I wish I could play the fiddle,' said Anna savagely.

Bridget sighed, but kept her impatience to herself. 'You are who you are,' she said. 'I can't play the fiddle. Nor can Emily. Nor can Fiona. It changes nothing.'

'I want to know,' said Anna, pacing round the room, playing the mugs on the table. 'Whose footprints were they on the path beyond the loch? Where is the summer when the forest is locked in winter? If you know the answer to that, why are you hiding it from us?'

'I'm hiding nothing. But there are no words.'

'I belong to this village,' said Anna, standing still suddenly and facing her. 'I'm a woman of Clachanpluck. I have every right to take part in these things. I have every right to love a man and be loved back. You take what you want so easily, and you never think about anybody else. Don't you care? Would you care if I were of your household, if I were your daughter? Would you care that I had none of these things then?'

'I do care,' said Bridget patiently. 'But I have no power over you. No more than Davey, or anybody else. The forest is open to you. If you follow the path other women have followed you're bound to see their footprints. There's no mystery about that. You have no one to face but yourself.'

'I thought you would understand. I thought you were the wisest woman in this village, and that you would understand.'

'Perhaps I do. And so I know I can't offer you anything. What do you want? Advice? Sympathy? You know quite well they'd be no use to you. You don't want anything from me or anyone else. You have yourself.'

'But that's not what you do!' cried Anna passionately. 'You want people. You do!'

'Yes,' said Bridget, 'And no. I'm not perfect. But there are people I love well, and I'll be sorry to lose them.'

'Why will you lose them?' asked Anna, momentarily diverted.

'Each of us is alone. Though it's hard. I . . .'

The door opened with a bang, and Alan and Molly came in with a rush.

'He fell in the ditch,' Molly was shouting. 'Right up to his middle. The ice broke, and . . .'

'I'm wet!' wailed Alan.

'You are indeed. Look at the bairn! Come over to the fire now. Come on, take your boots off.'

'I can't undo the laces. They've stuck!'

'Just pull now,' said Bridget, taking hold of a mud-caked boot. 'Hold my shoulder. Keep still, silly boy. Molly, hold him still.'

'They're full of water.'

'Tip them out the back door, Molly. Let's have your trousers.'

'He's probably got frogs in his pockets.'

'Not in winter, stupid. My shirt's wet too.'

'You'll have to take everything off. Hang that up, Molly.'

Anna retreated to the far side of the table until Alan stood shivering on the hearthrug, clad only in his vest. Bridget wrapped a large towel round him, and began to gather garments from the clean washing.

'Each of us is alone,' she went on, as if there had been no interruption at all. 'The fiddle player is probably more alone than any woman in this village.'

Anna looked up at that, and was about to speak, but Molly forestalled her. 'The fiddle player isn't alone,' she remarked brightly. 'She's in bed with my uncle Davey.'

'How do you know?' demanded Anna sharply.

'Because I saw her. I went in his room this morning because I wanted a piece of string.' Molly paused, delighted at becoming so effortlessly the centre of attention. 'And she was in his bed right on top of him. They were all mixed up together.'

'What did you want a piece of string for?' asked Alan with slight interest.

'I'm going,' said Anna stormily. 'Thank you, Bridget. I'm going now.'

'Where?' called Bridget after her.

'Into the forest,' called Anna fiercely, and the door slammed behind her.

18

The mist lay low on the loch, and grey clouds gathered over the hills, threatening rain. The air was raw, no longer freezing, but with the chill of sleet in it. There might have been no farther shore, only an eternity of sky and water. Slowly a shape issued out of the mist, gliding into visibility like a ghost slipping through a crack between worlds. The silhouette grew larger, more discernible; moving at an angle, it presented a different outline. There was a faint regular plash, a dipping in and out of water. The watcher on the shore moved nearer the water, standing in the damp shelter of a clump of alders. The mist in the trees had constellated into sodden drops which, falling into melting snow, in turn dissolved to water and blended with the rising loch.

The little boat touched the shore just as the first drops of rain began to spatter on the still surface. The mist had drifted in with the twilight, drawing a curtain of darkness between water and wet sky. At the water's edge the snow had soaked to sodden slush, so that the boat stopped with a swish, drifting in a mixture of water and melting ice. The rower shipped her oars with a faint thud and stepped out carefully into ankle-deep wetness. The chill pierced her boots, but she stepped quickly ashore, slipping on slush-covered stones. There was a bump of wooden keel on rock, a crunch of shingle, and a small exclamation of pain.

'Emily?' The watcher detached himself from the shadow of the alders, a dim figure half visible in the gathering dusk. Startled, Emily slipped again.

'George? Is that you?' Her voice was unnaturally high-pitched, like a string wound too tight, sounding a false note.

'I thought you'd be back this evening,' he said, and came down to the other side of the boat. Automatically she lifted it with him, and they carried it carefully over the treacherous ground, upturning it on snow-patched yellow grass. With desperate concentration Emily tucked the oars neatly under it, and then, as if the act had taken the last ounce of her endurance, she sank down on the boat and dropped her head down on her folded arms.

'Emmy?'

A shudder ran through her. George came round the boat and sat gingerly down beside her on the wet planks. He put his arm round her shoulders. Her body was taut as a strung wire, and she seemed hardly aware of him. She had got herself home, but it had cost her too much. 'Emmy?'

He felt her shudder again, then the tautness suddenly snapped and she began to cry with wild frightening sobs, without any turning to him for comfort. It was like a voice crying out of silent space, expecting no echo or response in any human world, crying out in anguish for a loss that he had never known. George did not pretend to understand, but he held her through all the layers of wet clothes that divided them, and waited. Emily slithered off the boat and crumpled up in a heap on the sodden turf. He went down with her, and put his arms right round her. The ground was wet and freezing against the warmth of his body. He felt her go quite rigid in his arms and hugged her tighter to him. She wasn't breathing. He spoke her name in sudden fear, but the sound was lost. He winced and hid his face in her hair as she arched away from him and screamed.

He held on and she screamed again, screaming without stopping. George had never heard anyone scream like that. Screams assailed him like blows, vibrating right through him as if he were screaming too. The sound seemed to swallow up the air, the loch, the whole world. It was like a cry of agony out of the whole forest. It was all the pain of the world that he was holding on to, and it terrified him. But it was also Emily, so he would not be afraid of it. Wet snow was soaking through his clothes, seeming to penetrate his very skin. She was cold and unreachable even in the circle of his arms. George pulled her head down on to his chest under the shelter of his wet jacket, and she turned her face into his jersey and screamed like one possessed.

She had got home. She had made it. It was George. Somewhere in the recesses of nightmare she knew that for sure. Otherwise she would never have turned to face this. This thing that haunted her, pursued her, threatened to drown her. She'd got back. Out of the earth. Across the water. The boat was beached. George was here, and his presence proved she did exist. Her own world was not the figment of a dream. It was safe to face the thing now.

To face the dark. But the dark was not behind her, it was within her. Pain rose up inside her to meet the pain that pursued her. She never knew she held so much pain in her. It rose up, threatened to choke her. It would stay dammed up no longer, could be held back no longer. A cold birth. To stop it now would destroy me. To let it go is to lose myself.

'It's all right,' said George, hoping words meant something. 'I'm here.'

Screams echoing across the loch. Piercing terror absorbed in moist air. Screams not her own, the terror of another person, another time, but her whole body open and vibrating to it. A purification not hers which flamed inside her, threatened to consume her, but the fire that touched her belonged to another world. To feel it like this, like being part of the earth itself. There is no separation. Whose pain do I carry now? Whose screams are these, that echo through this night and all the nights? I don't know who I am. I am nothing, only a torch that is burning itself to death.

'Emmy,' said George. 'Emmy, I'm here. You're home now.'

It was George. It had been George all the time. And she was not burning, she was freezing. It was much too cold here, and soaking wet. Damp rough wool rubbed her burning face. She was choking on sobs and shuddering. She was on her own side of the loch, in Clachanpluck, and there was snow melting in puddles underneath her.

'George?' said Emily at last, in a small cracked voice.

'Emily.'

'I feel sick,' said Emily.

'I'm not surprised. Can we get up now? It's pretty wet.'

She could hardly stand. He pulled her to her feet, and felt her shaking in his arms. Her teeth were chattering uncontrollably.

'Better get you home,' said George. 'Come on.'

He pulled her arm round his neck, and put his own arm round her. 'All right?'

'Of course I'm all right,' said Emily crossly, shuddering.

'Yes,' said George soothingly. 'Come on.'

She wasn't all right. She was shaking like a birch tree in a gale. She's probably caught a chill, thought George, and hurried her through the slush and mud along the cart tracks of the road from the north.

'It's something out of the past,' said Emily hoarsely, her teeth chattering still. 'I think it's the past. Or perhaps only a possibility. But we carry it into our own time. If a space is left for it, we can make ourselves the inheritors of a dream we never chose.' She slipped, and George staggered and regained their balance. 'Do I make sense to you? Do you understand me?'

'I could never doubt you for a moment,' said George.

'We affect one another. Time is not a strong enough thing to prevent that. Time is no healer. Not if the patient is no longer there. Do you understand me, George?'

'I love you,' said George.

'Everything we do makes everything different,' said Emily. 'I'm afraid of what I have done.'

'What are you afraid of?'

'I'm not sure I'm really here. I could be looking down on us from a long way off. Do I even know my own body?'

'I can do something about that,' said George.

'We used to be punished,' she went on breathlessly. 'They used to punish people for going outside their own minds. Torture them, lock them up, kill them, anything to prevent them going outside themselves. Why were they so afraid of the dark, George? Why should not everything be the same?'

'It's all one,' said George. 'Come up a bit.' He pulled her arm round him tighter. 'That's better.'

'No one believed them,' said Emily, and there was fear in her voice again.

'I believe you. So you don't need to worry.'

'But I do,' said Emily with sudden energy, stopping in the middle of the road so that George had to stop with her. 'Don't you see I've failed?'

'No,' said George. 'How have you failed?'

'Not to find what is hidden in the heart of the darkness. You know that my charge is Clachanpluck. But I've failed to stand against the nightmare, George. I'm afraid of what will happen. Who will carry the burden of the past, if I have failed to prevent it? What's going to happen now?'

George turned and hugged her to him, and laid his cheek against her forehead. 'You're hot,' he said. 'Probably feverish. I think you should have a hot bath and go to bed.'

At the door of her house he stopped. 'Do you want me to come in?'

'I'll be all right,' said Emily. 'Thank you.'

'I'll stay if you like.'

She seemed uncertain. 'I don't know. I think I need to see my family.'

'You might be right.' He held her close to him again, and kissed her. 'I love you,' he said. 'If you want me to come, send a message.'

She hugged him tightly. 'I love you,' she answered. 'I think you've probably saved me. I'll do what you said, and go to bed. I'll be all right now.'

'I never doubted it.'

'George?'

'Yes?'

'I'm sorry.'

'Nonsense,' he said, and kissed her again. Then he let go of her, and waited until she disappeared inside the house door. He turned abruptly, and went up the street to his own house.

Only Fiona was in the kitchen. She was sitting by the fire cutting out small pieces of material, but she jumped up at once when she saw her mother. 'You're back! I looked for you. Are you all right?'

'I'm cold,' said Emily. 'Where are the others?'

'At the ceilidh. It's the seventh night. Had you forgotten?'

'I don't know,' said Emily, and sat down by the fire.

Fiona regarded her shrewdly. 'You don't look very well,' was all she said. 'Are you hungry?'

'Probably,' said Emily. 'I don't know.'

'We kept you some stew,' said Fiona, and, putting her pieces into a bag, she got up and pushed a pot into the centre of the stove. Then she got out bread, and a plate and spoon, while Emily took her boots off.

'You looked for me?' repeated Emily wearily. 'Today?'

'I didn't like the moon. I took a boat across the loch.'

'So you know that,' said Emily, half to herself. 'No, it was a strange moon.'

'I found your boat, but you weren't where I expected to find you.'

'No,' said Emily.

'I found this,' said Fiona, 'and after that I came home.' She took something out of her shirt pocket, and handed it to her mother. Then she turned away and ladled stew on to a plate.

Emily turned the small thing over, and let it lie in the palm of her left hand. It was nothing so very unusual. Only a small blue flower, which one might find anywhere in the woods or hedgerows, growing in thick matted clusters. A speedwell. It had wilted now, through being in a pocket for several hours, but it was still alive and moist. Emily sniffed it. It had a very faint scent of crushed green leaves. Nothing unusual about it at all. Only the time.

'Do you want to eat this there?' asked Fiona, 'or at the table?'

'Here,' said Emily. 'Thank you very much.' She laid the flower down very carefully on the arm of her chair, and took the plate from Fiona. She realised suddenly that she was ravenous, and said nothing more until she had wiped the plate clean with the last piece of bread.

'Anything else?' asked Fiona, who had resumed her patchwork.

'No thanks. So you never went to the ceilidh?'

'No. I wanted to know if you'd got back.'

'Thank you. I appreciate it. Shall I make some tea?'

'Why not? There's boiling water in the little kettle.'

Emily warmed the pot, and measured in chamomile tea. 'The summer dwells in the heart of the winter,' she said, 'and the promise of the summer is the return of the dark. Water flows down from the hills, and the past is endlessly washed up on the shores of the sea. I never left this place, Fiona. I brought no new blood into the village. I've nothing to offer you but the forest, but you'll find your own way through that.'

'I don't want anything else.'

'I thought once that my time would be the time that changed everything,' went on Emily. 'I thought that in the present the past might be healed, and not carried on into the future. But it can't be done. Time is no healer. There have been moments of insights and happiness, and there has been pain. Nothing changes the pain of the past. But I don't want you to live it all again.'

'I think I'll have to deal with the world the way I find it,' said Fiona. 'There's nothing you can do to change it for me now.'

'No,' said Emily. 'I'm sure you will.'

Fiona put her mug down. 'What happened to you?' she asked.

'What happened to you?'

'I showed you. I gave you that.' Fiona pointed to the speedwell lying on the arm of the chair.

'I can't show you anything,' said Emily, 'But I can give you something in return.'

Fiona looked up, a question in her eyes, and her scissors were still. Emily reached inside her damp collar and pulled the gold chain over her head. She held the sapphire in her hand and it flashed momentarily in the lamplight. Then she handed it to her daughter. 'For you,' she said.

Slowly Fiona reached out and took it. Emily watched her cradle the stone in her small capable hand. Fiona held it up, and it twisted on its chain, so that bright sparks winked from within it. 'Thank you,' she said, and hung the chain round her neck. It felt awkward, an unaccustomed weight. She stuffed the stone down her jersey so it couldn't be seen.

Emily stood up. 'I'm going to have a bath,' she said. 'Is the big kettle hot?'

'Should be. I'll fill this one again.'

'Then I'll go to bed. You won't go to the ceilidh now?'

Fiona shook her head. 'I might go for a walk later.'

19

In the beginning was the land. The land was sufficient to itself, and flourished through timeless years in the strength of its own dream. The land nourished itself, drawing water down from the sky and offering back the same water to the sea. The land turned to the sun by day, and to the dark by night, and knew itself in the light and in the darkness. The land was born of the living rock, was sheltered by the living air, was endowed with motion by the spinning of the turning world. Earth and air, fire and water, drew together and offered their own being that the land might be.

In due time the land brought newer beings to birth, beings of the same substance as itself, each one partaking of the first elements, but each unique, individual, diverse and singular. Each one knowing itself and delighting in knowledge, but belonging to the land. From the land they came, and to the land they returned, and not one was ever lost. There was birth and death, and the birth and the death were one. The land flourished, expressing in its own creation all possibilities of form, colour, expression and desire. There was nothing conceived that was not fulfilled, and no fulfilment that was not change.

When the people came they were not different. They were brought to birth by the land, and they in their turn gave birth and multiplied. The land nourished them, and they took nothing from the land that they did not return to the land. Above all creatures they delighted in knowledge. They took so much of the gift of knowledge that they were given, according to the law of the land, a greater gift. They were given not only the power to know, but also the power to perceive, and to change the world for themselves. The power of words was theirs, and by a word they could change everything. They were given a rainbow, to turn the world another colour; a mirror, to reflect whatever they chose to see; a language, that could make the world the thing that they had described.

The gift aroused their curiosity and their ingenuity. They played with it all ways, and explored everything, and the possibilities were limitless. Their quest brought them to the point on which the world turned, and they saw it, and created Space and Time. They took Space and Time and tossed them around the land, until the land was bound up and imprisoned. Where there had been only infinity, there were now lines, and limitations. And because there were limits, the people began to fear what lay beyond them, and their minds were soon weaving again, creating possibilities out of what lay beyond the boundaries they had made.

And having created a threat, they proceeded to create a fulfilment, for the beings beyond the boundaries hammered at the boundaries, pressed against them, and pushed through. The frontiers of Space and Time cracked and broke under the strain, and the people were aghast, for they thought that their world was ended. The world that they had made themselves was ended indeed, and lay in ruins round them. In their terror they thought everything was destroyed, and the power of the thought became words, and the power of the words became truth. Thinking that all was destroyed, they set about destroying it. Thinking that all was lost, they gave their energies to losing it. Thinking there was no longer birth or death, they discounted both, and created annihilation.

The nightmare reigned, and there was only one hope left in the world, the hope of the land. For beneath every created thing the land lived on. The dream of the land was untouched by the dreams of the people, because it had never been the same. The land was not confounded by Space and Time, because it had not created them. There is only one crime in the world, only one wickedness, and that is the turning against the land. The land is the creator of all, and nurtures all, and there is only one way to destruction, and that is the destruction of the land.

We are the land. The elements that created the land live in our bodies. We are born, we bring to birth, and we die, and the land takes us. There is no difference. What is done to us is also done to the land, and what is done to the land is the thing which is done to us. There is nothing else.

By the time Anna came clear of the forest on the road to the west the storm had broken. Black ragged clouds swept down on the wind so that moon and stars were alike extinguished. She held her hood tight round her face with one hand, the other clutching a dark lantern that flickered like a will o' the wisp. A swell like the sea was rising in the trees, and the sound of waves swept across the whole forest. The wind was much stronger when she reached open ground, so the lantern swayed in her hand. She used both hands to steady it, and at once the wind whipped her hood back, buffeting her bare head. Wild clouds above her parted a little, illuminated by the white light of the hidden moon. There was a brief hint of hills on the horizon, then the light was gone. She was right out on the moor now. There was no telling what lay beyond the tiny circle of light shed by the lantern. She could feel nothing but the beat of the wind.

Fiona had crossed the loch today. Anna wondered briefly whether she was back. It would be no night for crossing the water if she'd not reached home by dark. I wish I'd gone with her, thought Anna, then I wouldn't be alone now. The wind drove against her with fresh force, as if trying to push her back the way she had come. Anna struggled against it, painfully following the winding course of the track.

She nearly missed the turn off the road to the bothy. The summer pastures were sheltered in a high valley between the hills, formed by a little river which flowed north to the heart of the forest. The track was still snow-covered where drifts had blown over it, and it was difficult to make out the way at all. A shower blew over her, and when it passed she raised her lantern and surveyed the pool of light it cast. There were trees, a small copse in the sheltered banks of the burn. She recognised them, and found the track where it should be, to the left of them. There was a snowdrift right across it. Anna made her way over to it, and her heart thumped. There were footprints across the drift, travelling away from the road, north to the pastures.

She lost them again on the far side of the drift. The snow was melting fast, and the track was turning to puddles and runnels of water. Anna splashed across, following the familiar curves of the track in their winter disguise.

It was only a mile to the bothy, but it felt far longer. The wind disorientated her; it kept blowing her off-course eastwards and, unconsciously yielding, she let it take her. When the bothy at last rose up out of the dark it startled her, as if she had given up all hope of reaching it. The stone walls were squat and blank, its only window was round the other side. Anna fought her way into the lee of the house and leaned against the wall in the welcome calm. She breathed in still air that did not whip her breath away before she had caught it. Then her heart jumped again. There was a whiff of woodsmoke. There was a fire then, in the bothy. Bridget was right.

Then he had lied to her. Relief turned to anger as soon as she registered it. He was safe enough, and he had known he would be all the time. And if he hadn't been, said Anna to herself bitterly, what could I have done anyway? Have I only come up here to reassure myself? And even if the fire is lit, he could still have done himself harm. But he said he was going into the forest. He lied to frighten me.

Anna leaned against the wall in a turmoil of confusion. I'm not responsible for him, she told herself yet again. Only he wants me to feel as though I am. But suppose he did do what he threatened? How could I live, with his death upon my conscience? He never meant to do it. He knew how to frighten me, that's all.

How dare he have such power over me? Anna clenched her fists in a sudden spurt of rage. How dare he bring me up here? He has no right to demand so much of me. I don't belong to him, and I never lied to him.

But then he never asked me to follow him. But he intended me to. No, thought Anna wearily. If he intended me to, he would have said where he was going. He only meant to frighten me. But I've come. She considered going back. The storm was no threat to her, in fact it fitted her mood, and she was soaked already. But then I'd go home and go through all this again. He still has that gun. What I should do now, is walk in there and insist for the last time that he treat me with respect, and himself as well. No sooner had she thought of doing it than she recoiled from the idea. She realised then that she was frightened of him.

It was only Patrick. Patrick, who she'd known all her life. And he had loved her. It was ridiculous to be afraid of Patrick. She was the strong one, not him. She didn't need him. She wasn't remotely suicidal. Hurt, perhaps, but not desperate. An image flashed into her mind of Davey and the fiddle player. It hurt, more than she could take in at the moment. But Davey had given her exactly what she had asked for, and if there were pain attached to it, she would have to accept that too. It would be unforgivable to ask for more.

But she'd run away from all that, and chosen to confront Patrick. And now she realised that she was afraid of him. Foolishness, she told herself fiercely. I'm far stronger than he is. I can accept that I'm on my own, and he can't. I know exactly who I am. Patrick can't hurt me.

Anyway, the longer she stood here, the worse it was going to get. If she wasn't going back she was going to have to go in. As if in support of her thought, the candle in the lantern flickered and flared up higher. It would soon be out. Anna looked at it in dismay. The flame turned red and rose almost to the top of the glass. There was small pool of darkening wax at the bottom. Anna clutched the lantern firmly, walked round the house before she could think, and pushed open the door.

There was flickering firelight inside, and sudden movement. A voice came out of the shadows, sharp and angry. 'Who's that?'

'It's me,' she said firmly. 'Anna.'

There was no answer. She shut the door and stepped into the room. It was quite bare. There were benches pushed up under the window, and bunks against the end wall. Hay was stacked behind the door. She held up her lantern.

Patrick was standing in the shadow cast by the hay, not six feet from her. He looked wild, his body charged with tension, like a cat about to spring. A flicker of panic stirred inside her. But it was only Patrick. He didn't move. Caught off balance, he was waiting for her to react. His clothes were torn and dishevelled, his face unshaven. There was mud splashed all over him, as though he had run blindly through marsh and bogland.

'Patrick?'

'What do you want?' His voice shook. She had been prepared for an explosion of anger, but not this. His fear frightened her, but it was too late.

'You threatened to shoot yourself,' said Anna steadily. 'So I came.'

There was no reaching him. He recoiled from her, as if he hated her. He's going to throw me out, thought Anna. He could, too. She stepped tentatively towards him.

'I told you to stay away.' The words seemed to be wrung out of him. She'd been wrong, it wasn't hate. There was a simmering tension in him, barely suppressed.

'I was frightened for you. You said you'd shoot yourself.' It was taking all her courage to stay steady, as if one false step might break his control, or hers. But something had to happen. She waited, like a player who has made a desperate move.

'I intended to.'

He met her eyes unwillingly, glaring like an animal at bay. But I have no power to hurt him, thought Anna. How can he be afraid of me? What power can he think we have over one another? She realised that she was desperate for him to look at her, to admit that she was human, to give her one word of acknowledgment. He's not seeing me, she thought numbly. I don't exist for him. That's why he hates me, because he has no power over who I am. She felt herself trembling, but she spoke to him as clearly as ever.

'Then you must understand why I followed you. There's no way I wanted to be responsible for that.'

'What on earth do you mean by that?' The sudden sneer pierced her defences, but she stood her ground.

'If I have hurt you,' said Anna, 'I don't want you to hurt yourself even more.'

His eyes dropped. She could see now that he was trembling violently, and his face was wet with sweat. Dangerous. The word slid into her brain and shocked her. It's only Patrick, she told herself again, but she knew her fear was real.

'You're destroying me,' said Patrick in a low, goaded voice.

'No! I have no power to do that!' He couldn't have insulted her more, and she saw at once that her anger had registered. There was no being gentle with him now. She had him cornered, whether she meant it or not, and he was ready to attack. 'I don't want a fight,' said Anna, as calmly as she could.

'You've made it a fight!' He stepped towards her, and she retreated instinctively. 'And you can't get out of it like that.'

'Shut up!' She was shouting at him, furious at having been so frightened. 'How dare you threaten me! How dare you! You have no rights over me!'

He flung away from the wall, out of the shadow, and faced her. He shook his fists over her, rigid with passion. 'How can you!' he screamed back at her. 'You followed me! Haven't you hurt me enough?'

'I came because I cared about you! I never hurt you! I was thinking about *you*. So don't you dare to threaten me.'

He looked at her with disgust, letting his arms drop for a

moment. He spoke quietly again, but his voice was shaking. 'So Davey ditched you, did he?'

The last vestiges of her control vanished in a rising tide of fury. It swept her up and whirled her into a world of red mist and fire. Fear was consumed to ashes, and before she knew what she was about she had launched herself at him and was hammering him with her fists.

He was a lot stronger. He grabbed her wrists and twisted them, so she doubled over with a cry of pain. She fell hard on the flagstones, but was up at once. 'Don't you dare!' she screamed. 'Don't you dare touch me!'

He had her wrists again. She twisted round and tried to bite his hand. He held her down. His body was hard against hers, unfeeling and unassailable. He was panting fast. She struggled and kicked his shins hard. Patrick lifted her right off the floor and threw her against the hay. 'You asked for it!' he hissed at her. 'You asked for it! And you'll get hurt!'

'No!' Her face was wet with tears, her jacket half torn off. It was all unreal, beyond experience, like a dream. Anna pulled herself up. 'I won't! Patrick! Listen to me! Listen!'

He was coming at her again, standing right over her, arms flailing, so she cowered back against the hay. 'And he was my friend,' screamed Patrick. 'You just want to destroy me! How could you do that to me?'

'I didn't do anything!'

'That's a lie! You were with him midwinter night. Everyone knows!'

'You know nothing.' She pressed back against the hay, trapped, but still raging at him. 'I'm not yours! What right have you over me?'

'What right have you to destroy me?'

'I never did anything to hurt you,' said Anna. She was suddenly exhausted, her anger cold as ashes. 'Patrick, let me go.'

'Liar!' He was white with rage, and coming at her. Anna recoiled, arms over her head in protection. 'Liar!' Anna buried her face in the hay. He pulled her to her feet with rough hands, jerking her upright, forcing her to face him. 'You'll pay for that!'

Desperate, Anna whipped herself out of his grip and climbed up the hay. She was looking down on him now, poised for flight, or for attack. Dimly she was aware of hailstones sweeping over the bothy, drumming on the roof with insistent beat. It was nightmare, inhuman. No human could treat another so. Like being torn out of her own world into a dream from which she could not wake. There were no defences, nothing she had ever heard of that would help her deal with this. This was panic, like another dimension, an element wherein she was powerless, and everything was impossible. She couldn't comprehend it. 'What do you want?' whispered Anna, into the chaos.

'You know what I want.'

A riddle? Her mind was spinning. What did she know? Answers eluded her, coherence fleeing before impossibilities. A new threat. She couldn't grasp it, there never was such a thing, not in her world. And yet he meant it. He wasn't human. It was not possible. Panic caught at her, rose up, suffocating her. 'You can't,' she wasn't even sure if she'd said it. 'No, you can't.'

'Tough. You were willing enough with Davey.' The words penetrated. He could do it. A whole world disintegrating, all a monstrous lie. Words that meant nothing. Meaningless, because not human. Only the nightmare, and nothing she could do.

He knew he had her. Only a dream, no reality left to her. He was coming towards her very slowly. She could see him so clearly. Two buttons lost off his jacket, grey jersey stained with mud, a scratch across his chin. Her mind flickered over details. Everything irrelevant. It was not happening. This thing could not happen. He pulled her down off the stack, not even roughly. Anna felt herself falling, falling for ever. She tried to force herself to think, to react, to take charge again and bring them back into the world.

'Patrick?' she wasn't even sure if she'd said it aloud. It made no difference at all.

He pinioned her against the hay, pressing her shoulders back with unmerciful hands. His face was blank, not seeing her. Not the face of violence, just for a moment, but of despair. A pang of hope shot through her, and died again. 'What difference does it make?' said Patrick wearily. 'You were mine, or should have been.'

'No!'

The moment was lost. There was a surge of energy through him again. She was alert, struggling to break away. He hit her hard across the face, pulling her back. Quite suddenly he was screaming again, screaming in her face, forcing her back against the hay. She fought wildly, uselessly. Patrick grabbed her and shook her and shook her until she couldn't see and the bothy itself spun round her head and dizzied her. She tried to drag his hands away. 'No! No! No!'

He was hitting her, hitting her again and again, and she couldn't pull away. There was no up nor down, no way she could twist out of his grip. It was all spinning round her, her clothes tearing, he was pulling her clothes off her, shaking her. 'No!' Impossible to fight. Blood pounding in her head. She couldn't see, couldn't think. Only blows, and pain in front of her eyes, his whole weight on her, she couldn't push him off, couldn't fight him any more. Not what Davey had done. No! No! No! Couldn't say it out loud. Couldn't stop him. He was right inside her, she couldn't fight him any more. Nothing to do, not any more. There was a whimpering in her ears like a sound made by somebody else, and unbearable pain left in her, her body torn apart. His weight was gone, there was only the pain, and a flickering in front of her eyes that was pain. Not only pain, but firelight. Firelight, hay scratching her, her whole being throbbing with pain and blindness.

Anna lay crumpled up in the darkness, and the whimpering that was the only sound in the empty bothy was all she was aware of for a long time. The flickering died down and faded to a red glow. There was a creeping cold felt by a body that did not seem to be hers. At last her eyes focussed, and there was a faint outline of rough stone walls and rafters above her head.

Not the same world any more. Not the same body. Nothing. Life blotted out, shattered and flung into the dark. Anna. 'Anna,' she whispered at last out loud, like a requiem for a woman destroyed. 'Anna.' There was no answer at all. Only the rain on the roof, and the slow dying of the fire, and darkness.

20

'So what happened last night?' asked Emily, leaning back on her pillows and eating toast.

'It was fine,' said Davey. 'Not that I had a chance to notice much, apart from the music. Half the band didn't turn up. In the middle of midwinter. I don't know what's going on in this village.'

'But you had Naomi?'

'Oh yes. It's not going to be the same without her,' said Davey, spreading butter lavishly.

'How was Molly?'

'Fine. She likes parties, that one.' Davey sat down on the end of Emily's bed and reached for the teapot. 'She's been all right. We only had one row.'

'Oh dear.'

'No, it wasn't bad.' Davey took a large bite of toast, and said as soon as he was able, 'About clothes. And boots. She seems to have no idea about keeping dry.'

'Children don't,' said Emily. 'They shouldn't have to be bothered with it.'

'I didn't. But how she thinks she'll get things dry by leaving them in a heap in the passage where everyone falls over them I don't know. Her boots are soaking. All she has to do is put them next to the fire. She just doesn't think.'

'You never used to either.'

'I'm sure I wasn't that bad. Was I?'

'Yes,' said Emily. 'Do you want the last bit of toast?'

'You have it. Oh, and she made a bird – a swallow. Maybe I shouldn't tell you. It might be a surprise. Andrew helped her. She whittled it out of a bit of kindling. She's a clever girl, that way.'

Emily grinned. 'She is, isn't she?'

'And I helped her hang it from her ceiling with a bit of string,' said Davey. 'It looks quite lifelike – nice and cheerful, at this time of year.'

'That was very good,' said Emily, finishing her tea. 'I'm going to get up.'

'The idea was you stayed put. We won't fall apart.'

'I can't stay in bed all morning!'

'You put me to shame,' said Davey. 'What's that?'

Emily looked at him enquiringly. His ears were much sharper than hers. Then she heard it too. A faint repetitive tone, low but resonant. It rang out again, and then again, louder.

'It can't be,' said Davey. He jumped to his feet and ran to the window. He opened it and leaned out. The village street was deserted, wet and gleaming in the sun after the night of storm and rain. The bell pealed again, louder, and another answered it from the other end of the village.

Emily shoved him aside and hung out of the window. 'Oh no,' she whispered. 'What is it? Davey, what did I do?'

'You?' he said, uncomprehending. 'You didn't do anything. I don't know. I'll go and see.'

Emily pulled off her nightgown, ripping the last frail seam that was still holding it together, and began to pull her shirt on. 'The bell!' she said. 'Davey, find the bell.'

'Where?'

'In the storeshed. At the back. I'm coming.'

Emily dragged her trousers on, and the bells outside rang out louder. A third bell joined the two, from another part of the village. She heard Davey's footsteps running down the stairs. And more footsteps outside, running. Someone banging on the door. She seized the rest of her clothes, and hurried down to the kitchen, tripping over her socks. There was no one there. Emily grabbed her boots from the hearth and began to lace them furiously. There were voices in the yard. She heard Davey call out. And another tone. The bell from her own house, low and clear, resounding across the yard so that the kitchen walls seemed to hold the sound and vibrate to it. There was a wild pealing outside now. Bells all over the village, ringing out, pealing wildly together in panic, or in warning. Emily seized her jacket and flung open the door, and cannoned straight into Bridget.

'What is it? Bridget, oh, what is it?'

'Rape,' said Bridget. 'There's been rape.'

158

21

This is a little as it must be in summer, thought Naomi. The land was still soaking, open and receptive to the wet of the night. The wind had quite died away, and wet trees gleamed in the low morning sun. The gale in the night had been wild, almost frightening, carrying showers of hail that swept over the huddled houses, drumming on the slate roofs. She'd been thankful to have a warm place to shelter out of the night. But this morning was showing her another face. The sky was blue as blackbirds' eggs, clear and limpid, the last tattered shreds of cloud carried high over the hilltops. The bare trees glinted in a light that held the promise of warmth, though there was no warmth; a hint of summer heat on green leaves. The last snow had vanished, and the tired grass lay flattened by it, brown and sodden. But on the rock where she stood lichen shone in vivid patterns, yellow and white and green against the grey bones of the hill. The little trees that gathered on the slopes of the hillock were tough and spiky, hawthorns, they looked like, and maybe a rowan or two. It was hard to tell in winter.

I am happy, thought Naomi. Who could not be happy on a day like this? It holds all the promise of summer in it. I've let myself love a man again, and nothing dreadful has happened. I am alive, and I have Davey and I have my music, and we can do both together until the spring comes.

She lingered a little longer on the hill, looking down on Clachanpluck. Wet roofs reflected back the sun, and the trees that protected the houses made still patterns of branch and twig against the farther forest. Coils of early smoke rose vertically into the shimmering air. People would be busy down there now, doing the things that they did every day, but still responsive to the loveliness of the morning.

There was a sound from the village, a low resonant tone that reverberated softly across the open fields. It was followed by another, a steady deep-toned chime that seemed like an echo of the first. The slow tones rang out steadily, and were joined by another, a higher note that fell in perfectly with the first, so that Naomi recognised the sound for what it was, the tolling of a bell.

She stiffened, and stared down at the village as if the slate roofs and curling smoke might spell out an explanation. Bells? She had seen no bells. A fourth tone chimed in with the other three, less harmonious, ringing out sharply and bringing the whole into an alarming clamour. Then a fifth, low and steady, a firm bass note tolling against the wild clanging of the other four. Five. There were more bells now. Naomi found herself automatically tuning to them, counting. Six. Seven. There was no gentleness in the sound now, no harmony. Just a wild clamorous jangling of noises, terrifying, flinging out a message into the forest, a proclamation of panic, or of warning.

Naomi stood rooted to the rock, mouth open, panic-stricken. There were no bells in Clachanpluck. No one had mentioned any bells. She found herself thinking back wildly, illogically. There had definitely been no bells. She visualised the yard at Emily's, the barns and the hayloft door where she had first seen Davey. Was there a bell tower there, any place to hang a bell at all? She couldn't remember. But she would have noticed if they had had a bell.

There was no stopping the sound. Naomi pressed her hands over her ears. They were so discordant now, so demanding. The sound seemed to swallow up the morning, and the echo of it was flung back at her from the forest on the slopes opposite, redoubling the noise. There seemed to be bells ringing out from all over the forest, until the whole valley and every fold in the hills was pulsating with the sound. The forest was on fire with bells. They were everywhere, surrounding her, and there was no escape. Naomi turned her back on the village, and looked out eastwards. Half a mile away was the road to the east, to Carlingwark, and only bare fields and spinneys between her and it. I could leave, thought Naomi. I could take the road out of here and never come back again. A frantic impulse stirred in her to run, to escape from Clachanpluck for ever, and take to the free road, unburdened as when she came.

My fiddle, thought Naomi. I don't have my fiddle.

The fiddle was in her room down in Clachanpluck. Naomi turned her face west again, and the sound of the bells seemed to hit her like a breaking wave. What was it? How long would they ring them like that? I have to get my fiddle, thought Naomi, and pressed her hands harder over her ears to shut out the consuming sound.

She hesitated no longer on the hilltop. There was no shelter here. The bells were pealing all round her, echoing back from every outcrop and hillock, and there was no escape from them. The only way out was away, but not without her fiddle. Naomi pulled herself together, and began to climb down the wet rock on the path towards the village.

Below the rock there was a small area of woodland. Naomi dived into the shelter of the trees, threading a path through dead brown bracken. The bells were a little muffled in the hollow, but not much. The trees themselves seemed to reverberate with the sound; the deep tolling of the bass bell seemed to echo through the very earth on which she trod. She splashed through boggy ground, where a burn swollen with meltwater had burst its banks, and out again into the open fields. A flock of sheep huddled together and ran as she emerged precipitously out of the wood at their backs, scattering across the hillside as she ran through their midst unheeding. She came up to the back of Emily's yard, under the great beech trees that overwatched the household, and climbed the stone wall behind the barn. The bells were overwhelming now, ringing out turbulently as though they would never stop, dominating the whole air, the whole forest. Naomi paused for an instant. The bell with the deep tone was ringing out from the yard itself, the steady bass note that roused echoes from the very earth. No! thought Naomi. Not that way. She dodged round the back of the barn, finding a small passage between the back of the storeshed and the wall. Her way was blocked by the round stone shape of the kiln at the back of the storehouse. Naomi climbed up on the yard wall and encircled it, and jumped down behind the midden on the other side. There was a narrow doorway into the kiln. She slipped inside, and found herself surrounded by piled logs and peat. She scrambled over the stacked fuel, and into the passage by the storeroom. Even here the rooms and passages were permeated by the clamour. Her head was ringing with it. It was unbearable. Naomi thought of turning back, out into the fields where at least the air was free and clear, carrying the sound away into the mountains. Here was all confusion, wild discordant noise and small spaces, jangled echoes and sound traps, clanging and confusion all round her. I can't bear it, thought Naomi, and almost turned back. My fiddle. I have to get my fiddle.

She opened the kitchen door cautiously, but the room was deserted. She was across it in a moment. The fire was almost out, ashes scattered on the hearth. She opened the farther door and was up the stairs three at a time. Her room was empty. Her fiddle was by the bed. She took its case from its place in the corner, and packed the fiddle away with trembling clumsy hands. She tied up the case in its bundle and tucked it under her arm. Then she looked out of her window. It showed her nothing. Her room looked out on to the storeroom roof, out over the field to the beech trees beyond. There was nothing out there, only the clanging of the bells. Naomi ran back to the door, and went hurriedly back down the stairs.

Through the kitchen, round the back of the kiln, past the storehouse wall. The barn was in front of her. There was a flicker of movement under the beech trees, a shadow of passing forms, or a cloud across the sun. Naomi drew back into the safety of the barn wall and found herself in a doorway, the small door used to load feed straight on to the cart across the field wall. The beech trees stirred, although there was no wind, their branches rustling like the waves of the sea. There was a flickering below them, like flame or dappled sunlight. Naomi clutched the fiddle to her chest, and pressed back against the door. It gave under her weight, and she found herself backing into the barn. Hay was piled up behind her where it had been taken out this way. Naomi glanced out again, then pulled the door to, and scrambled up into the absorbing hay. It was still heaped right up to the ceiling at the back. There was a small space between the top bales and the rafters, and a chink of sunlight filtered through at the top, where the roof joined the gable. The bells were muffled here, muted by the high piled hay. Naomi wriggled into the space under the roof, still holding her fiddle tightly to her, and lay flat across the hay on her chest. She laid the fiddle safely beside her, and pressed her hands over her ears, shutting her eyes tight, her face buried in the darkness of the prickly hay.

It was the silence that brought her back to herself at last. It took her a little while to be aware of it. There was only a dim consciousness that the world had changed in some way, that everything was different. Naomi felt herself gradually resurfacing, like a person returning from the drowned.

There was hay all around her. It prickled her intolerably, so that her body felt raw and itched all over. It was warm and uncomfort-

162

able. She put out her hand and felt the fiddle case still beside her. So that was all right. Then she realised that what was different was the silence.

It was like a tangible element, a soft creeping thing that had made its way inside the chinks in the haybarn, bringing contentment, and had curled itself up like a cat in this dim warm place, and slept. Silence surrounded her; the very air was charged with it. Naomi sat up, with small rustlings, and reorientated herself. In the silence it was possible to see properly again. The chink of sunlight had vanished, and only grey winter light filtered through the chink in the roof. There was no sound from outside at all. Perhaps the whole thing had been a dream. Naomi scratched her itching legs absent-mindedly, and tried to let her thoughts settle into some kind of recognisable pattern. She had wanted to run away and leave, but she had been stopped, as surely as if the village were enclosed with high walls and defences, and stood besieged. She tried to remember, but her mind's eye saw only the beech trees, and the shadow of a cloud scudding across the face of the sun. But there had been no possibility of a way out.

The bells had stopped. That was something to be thankful for, at least. If there were any bells. Perhaps it was all the figment of a dream. Naomi rubbed her eyes and tried to pull bits of hay out of her hair. So where was everybody? Would she find everything as it was before? Would they even notice this thing had happened? Or would they act as they had done before, as if it had not? Only Emily had been willing to share her thoughts with her, and she had not seen Emily for days. Naomi felt a sudden longing for company, to be with another human being like herself, to look into someone's eyes, and see respect reflected there, and reassurance. I'm not the only woman in the world, thought Naomi. No one has tried to hurt me. So what am I afraid of?

She picked up her fiddle and laid it across her knees. She sat looking at it thoughtfully for a long time. Then, having reached a decision, she put it carefully back on the hay behind her, well away from the hole in the roof. Then she brushed her clothes down perfunctorily, and began to descend the stack.

The yard was deserted. The mud endemic to it was churned up with hoofprints and footmarks, but that told her nothing, for it was always so. There was no saying if anything unusual had occurred. Naomi hung back for a moment, then she went up to the kitchen door, and entered the house.

Andrew was there. Not alone. There were two other men with him. Naomi recognised them as neighbours from further up the street. They stared at her as if they couldn't believe what they saw. Andrew stood up. She could see he was upset to see her, almost horrified. 'What's this?' he said huskily. 'Why are you here?'

Naomi stood open-mouthed. It seemed such an extraordinary question. She saw one of the other men make a sign with his fingers, a sign against evil. He did it covertly, but there was no mistaking at whom it was directed. It was like a blow in the stomach. Breathless with shock, Naomi shut the door again, and stood out in the empty yard, shaking.

A robin hopped in the mud beside her, picking at crumbs tossed out that morning. She knew him well enough. He was the house robin, fat and round and well-liking. Naomi stared at him, her brain still reeling. 'I don't understand,' she whispered, 'I don't understand.'

So where was Emily? And Davey? And the others? What was this? She dared not go back into the house. She saw the faces of the men again, fear writ large in their eyes. And that sign, made against her. There was no going back. Who would explain this to her? Who could she trust to make it clear? An answer spun into her brain; with a last glance at the heedless robin she left the yard, and sped up the road towards Bridget's house.

The road was not empty. There were men there. Small knots and groups of men, standing in doorways, sitting on the parapet of the bridge. Naomi drew back, but they had seen her. Nowhere to go back to. There was a heavy silence in the street. Not one of them moved, or spoke. Naomi felt herself shaking, but she made herself breathe, and walked on.

Every man in the village seemed to be in the street. She fixed her eyes on the top of the hill, where the crossroads was, and walked firmly past them. They made no pretence of being uninterested, but watched her silently. Not one of them moved. But when she had passed she heard a whisper behind her, low voices muttering together. She felt a shiver in the small of her back, eyes fixed on her, signs of protection made against her. Her skin was creeping with cold fear, and damp sweat trickled from her armpits and between her breasts. But she held panic at bay and made herself walk steadily, past all the eyes and silent forms in doorways, every man and boy watching her as if she were a prisoner doomed to die.

There was no one at the crossroads. Naomi gave a shudder of relief, and turned into the inn. She went round to the kitchen door, and stopped. She was still shaking, and could not trust herself to speak if she had to. She pressed her hands against her face, and tried to breathe properly. Then she held up one hand. It was shaking uncontrollably. The ridiculous thought rose, you can't play the fiddle like that. With an effort she steadied herself, and knocked at the door.

There was a pause which seemed interminable. No welcoming, 'Come in,' but footsteps. Slow footsteps crossing to the door. It opened in front of her. Not Bridget. George. He stared at her, apparently thunderstruck.

'Can I come in?' asked Naomi. Her voice was shaky, but to her relief it still functioned.

Automatically George opened the door wider. But he still said nothing, and he went on staring at her as if she were a ghost. Naomi crossed the threshhold. The kitchen was clean and tidy, no activity going on inside at all. Alan was there, on his own, squatting on the hearthrug by the fire.

'Isn't Bridget here?'

They both seemed bewildered by the question, and slowly Alan shook his head. 'No,' said George blankly. 'No, she's not here.'

It was too much. Naomi felt the tears rising, but that would do no good. She forced them back, and tried to speak without sounding pleading. 'Then where is she? What's happening here?'

There was a long silence. The little boy on the hearthrug never took his eyes off her, sitting unnaturally still, doing nothing. That's not like Alan, thought Naomi, with another flash of clear but irrelevant thought. George was still holding the door, but he slowly pushed it shut, moving like a man who thinks he is dreaming. 'Didn't you hear the bells?' he said at last.

'Of course I did. But I didn't know what they were. How could I be expected to know?'

'You didn't know,' said George. It was a statement, not a question. He seemed to be saying it to himself, as though it were a new proposition, a problem that had been set him to which he had to find the answer. 'I can't help you very much,' he said eventually. 'You shouldn't be here. But I can't change that.'

'What was it?' asked Naomi, and made herself ask the thing that terrified her. 'Was it me?'

'You?' said George, startled. 'You? No, of course it wasn't you. But I don't know what you should do now.'

'Then what was it?'

He seemed to find it hard to look for words, as though he had to tell her something that was impossible. A thing that should not have happened, or a matter for which there was no common language between them. 'There was wrong done,' he said at last. 'My words aren't the same as your words. But the women have gone.'

'Gone?' A new terror, but a flicker of understanding at last. A wrong done? If there were only someone here who spoke in a language I could understand. What would Bridget tell me? What would she call it that I would call it too? Rape? Has there been rape? She looked at George again, and recoiled from him. She didn't want him to explain to her, didn't want to hear his words. There was nothing he could do for her. Naomi felt suddenly totally alone, more alone than she had ever felt in her life. This was not solitude. This was the loneliness of a different species, of one who seems to be alone of all their kind in the world. She looked at George, and thought of Davey. I want to get out, she thought. I want to get out of here.

'What do you want to do?' asked George, echoing her thoughts.

'My fiddle,' said Naomi. 'I have to get my fiddle.'

He considered that. 'Is it at Emily's?'

'Yes.'

'I'd better walk down with you.'

She didn't want him to, but knew she could hardly do without him. He was right. The men were still in the street, and the same muttering broke out behind them as they passed. George kept his distance from her, but walked in step with her, until they reached the yard gate. 'You'll be all right,' he said. 'Andrew's there. And Davey.' Then he turned abruptly, and left her.

Naomi didn't try to go into the house. She made a beeline for the haybarn, and climbed up again and found her fiddle. She clutched it to her chest like a talisman, thinking hard. She remembered the flickering under the beech trees, and the street with the knots of men. The pealing of the bells, and the silence. No way out. She realised she was cold with fear, still shivering. Taking her fiddle with her, she found herself a warm corner in the hay, and huddled there like a hunted creature, out of sight.

22

The hunted man crouched in the heart of the forest, his ear to the earth, listening. It was midwinter and there should have been silence, but there was no peace in the cold ground. The forest was alive, aware of what had been done, and watchful.

He stood up slowly, his eyes wary, glancing all round him, ready to run. The trees were still, pale larches bare of needles, a silent wall of matted wood behind him. Needles carpeted the ground, so the land was soft and bare beneath their covering. There was a rough clearing in the trees before him, thick with dead bracken crushed under the weight of vanished snow. Beyond, forest trees towered over him, oaks with huge branches that defied the weight of the air, grey beeches rising in pale columns to an arching canopy above. There was a rustling in the larches and he swung round sharply. But it was only a couple of crows that flapped out of the trees in ungainly flight, disappearing over the treetops.

There were more sounds, drumming, a faint steady thud of hoofbeats. He stepped back into the shadow of the larches. Three deer, two hinds and a stag, came out at a gallop, leaping across the bracken in long graceful bounds, passing him, unnoticing. Something must have startled them. He crouched down again behind the thin cover of the bracken, torn brown jacket blending with the pale brown of winter larches.

There was a thickening in the air under the trees. A heavy stillness like a summer night before the storm, when the stars are blotted out and dark clouds drift across the heat-held sky. A closeness in the air so he found himself fighting for breath, lungs leaden in his chest. A weight that spread downwards and settled itself in the very tips of the larches. Instinctively he dragged his hood over his head, shielding himself from the heaviness above. But there was no movement, no sound, merely a persistent drifting in, and quiescence all round him.

And voices. He raised his head quickly, eyes wide. A far-off keening of many voices, thin and agonised, like a persistent wailing out of another time. The sounds rose from beyond the forest, bodiless, and then behind him, so he turned again and stared wildly into the shadows of the matted larches. There was nothing there, only an opaque shade, unnaturally dense, as if the sky had crumpled and fallen to the earth, entangled among the branching trees.

The forest was foreign to him now, another place. He had loved it all his life, and cared for it, and now he was cast out, blinded, staring at familiar forms and shadows, recognising nothing. There was no exile more bitter than this, to be no longer part of the land. The land was rising against him, trees crowding in, delivering sentence upon him, the earth ominous and unyielding under his feet.

Now there were footsteps, running footsteps, and the wailing drew nearer, voices belonging to no bodies, closing in upon him; a harsh chanting with no music to it, only the embodiment of pain. The footsteps under the trees coming closer, from all sides of the clearing, through the thickness of the larches behind him. The dark drew down, thick and substantial. The weight of it made him stagger, it dragged at his lungs in painful breaths, engulfing him.

I never did this thing. It was something done to me. I never wanted to hurt her, but I was hurt. Is that a crime, is it a crime to be in agony, and not know what I do? There is only one crime, and that is the crime against the land. What is it that you think that I have done?

The shadow was detaching itself from the trees. There was darkness across the clearing, night falling when there should be no night. There was rustling again, and movement. Hoofbeats, footsteps, the shapes of figures, animal or human, crossing the clearing. A thing not part of the forest he had known, but not alien either. An element recognised for the first time, like the shadow of his own image. Patrick watched, mesmerised. The bracken stirred, there was the sharp sound of a breaking twig. His skin prickled, and he drew in a sharp breath. Then he turned his face towards the larches, and fled.

It was impossible to run through the larches. They grabbed at him, caught his clothes with spiked fingers, tore at his face, pushed him down. The only clear space was under. Patrick dropped to his hands and knees and pushed his way through dying wood, the debris of the years littering the floor of the forest. Low branches whipped his face, and he could not look up. The keening was very close behind him now. There was movement at the edge of the trees, on the fringes of the clearing where he had just been standing.

I did what I could when I fled from her. I didn't trust myself either. Is that a crime, not to trust myself? I did what I could, but fate followed me. I never meant to do it. I love her still. She was mine. The crime is only the thing that she says that I did.

There was free air in front of him at last. Patrick came clear of the clinging larch trees and rolled down a bank before he could regain his footing, fetching up against the huge trunk of a long fallen tree. He clawed himself upright, holding on to the trunk. It was rotten and disintegrating, and gave under his clutching hands. A dead branch snapped off with a dull crack. Patrick scrambled over the treetrunk and fled into the tangle of undergrowth beyond it.

It was thick with briars and dead bracken. The trees were young oaks and birches that didn't keep out enough light. Patrick forced his way through, no longer knowing where he was. This was his own forest, but it was betraying him, indicating nothing. There was mud under his feet. He slipped in sudden wetness, and heard the plash of paddling feet ahead of him. Feet crossing marshy ground, and a rustling just out of sight. The voices had died down. There was only the hint of mournful crying far away over the moors, or perhaps it was only the curlews calling, or the crying of a lost soul out of another world.

Patrick listened. His hands and face were torn and scratched, his clothes ripped to rags. No longer a being of the forest, but something inimical, hunted and apart. He watched black shadows drifting over the trees, blotting out the day. He saw the trees swaying in a wind he could not feel, soundlessly. There was no more soughing of the wind in the trees for him. With sudden realisation he registered silence. No rustling, no movement, no call of bird or sound of branch on branch. No running water or drift of leaves. He could hear nothing, and the shadow loomed over him, deadening the air. Patrick watched the branches moving to a music whose strains he could no longer hear, and realised that the forest was lost to him. For the first time he sank to the ground, and wept.

There was no sound in all the world but his own sobbing. Like a being whirled into a vacuum, out of the world, he was torn away, cast out. There was still earth under his body, but no longer his earth. The forest was closed to him. Patrick lay still at last, and listened to the silence.

It was not a sound that he heard, merely a coming closer. The shadow was very near to him now. The movement was not so much a thing heard as a vibration that ran through the earth beneath him. He was aware of them all round him, a slow circle moving inwards. It was too dark to see. But he was conscious of eyes holding him, drawing in. Patrick stopped weeping and stood up. They were very near. So near, if he stretched out his hand he might touch them. Perhaps he could feel their breathing, a rhythmic pulsation very close to him, enclosing him. There was no escaping from them now. No possibility of flight. He could not move at all. The inevitable steadied him. He stood upright, accepting at last.

The darkness was all round him, part of him, his own being was swallowed up in it, intertwined. He felt himself dissolving, losing substance. No longer resisting, no longer separate. There was a man, but I am not he. No longer. Only the dark.

A shot cracked out, an explosion of sound, and he was part of it. A flash of light, and a falling apart. Disintegration. And the welcome dark.

Earth received him. Damp earth under him, and his blood flowing down to it. Blood soaking down into the earth, and then only the dark.

23

Emily felt more tired than she had ever felt in her life, quite drained of all energy and emotion. It was worth it; she had done everything that was necessary. In a curious way she even felt vindicated. It had been difficult to come to terms with what she had given to Fiona. To give away her own power was impossible, but the mere transference of a symbol had signified more than she had expected. There hadn't been any time to think about it. She had left Fiona knowing that she had done right by her, but with a passive kind of melancholy that didn't feel like herself at all. Because she is older, she had thought, does that mean that I am growing old? I haven't finished with these things yet. And then there had been a crisis, and she had done what she must do, and never wavered. It was hard to feel anything now. The day was grey and empty, the house quiet, as though still shocked into silence by what had happened.

And there was still something else not dealt with. I should have thought of her, thought Emily dully. I should have thought about her before this. There has been so much to do, and I am too tired to think. But she is my guest, and it should have been my responsibility.

Besides, I love her. Emily stood abruptly. She didn't want to think about that; there had been quite enough emotion. She went over to the window and looked out. The street was empty. A thin rain was falling, and the earth looked worn out and grubby, crushed by the departed snow. The road was badly potholed after the frost, swamped by brown puddles and churned mud. Draughts edged in around the closed window, icy on her warm skin. It had to be done, thought Emily drearily. I want to talk to Bridget, but Anna wants her more. I can't rest from this yet.

She sat down on her bed again, arms huddled across her chest, trying to keep warm. I have thought about them all, except one. I could have done no more. I owe her an apology. But when I dreamed about her it was a nightmare. And yet she has given us so much. I should have remembered that she was afraid of the forest, but I had to think of the village. There has been no time to think of her till now. And now I want to sleep.

Emily got up again and paced to and fro, her hands up her sleeves. I can't work it all out. I should have known. Whatever the connections were, I failed to see them. That was the first time in my life I was afraid of the dark. 'I wish it were summer,' she said out loud, inconsequentially. She was staring out of the window again. The rain was harder now, the puddles flecked with heavy drops, and the roofs across the street black with water. It will take a long time to heal, thought Emily. Perhaps it will never be healed, not in my lifetime. What will I find that I have lost, when the village is properly awake again?

She has nothing to lose. Why do I have to worry about her? None of this had anything to do with her. But she must have been very much afraid. Perhaps she is still afraid. But she is still here, there must be a reason for that. If it were nothing to do with her, she would have run away. She stayed, so I owe her something. An explanation? There isn't anything I could explain.

A figure shrouded in a hooded jacket splashed past on the road below, stooping under the weight of a load of hay. A dog circled round, skirting the puddles, making short dashes ahead and doubling back again, ears cocked impatiently. I wonder if anyone fed the chickens, thought Emily. It's no use, I have to go and see her. It's not a thing anyone else can do, any more than what I did last night. You can't hand over responsibility as if it were a trinket. It's between her and me. Emily turned away from the window again, and left the room.

She knocked at the door on the other side of the landing. There was no answer. She was just about to knock again when Naomi's voice, rather muffled, said, 'Who's that?'

'It's me,' said Emily.

Another pause. 'Come in,' said Naomi.

Naomi was sitting on her bed, her quilt wrapped round her. There were dark shadows under her eyes, but she seemed composed enough. Emily wondered if she had gone to bed at all last night. She stood awkwardly at the door. 'I owe you something,' she said. 'An apology, perhaps.'

Naomi shook her head slowly. 'I don't want your apologies.'

'I don't understand.' It hadn't occurred to her that Naomi might be angry. Emily felt a pang of shock, and realised that she was exhausted.

Naomi shrugged and said nothing.

'Are you angry with me?'

'Why should I be angry?'

Naomi sounded as tired as she felt. Perhaps she was wrong, it wasn't anger. Then what? 'I forgot you,' said Emily, and the words seemed ridiculously inadequate even as she said them. 'I had to think about Clachanpluck.'

'Of course.' Naomi wasn't giving anything away. Emily suddenly noticed that she was shivering under the quilt. It was certainly very cold in here.

'Look,' said Emily desperately. 'I'm no good at this. I don't know what you feel. I don't know what you're thinking. I have no imagination and I'm entirely obtuse. You have every right to be angry, or whatever you're being. But I wish you'd tell me what it is.'

'I don't believe you.'

'Don't believe what?'

'You're not obtuse. You just choose not to think about it.'

'I am thinking about you. That's why I came.'

'I don't mean that,' said Naomi impatiently. She shoved the quilt away and stood up. She was very pale still, but her eyes were bright. 'Listen to me,' said Naomi with sudden vehemence. 'I don't need this. I don't want you apologising to me as if you were a public deputation. I'm a human being. You scared me out of my mind, you and your village. I'd have run away, only I couldn't. You know why I couldn't. It's your forest. I don't know where you've been. I don't know what you did. But I know you've got feelings, the same as me. And I'm sick of you trying to pretend you haven't.'

'What?' said Emily, in complete confusion.

'And don't come that over me. Treat me like a person. I'm not a bloody tree!'

'But it's true!' Emily was almost shouting back at her. 'I don't know what you're talking about. What do you want me to do? It's my village. I had to deal with it. People were hurt. Don't you care? Don't you care about this place at all?'

'Fuck the place. I care about you.'

'I don't know what you want.' To her fury she realised she was near to tears of frustration. 'I came to try to explain. We had to do what we did. There was a rape.'

The flurry of words was silenced, savagely cut off. They stared at each other with frightened eyes, appalled at their own failure to understand one another.

'I know there was,' said Naomi huskily. 'George told me. You don't have to explain anything to me. It's not between you and me, not that.'

'Then what?'

Naomi sighed, and brushed her hand over her eyes, as though trying to keep herself awake. 'We don't seem to speak the same language, do we?'

'I don't know.'

'I was frightened,' said Naomi very slowly, as if she were speaking to a foreigner. 'I was frightened because any woman would have been frightened. You have done nothing to hurt me. On the contrary, what you did to save your world saves me too. You must never apologise to me for that. I am angry for quite a different reason.'

'Tell me.'

'I'm trying to.' Naomi took a deep breath and carried on. 'I am not a woman of Clachanpluck, but I am still a woman. I wish that you could see who I am.'

'You think I haven't?'

'Because you only see yourself in Clachanpluck. It's like looking in a mirror. What you don't see in me is what is the same as yourself.'

Emily pressed her hands against her eyes. 'I only got back an hour ago,' she said. 'I've been with Anna. We knew what to do in the forest, and we did it. But I don't know how to reach Anna now. All I know is I know nothing. I've never even used the word. They taught us it was unmentionable, a horror out of the past it was sacrilege to name. The threat of it never touched me for a moment. I can't grasp what it means. How can we live on our own terms if such a thing is real? Who are we, if this can happen to us? How can I answer that? How can I help her get out of a place I was never in? How can I give her back her own image of herself? What can I do? What would you do, Naomi?'

'Me?' said Naomi, astonished at the question. 'Why do you ask me?'

'You might see more clearly. You are a woman too, but not of Clachanpluck. I failed to see the connections. Perhaps I could have made things different.'

'No!' Naomi took her by the shoulders and shook her, but not roughly. 'No! You must never say that. You're betraying yourself. Betraying all of us, including Anna. You can't take responsibility for this. You can't say any woman made this happen!'

'He was a man of Clachanpluck,' said Emily, and put her hands over her face.

Naomi pulled them away relentlessly. 'So what?' she said fiercely. 'He didn't rape Clachanpluck. He raped Anna. He didn't threaten Clachanpluck. He threatened every one of us. Including me. Emily, when I didn't know what had happened, I was terrified. There were only the men, and I thought it was because of me, because I didn't belong here. I thought that I was responsible, and I didn't even know for what. Don't you see? It stops us seeing each other. Look at me!'

Emily looked at the floor. Naomi held her wrists so she couldn't hide her face, but Emily wouldn't look at her. She is ruthless, this woman, thought Emily, she seems to have no compassion for us at all. 'Of course I know,' she said wearily. 'That's why we went away. It's why we could never let him back into the forest. Men may think it cruel, but there was nothing else to be done.'

'I do understand, you know.'

Naomi's voice was unexpectedly gentle, and Emily allowed herself to look up. Naomi was right in front of her, closer than she had realised. There was naked affection in her face, no ruthlessness at all. Emily was shaken. She twisted her wrists out of Naomi's clasp and took her hands. 'I'm glad you couldn't run away,' she said. 'You were needed.'

Naomi shook her head slightly, and took Emily in her arms. Emily held her tightly. It was pure relief, confusion falling into place at last. Naomi realised she was as tired as Emily, still keyed up and defensive against this village that had so nearly seemed to turn against her. But not now. Naomi shut her eyes, and sighed. A knot of fear seemed to dissolve inside her, and she shuddered. 'Are you all right?' asked Emily, looking up.

'I can't believe the questions you ask. I don't think I have anything to say.'

Emily smiled. She felt so right, this woman who had landed in her life from nowhere. It was easy to hold her, like holding the image of herself. When she looked at Naomi, their eyes were on a level. Naomi's were greenish, slightly flecked with hazel. They were alight now with affection, or relief. There were still deep shadows under them, and under a faint sprinkling of freckles her skin was unnaturally white. 'You look worn out,' said Emily, 'and so am I.'

'It's not the most peaceful night I ever had.' Naomi spoke flippantly, for fear of saying too much.

'Would you like to sleep? Because I would.'

'Here?'

'If you want me.'

'I'll tell you that in the morning, when I can think straight.'

'It is morning.'

It felt extraordinary to be smiling again, almost dangerous after so much pain. But Naomi was smiling too, green eyes crinkled with tired amusement, and a warm body against hers, blotting out the cold. Naomi looked back at Emily, and held her close. She was strong in her arms, this woman, even though she was exhausted. Naomi looked at the steady blue eyes and sunburned skin. This close, she could see there were tiny broken veins in her cheeks, from being out in every weather. Whatever she did last night, thought Naomi, it's taken nearly all her strength. She stood back, still holding Emily's hands. 'Come and sleep with me then. I think we deserve it.'

Naomi's bed was cold, the sheets clinging and clammy. They pulled the quilt and the blankets tightly round themselves, and twined themselves together to get warm.

'Naomi?'

'Yes?'

'I love you. I'm going to sleep.'

'So am I. I never thought I'd be warm again.'

'That's all right then.'

'But it's not all,' said Naomi, half asleep. 'I'll tell you the rest tomorrow.'

There was no answer. Naomi wriggled herself more comfortably around Emily's sleeping body, and shut her eyes. Uneasy images danced before her brain, a moving forest, swallowing up them all, except herself, and a street full of men, silent eyes watching, dangerous, and a woman running through the storm, lost among the indifferent trees. Naomi jerked and half woke, muttering. Emily stirred and pulled her round so Naomi's head was resting on her shoulder. The nightmare receded. There was still the forest, but it was benign, summer sun slanting through a curtain of young leaves, and a soft path through the leafmould, trodden by the feet of people like herself, another woman like herself. Naomi stretched herself in the unaccustomed warmth, and slept.

24

Midwinter spring is its own season
Sempiternal though sodden towards sundown,
Suspended in time, between pole and tropic.
When the short day is brightest, with frost and fire,
The brief sun flames the ice, on ponds and ditches,
In windless cold that is the heart's heat,
Reflecting in a watery mirror
A glare that is blindness in the early afternoon.

'I don't want it,' said Davey.

'No one does,' said George. 'So I said I'd take it to Carlingwark. And there's the messages. Will you come?'

Davey sighed heavily. 'Ay,' he said at last, 'I'll come.'

'Bring that, then.'

Davey picked up the gun, which had lain on the wall between them, and went round by the gate out of the yard. George went to the pony's head and unlooped the reins. Then he jumped up into the little cart. Davey handed up the gun cautiously and climbed up after him. 'Come up then,' said George to the pony. The cart started with a jerk, and rumbled over the cobbles.

There were only a few people in the street. A neighbour called out, and George stopped. She came hurrying over, and said, 'While you're there, George, could you get me a ball of twine? Not if it's a trouble. I know what you've got on your hands, but we're needing it badly, if you do remember.'

'I'll try,' said George. 'No promises.'

The pony plodded uphill to the crossroads, and the iron wheels creaked over the stony road. The pony turned left automatically, for this was a familiar journey. Only its driver was different, but habit was strong. The road to the east was clear of trees, running directly through fields separated by hedges and stone dykes. It ignored the inevitable hillocks, taking a line straight over them like a switchback. The pony strained to the top of each steep slope, then jogged down into the next dip, so George had to put the drag on the wheels each time.

It was one of the hard frosty days of early January that held all the promise of spring. The sky was clear, and sunlight touched the fields with a forgotten warmth, a warmth only in vision, for the ground was still bound by frost, but there was a glint of gold in it which was like riches to starved eyes. The air was sweet and clear, with a faint promise of growing things to come. Tight buds were forming on the hawthorn hedges that lined the road, presaging a gentler flowering than the white touch of snow. There was the rest of a long winter still ahead, but this was a foretaste of what lay beyond. In spite of himself Davey was cheered by it, and an irrepressible happiness warmed him. The darkness of the time had touched him closely, but his world still turned. He did not say so. George seemed wrapped in more sombre thoughts, which were perhaps more proper to the occasion.

Silence continued between them until the fields of Clachanpluck were left behind, and they were once more jogging through woodland. This was not the forest. There was nothing perilous or uncertain about this place. It was a pleasant stretch of wood, protecting the village from the human world outside. The road was better used than any of the other three roads out of Clachanpluck. It was a wide, prosaic track, suggesting company and market places. It presented no difficulty to a pony and cart in this weather, now that the ground had hardened, and the muddy dips solidified again. Sometimes the cart skidded a little, driven off course by the frozen tracks of other passings, but the pony was canny, and required little assistance. George kept a light hand on the reins and allowed his thoughts to drift. It was a relief to be out of Clachanpluck. He acknowledged the feeling, with some surprise, as one entirely new to his experience. He wondered whether to mention it to Davey, but Davey was absorbed in his own thoughts. He must have been badly scarred by what had happened. George forebore to disturb him.

It was Davey who broke the silence. They had negotiated a bridge over a burn, and had got out while the road curved steeply up the bank round a sharp outcrop of rock. The two men walked side by side at the pony's head until the going became easier.

'What do you reckon to do with it?' asked Davey.

'Sell it,' said George. 'His family could use the money. They've lost a good smith.'

It was like the sun going in. A good smith. And a good friend too, thought Davey, and allowed a name to form in his mind for the first time since it had happened. Patrick. Davey shut his eyes for a moment, and struggled with feelings that he didn't want to know. When he opened them again he glanced at George warily, in case he'd noticed. But George was looking at the sky. 'It's not going to last, this weather,' he remarked.

'No,' said Davey.

'I don't know if we'll find a buyer,' went on George. 'I'm not up in these things. We can only try.'

Davey stopped in his tracks. 'We can't take it back,' he said.

'We might have to.'

'No!'

The pony, seeing that they had both stopped, and the top of the hill was safely reached, stopped as well, and half closed its eyes, shifting its weight on to three hooves, resting.

'I know what you mean,' said George. 'But we might have no choice.'

'I never used a gun,' said Davey. 'He offered to teach me.'

'Ay.'

Davey fought off the feelings that threatened to overwhelm him. There was no safety in the village. Too much had happened, too much was expected of him. He was free of it now, and it would be forgivable with George. After all, George was also a man. Davey tried to be silent, but he had been silent too long, and the pain was too great.

'He was a musician,' he said, as if the words could be held back no longer. 'He could play the drums, and the pipes too, though he was shy about that. He was a good friend.' He was aware of George listening, and rooks chattering in the trees below the road. 'He was my friend,' said Davey, and heard his voice crack. 'I loved him.'

'Ay,' said George, and took Davey's hands in his own. Davey turned his head away. A tear glinted on his cheek, and dripped on to his jacket. 'It's not a bad thing,' said George, 'to weep for a friend.'

'But I can't,' said Davey in a choked voice. 'I'm living with what

180

was done. I love my family. I can't say anything about it to them. It would be an insult. I think that Naomi wants to go, but she's afraid of hurting me more. And I should let her, but I can't say it. And I loved him.'

'You did no wrong,' said George.

Davey took his hands away and smeared the tears away. 'You can't say that. It isn't like that at all.' He wanted to explain to George, but the words were drowned in grief. Davey fought to master himself, and glanced at George. It was his undoing. George was watching him. No man had looked at him with tenderness before. Sorrow flooded over him like a tide, and he cried unrestrainedly. The relief of it was hardly bearable, that he should be allowed to mourn without guilt. Everything was drowned at last in tears, pain melting into sorrow, a constricting weight lifted off him, dissolving into peace. He clung to George, blinded by weeping, and George held him, rock-like.

Davey raised his head at last. It was hard to meet George's eyes. When he did, he saw that George had been crying too, and he found himself smiling in sudden shared delight. 'It's all right,' said Davey, holding on to George. 'It will be all right.' He chuckled, and wondered if George thought he was hysterical.

'I love my family too,' said George. 'But I was frightened. I was frightened of what was done.'

'I dared not say so,' said Davey, and shivered. 'Patrick was my friend. He wasn't so different from me.'

'No,' said George.

'I never heard of it happening before. Not in my time.'

'Nor in mine.'

'I thought it never could. I thought it was only a shadow, a memory out of the past.'

'I think we still carry the past within us,' said George. 'It doesn't go away.'

'The past wasn't all bad. Did you know . . .'

'What?'

'No, no. It's foolish. Nothing.'

'Tell me.'

'I have a book,' said Davey. 'Did you know there were once hundreds of different kinds of roses that no longer exist? It was all done by grafting. A forgotten art. We may gain something, but we lose too.'

'No we don't. It's only change.'

Davey shivered. 'I'm scared of change.'

'Why?'

Davey seemed to search for words. 'I don't know. I can't explain. When my niece was little, she preferred me. She used to want to come with me, play with me, all the time. She's grown into a woman now. I used to think I knew her, but I don't.'

'No.'

'I can't stop thinking about it. What's happened. I can't say it to any of them. But if I had been different, that would have made everything different. It didn't have to happen. It didn't have to be him.' He looked at George almost pleadingly, as if begging for absolution.

'It's not just you,' said George. The cart creaked behind him, as the pony shifted from one foot to another. 'Shall we go on?'

Davey went round the cart, and they took their places again. George shook the reins, and the pony broke into a reluctant trot. There was a rattle of metal and the thud of something dropping behind them. 'Hang on,' said Davey. 'It's fallen over.'

'Better hold it.'

Davey reached over and took the gun again. He held it across his knees, and the sun glinted on the metal barrel. 'I suppose you couldn't use it yourself?' asked Davey.

'No. I've no need of it.'

Davey said no more. He glanced at George, but George's eyes were fixed on the road ahead. It was uncomfortable, thinking about what he had just done. To weep for a man condemned to die. Davey shuddered. 'George?'

'Ay?'

'You don't mind?'

'Mind what?'

'I wondered what you were thinking of me now.'

There was a long pause, and Davey waited anxiously. 'I was thinking about the way you put things. You're very like your sister.'

That was unexpected. Davey frowned over it for a moment. Well, they must talk to each other. He thought of Naomi as he had last seen her, playing long solitary tunes on her fiddle while the tears flowed down her cheeks unchecked. He had wanted to comfort her, but she was remote, unreachable. He realised that it had always been so. As far as he knew, George had not been to the house since what had happened. Emily was silent and subdued. It hurts us all, thought Davey. Nothing is untouched by it.

'I suppose I learned it from her, then,' he said eventually. 'I can't ever remember her different.'

'No,' said George. 'She was never different.'

Davey gave him another sidelong glance. He sensed an unhappiness for something he did not know. He recognised the pain, but George was a private man, and would never speak to him about Emily. But another piece of Davey's world was slipping away, another piece of solid ground disintegrating under his feet. If it were not well between George and Emily, what hope was there for him?

He was still subdued when they reached Carlingwark, but then his attention was demanded again. Neither man was used to trading, and they were painfully conscious of being supplanters. The man who would be looked for at every stall and workshop would not be seen here again.

'Will the news have reached them?' asked Davey, a new thought striking him.

'I don't know,' said George, and his face was grim.

The answer was soon clear enough. They were treated everywhere with civility and no overt curiosity, but no one went out of their way to speak to them. A hush fell in every place they entered, and their messages were attended to with unusual despatch. 'They know,' said George, as they emerged from the chandlers. 'They know too much.'

'It would be quicker if we divided the messages.'

George hesitated and said, 'I'd be glad of your company. I'm not very sure of this.'

'Then we go together,' said Davey readily.

He soon realised that he was of far more use in this situation than George. George made everything worse by turning taciturn, and retreating from all curious eyes with as much haste as possible. Davey stopped and talked to people, and there was a noticeable thawing. But no one asked them about Patrick.

The short day was drawing in, and long shadows reached across the street. A cold wind whined among the clustered houses. The market stallholders were beginning to pack up, and the shop doors were shutting against the wind.

'There's the gun,' said Davey reluctantly.

'Ay,' said George. 'I've not forgotten.'

They might as well have tried to sell a cask of lighted gunpowder. No one would touch Patrick's gun. After the first try the word went ahead of them so that doors closed hurriedly at their approach, and people turned their backs, vanishing into alleys and sidestreets. George stood with the gun in his hands, and looked at Davey with quiet despair.

'I don't think I can stand this,' he said.

For George, that was a frightening admission. Davey was already tired and confused, worn out by so many unaccustomed faces, crowds of people in a place that was not familiar to him. He didn't feel like himself here. He knew it better than George. He'd chosen to come sometimes, but only to the cattle market with Andrew, or with Patrick who knew what he was doing. In those times it had been a holiday, with time and leisure to browse among the pedlars' stalls and to chat to people about matters that cost no emotion. But for George it was worse. George hardly ever left Clachanpluck. This place disorientated him, and the bartering worried him, off his home ground. Looking at George now, Davey could see the strain in his eyes, and a whiteness under his tan. 'Let me try,' said Davey. 'You walk the pony a bit. I'll come back in half an hour.'

Gratefully George nodded, and walked the pony quietly behind the row of houses, along an empty track leading to the loch. The sun was beginning to set. They'd need to be gone in half an hour anyway, at the latest, if they were to be home by dark. The loch was clear and quiet. Two swans swam slowly across it in a wide arc, ripples undulating behind them, lapping the shore at George's feet. There were islands in the loch, dwelling places out of the far distant past. In the light of the low sun the trees on them were tinged with a light that was almost purple. There was a peace here, away from the business of the afternoon. A peace like the peace that had been broken in Clachanpluck. So much had been lost. He had his family, his life would go on, but the thing dearest to his heart had been lost, torn away and cast into a darkness that he dare not face. Davey was so like her. Same hair, same eyes. Same easy laughter and tears, same grasshopper thoughts, ideas leaping and landing unexpectedly, pulling him after them into an inconsequential dance. I have to face her, thought George. I'll have to face her. There was his sister too. She had said nothing, but there was a reproachfulness about her. Not much was hidden from her either. The thing had to be faced.

He heard someone approaching down the cart track, and looked up to see Davey, disconsolate, the gun slung across his shoulders. 'No luck?'

'No.'

Davey came and stood beside him. The swans had disappeared now into the rushes across the loch. A small breeze riffled the water, and the red rays of the sun caught the movement and turned it to a dancing pattern of colour, red and grey and black, rippling out across the still waters.

'I'm not taking it back,' said Davey.

'It's a valuable thing.'

'Patrick is dead,' said Davey. 'What's value?'

'It's not ours.'

'The burden is ours.'

'It's old. There's no craft for making such a thing as that left in the world.'

'Everything must change, if we are to live.'

'But the choice is not ours.'

'It is if we make it.'

'It'll take courage to do such a thing, and abide by it.'

'If there are debts, I shall pay them.'

'If credit is called for, we must both account for it.'

'You're willing, then?'

'I dare not, Davey.'

'I dare not do anything else. You won't take it. I refuse it.'

'Then we have no choice.'

'We have every choice,' said Davey vehemently, 'but we have to make it now.'

George reached and took the gun from him. It wasn't a thing he was used to holding. Wood and metal were smooth in his hands, surprisingly heavy.

'You saw his body,' said Davey. 'You know what it can do.'

There was a long silence. 'I agree,' said George. 'Is it you, or me?'

'I have a debt to pay,' said Davey. He took the gun back from George, and stepped away from him. He swung his arm right back in one strong movement, and flung the thing far out, so it went spinning over the loch, falling with a small splash into shimmering water. The ripples expanded, catching a brilliant red off the setting sun, ruffling the rushes that fringed the further shore. Slowly they subsided, and the patterns melted and vanished, and there was only the silent water, and the dying sun.

25

The first thing people made out of the earth was a garden. It is with a garden that the past begins, and in a garden that all is brought to fruition. In order to make gardens, people tilled the earth and nourished it, creating intricate patterns and designs, never neglecting the earth but changing it, bringing into being something which was neither of people nor of the land, but unique, a union of land and thought which was the most joyous creation of both. For the land is one being, and we are another, and too often we are aware of separation, but in a garden the hurt is healed. We make the earth part of us, and so become ourselves. If people had no gardens they would forget who they were, and turn their pain upon one another. There is safety in gardens, understanding and fulfilment.

There was a time in this world when the earth was abused. Trees were felled, whole forests put to the axe and brought to ruin. Grassy plains were ploughed and turned to desert, then the desert itself was exploited, penetrated by the lust of men, and despoiled. There was no place left untouched or respected, neither ice nor fire were left in purity. The very air was poisoned and defiled, and the waters were drowned in the waste of it.

Such a thing is inconceivable, unless the beginning of it is understood. For it begins with the loss of a garden.

There was once a garden containing every variety of rose ever seen in the world. The flowers of the rose are magical. They embody, more than any flower that grows, the union of the people and the land. There have been roses on earth through all the long years when there was neither past nor future, when the land was only the land. And there have been people who have turned their imagination to everything that has been given them, for both health and harm. The coming together of the people and the roses brought into being something new, flowers of white and crimson, scarlet and flame, plants that trailed or twined, turned to trees or shrubs or little bushes, more varieties than had been dreamed of in the world. The scent of the roses sweetened the long years of pain, but there was never a flower that grew without a thorn.

There was a rose garden surrounded by a hedge of yew. A garden surrounded by yew is a place out of time, for yew is the tree for whom time has the least meaning. Yew grows thick and evergreen, and whatever is held within its circle is a thing apart, protected.

There was a rose garden within a circle of yew, and the garden was made by a woman. When she had planted the roses and mulched the beds, and when the hedge of yew had established its slow growth, she was filled with delight, and she rested, and rejoiced in what she had made. But the moons passed, and the spring came. The earth stirred in its sleep, and all living things began to awaken and grow. The roses grew, and the yew hedge grew, but not only they. The soil in the garden was fine and fruitful, and nourished every kind of weed, dockens and nettles and willow herb and mares' tails, all the worst weeds that any gardener could dream of. For you have to remember that this was a very new garden. The woman saw how much work there was to be done, and her spirit quailed. There were not only the weeds. There was compost to make, and mulch to spread. There were flowers to be deadheaded, and the hedge to clip. And when the weeds died back there would be pruning, and grafting, and propagation.

So she thought about what she should do, and she consulted with the earth. The earth provided an answer that seemed both joyous and satisfactory. The earth gave her a man, to help with the work and share in her love, and to give her children when she wanted them . . .

'Go on,' said Alan. 'Why don't you go on?'

Anna got up and went over to the window, where she stood looking at the rain that beat against it, so that the garden beyond was lost in a wild splatter of water. 'I can't,' she said, and her voice sounded strange and choked. 'I can't think of the end of the story.'

Alan and Molly looked at each other doubtfully. Anna was grown up, and therefore presumably able to take care of herself. Alan wished Bridget would come back. He liked Anna very much, and she told good stories, but she seemed unlike herself, not so easy to be with as she was before. Molly frowned. Things weren't quite the way she liked them to be. It wasn't all right to stop in the middle of a story. If Anna couldn't go on, that was too bad. 'I can,' she said with shining confidence. 'Do you want me to finish it?'

Anna nodded, not looking round. 'Yes,' said Alan, supremely trusting.

'Right,' said Molly, and paused for thought. 'Well, this man came along, see, with a wheelbarrow, and other tools that were important. And he did a pretty good job. So then she decided she was sick of him, and it was winter again anyway. So she said, You can go home now. So he did. Great, she thought, it's much better on my own, and next year I'll make the mulch thicker and then I won't have so much weeding to do anyway. And if I want a baby I'll adopt one.'

'Is that the end?' asked Alan doubtfully.

'Yes. Why? Don't you like it?'

'No.'

'All right,' said Molly, offended. 'Think of a better one.'

Alan glanced at Anna, but she was still staring out of the window, and seemed to have forgotten all about them. It was probably better not to bother her, thought Alan. 'I can't think of stories,' he said.

'Course you can. Anyone can.'

'I don't know how.'

'You're useless.'

'I'm not!' said Alan, stung. 'All right. Listen then.'

'I'm listening,' said Molly, after thirty seconds.

'Wait!'

'I'm waiting.'

'Shut up and let me think. All right. Well, they worked the garden for quite a long time, and the woman had a few children, and some more people came along so there was another household it was all right to have more children with, and so they had to make the garden bigger. In the end it got too crowded.'

'So what did they do?'

'Shut up. I'm thinking. They said, Well, you can't all stay here. There isn't room. They had a fight about it. Half of them got killed, and the roses got squashed. That's why there aren't as many as there used to be,' said Alan, pleased at having produced a theory that was provable.

'No, they didn't!'

'Hey, whose story is this?'

'It's a stupid story.'

'It's not! You asked me to do it, so I did. And I haven't finished yet.'

'I don't want to hear the end.'

'Here's Bridget,' said Alan pacifically.

It wasn't Bridget. Fiona came in, looked round at them, and then saw Anna. 'Anna,' she said. 'I came to find you.'

'Let's do something else,' said Molly to Alan, disappointed.

Anna turned round slowly. 'Hello,' she said with an effort.

'I thought it'd be easier to come here,' said Fiona. 'Away from both our houses.'

'Yes,' said Anna. 'It's been safe here.' The words seemed to come reluctantly, as though she resented being dragged out of her own thoughts.

Fiona looked at the children on the hearth, who were now building houses out of logs from the log basket. 'Shall we go into the inn?' she asked. 'It's not cold. There was a fire in there last night.'

'All right,' said Anna, thinking that it hardly mattered anyway.

The inn parlour was warm and tidy. Someone had swept the floor and relaid the fire in the hearth. Clean mugs were lined on the dresser, upside down on a white cloth. Fiona knelt on the floor by the neat fireside, and Anna sat wearily down on the bench opposite her.

'I'm going to light the fire,' said Fiona. 'I'll just get a light. Bridget won't mind.'

I wonder if they planned this between them, thought Anna, but she didn't much care if they had. There was peace in Bridget's house that was lacking elsewhere. Anna leaned back, listening to it. Peace, with a suggestion of music about it. Perhaps it was music, single notes, clear and true, with the beginnings of a tune to it. A sad, grieving tune, but without bitterness to it, melancholy.

Fiona reappeared at the door with a piece of burning kindling. She stopped, listening too, while a thin coil of smoke wreathed upwards from the glowing wood. 'Who's playing the harp?' asked Fiona.

Always to be dragged back into the world. These practical people, always asking questions, demanding reactions, foolishness. If they would only leave me alone, thought Anna. There was music in the air, and she forces it into words, and involves me in a world where I have no wish to be.

'Bridget, I suppose,' said Anna unwillingly. 'There's no one else.'

Fiona fed the kindling to the waiting fire, and there was a crackle of burning spruce. Bridget must have laid the fire with the last of the midwinter hangings. Small flames leapt up, with sparks of blue in the heart of them. Anna and Fiona both stared into the fire. Music drifted down to them through the ceiling, tunes changing and merging into one another like the shifting images of a dream.

'I haven't known what to do,' said Fiona at last, to the fire. 'Not after the beginning, when there was something to be done. But now, it's harder. I can understand if you don't want to be with people.'

'I don't want to be alive,' said Anna.

She spoke so quietly Fiona wasn't sure if she'd caught the words. She knelt uncertainly in front of her friend, aware of her own uselessness. I know nothing about it, thought Fiona. What can I offer her? But there is a world still. I don't want to be cruel. I don't want to make her face it. But I think she's losing herself. I don't know what I should do.

There was merciful peace between them; only the music played on. Anna wondered distantly if Fiona had even heard. She seemed so far away, so unaware of the nightmare that wrapped Anna round, smothering her. Perhaps not unaware, but helpless, like a person who had never felt the touch of water telling her not to drown. Fiona was alive, unscathed, living in a world of light and substance, in a childhood innocence that seemed an insult if offered to her now.

Fiona reached out her hand timidly. She didn't touch Anna, but laid her fingers lightly on her sleeve. 'I know I don't know,' she said. 'I'm sorry. But I do care about you. That's all.'

Anna stared into the fire, as though it offered her the safety of withdrawal from Fiona's touch. But the fire only blazed up cheerfully, still crackling on spruce needles and turning all colours, already shedding a little warmth on their faces. 'I think I shall go away,' said Anna, from far off. 'There's no place here for me now.'

'There is.' There was a hint of the old vehemence in Fiona's voice. 'You don't have to take it on alone. It wasn't your fault.'

Anna shook off Fiona's hand as if it burnt her. She was shaken out of her dream, her face suddenly vivid with pain. 'How can you say that?' She was nearly screaming, and Fiona recoiled. 'How can you say that?'

Fiona stood her ground. 'But it wasn't,' she said again. 'It wasn't your fault.'

Anna went quite white, her eyes strained and tortured. 'But I did do it! Don't you realise? It was me that did it all.' The words came out like a shriek of pain, tearing her apart. 'I went up there. I went. I went because I cared what happened to him.' Her voice died to a whisper. She was looking straight through Fiona, unseeing.

'You didn't do anything wrong.'

Suddenly Anna was up and shouting at her. 'You don't know anything! You're just a stupid ignorant girl who never loved anybody! I've been raped, do you understand that? You don't, do you? You don't understand anything. Why can't you leave me alone? The least you can do is leave me alone. I don't want you! You know nothing! Go away! Go away! Go away!'

'I shan't,' said Fiona, trembling.

'Why not? You're torturing me! I thought you were my friend. Leave me alone! You can't do anything. Go away!'

'No.'

Anna ran at Fiona as if she would hit her, and grabbed her by the shoulders. Fiona shut her eyes, expecting to be shaken, but Anna's hands went suddenly loose, and she crumpled up so Fiona had to catch her. Suddenly Anna began to cry wildly, like a person lost and terrified, a highpitched keening wail. Fiona knelt beside her, frightened at what she had done, not daring to touch her.

Someone brushed her aside, and was on the floor beside them, taking Anna in her arms. I never heard the harp stop, thought Fiona stupidly, and in her relief she felt tears in her own eyes. Bridget knew what to do. She herself had made a mess of it, but Bridget would make things better, as she always had. The sound was terrible, so familiar, the same sound as had echoed out through the forest. I do know. I know too much. Fiona wanted to stop her ears. It was her own voice she was hearing, and all their voices, a wailing that was like a cry of pain out of the forest, mourning for all the terror of the past. I am part of this, thought Fiona. I also am responsible for this.

26

It was the hour before daybreak. A cold light slowly penetrated the byre until the lantern hanging above the stalls was merely a pool of yellow brightness, lightening nothing. There was a dank warm smell within of cattle steaming in the new-found warmth. The air was thick with the heavy scent of dung and the warm odour of freshly shaken hay. Slow jaws munched rhythmically, and milk plashed steadily into a bucket. The place was tranquil and dim, still withdrawn into the quiescence of night. The chill of winter was less biting in here. Though a draught like a touch of ice came in under the door with the grey light, it dissipated into a mere trickle of coldness through damp straw and rough partitions.

There was a shifting of hooves on straw, and the heavy breath of cattle through dry hay. Emily closed her eyes and went on milking, her head against the cow's warm flank. Not to think any longer, just to let confusion melt into unconsciousness, and the slow thoughts settle wordlessly. Her fingers worked steadily on greasy teats, letting the milk down in thin regular squirts. If there were only peace. This cow she was milking was an old one, clever and reliable. She had taught Fiona to milk with her, and then Molly. The necessary round, the uncertain hour before dawn, the waiting of the cattle at the gate, was the unchanging part of her life, like a loyal friend. There was no loss, no falling apart, merely the animals, and another day.

It did not diminish her grief, only transmuted it into something gentler. Time would not alter her loss, but the rhythm of continuing life would heal it. That was the only healing there would be; there could be no turning back, no searching after the thing dearest to her which she had lost. I am willing to grow older, thought Emily, I am willing to pass on what I have held for a little while, but I would like to have kept what I loved while I lived. Slow tears gathered in her eyes, and soaked into coarse warm hair. I can live without him, thought Emily, I can live without that kind of love, but I wish the parting had not been like this. The udder was empty. Desolation filled her, and she let her hands drop, her face turned to the comfort of a warm unheeding body. Then she stood up, picked up the pail, and, leaving the door open for the cow to make her own way back, she went through to the dairy.

The chill struck her as she crossed the threshold. The little room was very bare and clean. Emily dumped the pail on the scrubbed stone shelf and took down another, then went back to the byre to milk the goats. The first one required more concentation. She was a young one inclined to kick and knock over the bucket. Emily dealt with her with determined efficiency, then settled down to the second goat, who was willing to let her drift away into her own thoughts again.

There was a movement outside in the yard. A large form blocked the doorway, shutting off the light.

'Hey!' said Emily. 'I can't see a thing.'

'Can I come in then?'

Emily gave a small gasp, and stopped milking. The goat moved in protest, and she grabbed the bucket. 'Come in then,' she said, 'while I finish.'

The necessity of the milking steadied her. She concentrated on her work, and her hands stayed sure and firm, while the fact of his presence was absorbed and accepted. This wasn't going to be easy. She hadn't seen or spoken to George since the day it happened. She was aware of him standing quite still behind her, waiting with respectful patience for her to do what had to be done, before embarking on what he wanted. So he was still the same George, accepting the situation as he found it. Perhaps he would accept the rest too. Emily's hands shook, so she suppressed her speeding thoughts and turned to her task again.

When she was done, he opened the byre door for her and followed her through to the dairy. Then he helped her lead the goats back into the field and waited until they had trotted away.

'I wasn't expecting to see you,' said Emily.

'The reason I didn't come before,' said George, and hesitated, not looking at her, 'was that I dared not.'

'I'm glad you dared now.' She tried to keep her own agitation out of her voice. He was afraid, that was clear enough. He was keeping his distance, and his eyes never left the ground. He held his hat in his hands, twisting it round between his fingers. It'll lose its shape, she thought irrelevantly, then tried to collect her scattered wits. It was terrible that George should be afraid of her, but if he couldn't deal with it, she must.

George knew he must explain, but the words were eluding him. She was so quick with words, she would always have an answer and an explanation. But this he must say for himself. It was impossible to know where to begin. In the middle, he decided, at the point where it hurt most. 'We brought his body home,' said George.

'I know.'

'There was violence done,' said George, fumbling desperately for the means of making it plain. 'And again violence. It heals nothing.'

'No.'

'He was a good man.' If there were only words, thought George. Like having a tune in his head and no instrument to play. It was so easy for her. 'He did wrong. But so have we all, and it's all unchangeable. What's done is better let be.'

'No,' said Emily. 'Not that. It changes everything. The earth is not safe with that still held from it.'

'It's not so different,' answered George. 'Pain comes into the world with every one of us. Why must one man be punished?'

'It is different,' said Emily, knowing that even if she lost him for ever she must stand her ground. 'Because of who we are, and because of the land.'

'It wasn't only Patrick.' Expression was coming more easily now, fired by the heat of passionate pain. 'What did Patrick do beyond what we all do? Who can choose who is innocent, or who is guilty? Was what he did so very terrible?'

'It was the worst thing in the world.'

She spoke quietly, but quite intractably. It was probably costing her happiness to do it, but there was no other way. Clachanpluck mattered more, and they had only done what had to be done to safeguard what they held.

George looked at her with agonised incomprehension. 'I don't understand why it had to be that.'

'And you can't trust me to know it?' She knew it wasn't fair to ask that, but it hurt too much that he should stand against her and not be able to believe in her.

'I think you're living in a different world from me,' cried George despairingly.

'How could I not be? We're not the same, you and I.'

'Our language isn't the same,' said George. 'I didn't think it mattered. I thought there was always something without words which was the same.'

'There is. There is the land. But that doesn't help us to understand each other.'

'He was a good man.' This time it sounded like a cry of pain. 'Why does he have to bear this burden for us all?'

'He knew what he did.'

'I don't think so. He was in pain.'

'There is still knowledge, even in pain.'

'Could he not have been forgiven? Even she would have forgiven him.'

'He is forgiven.'

'But he still died for it.'

'Is death so very terrible?'

'Is rape worse?'

'There is only one crime,' said Emily, 'And that is the crime against the land. The land is within each of us. We only hurt ourselves.'

'You condemned him,' said George. 'You have condemned me too.'

'The past is over. It's only possible now to forgive.'

'Will that change anything?'

'Not the past. *Last season's fruit is eaten*,' said Emily, '*And last year's words belong to last year's language*.'

'What does that mean?'

A slow tear trickled down Emily's cheek, and she looked away from him across the fields to where a pale sun was rising in a pall of cloud. 'It means we have done what we can, and the future is for somebody else. A poor, patched up, broken thing we seem to have made of it. Not what I would have chosen to leave for my daughters. But it's what we did, George, and there is no place for regret in a world that changes. We could let ourselves fall apart now, or else start from where we are and play a new tune. Not to our music any more. That's done. But I'd still be glad of your company.'

George looked at her hopelessly. 'It could have been me,' he said. 'I don't think that I have anything to give you.'

'I think we know each other best,' replied Emily. 'And I love you better for all the years between us. All that I have of the future was what you gave me, and I don't want to lose you now.'

It seemed to slowly dawn on him that hope was possible, then he gave her a rueful smile. 'I gave you both of them,' he said. 'It's probably the most useful thing I ever did.'

Emily looked round at him, and smiled back. The sun had risen properly now, and her face was tinged with the warmth of day. 'So we can let the past go?' she asked, and held out her hand.

George hesitated and gave her his own. 'I can't forget,' he said. 'And I shall still be sorry for what was done.'

'I know that too. The past won't go away. But it will be all right, I know that.'

'I think it has to be,' said George.

Emily sighed, as though a huge burden had slipped off her back. She grinned at him with cheerful insouciance, as if she had nothing left to worry about at all. 'D'you want to come in now?' she said, laughing at him. 'I'll offer you a cup of tea, or make passionate love to you if you'd like that better.'

George took her by the shoulders and shook her gently. 'I've missed you,' he remarked. 'Habit, I suppose, seeing as I've no imagination. But I missed you.'

Emily put her arms round him and kissed him.

'I'll take you up on that,' he said, 'but not out here.'

27

'But they do blame themselves,' said Emily. 'We all do. It's a condition of living.'

'But it's dangerous,' insisted Naomi. 'Look at what's happened in the past. We dare not repeat it.'

'But don't you see? We just have repeated it. We've made our village a place where such a thing could happen, so we feel responsible for it.'

'No I don't see. Patrick committed a crime, and Patrick had to pay for it. And you have to let it go.'

'We can't. We've lived all our lives in a world where such a thing was inconceivable. Now it's happened. We aren't safe from the past after all. Time is no healer. All we can do is repair what has been done, again and again and again. We have to be responsible for it.'

'You scare me,' said Naomi.

'Why?'

'Do you suppose I was the only one that held myself absolved? I suppose you know I spent that night sleeping with your brother?'

'What's that got to do with anything?'

'Only guilt. You wouldn't see the connection, probably because it doesn't exist. Emily, will you explain something to me?'

'Wait a minute. I'm going to get some potatoes.'

When she came back Naomi was sitting on the table frowning into the fire. 'If I ask you questions,' she said, not looking round, 'you can always refuse to answer. I ask because there's no other way to understand. I don't want you to be offended.'

'You're not a stranger now,' said Emily.

'Thank you. Shall I help you scrub them?'

'Please. They can go in that pot.'

'I've asked you before,' said Naomi, examining a potato, 'and there were not enough words then for an answer. But that can change, I know. What is it that you think you are responsible for, here in Clachanpluck?'

There was a pause. 'Can I ask you something first?'

'If you like.'

'It's a personal question. I don't mean to insult you.'

'You can ask. I know much more about curiosity than you do. And I trust you.'

'Where is your own village?' asked Emily. 'And why did you leave it?'

She dared not look at Naomi while she spoke, for never in her life had she asked so intimate a question of anyone outside Clachanpluck. She scraped a potato until it shone white, and kept her eyes on the murky water in the bucket.

'You're not the first person in Clachanpluck to ask me that.'

'I thought we'd brought my brother up better than that.' Emily was indignant.

'Davey? Oh, indeed you did. Listen,' Naomi touched her friend's cheek so that she looked up. 'I trust you, Emily, and I shall tell you anything you like.' Having promised so much, Naomi seemed to be at a loss for words. She dropped another potato in the pot, but presently she spoke again.

'I have a son called Colin,' said Naomi slowly and unexpectedly, 'who is a little younger than Fiona. I left him as soon as he was weaned. Not because I didn't love him, you must never think that. I loved him more than anyone I have ever known. But I had already done him wrong, and I had to make a choice.'

There was another pause. Emily put down her knife, and waited with attentive respect.

'My village was much poorer than this,' said Naomi. 'The soil was thin and poor, and the salt wind off the sea meant that things couldn't grow the way they do here. It was hard to make a living from the land, and you know the danger that lies in the sea. The land was poor, as I say, and we had tiny fields, sheltered from the wind by stone walls, which we had to build thick to use all the stones that we picked off the land. I never saw a forest. There were no trees like those that you think are the whole world. I didn't see a proper tree until I was grown up. I was surprised how alive it seemed to be.'

Naomi put down her knife as well, and sat on the edge of the table, looking away from Emily into the fire. 'What we did have was music. The best music in the world comes from the country where I was born. I learned to play the fiddle when I was younger than Molly. The man who taught me was a man of my own village, who had travelled when he was younger, and collected music from all over Ireland. He passed it on to me. What I didn't know then was that it was not his music. We make nothing new. We take what is given us, and pass it on, and it is a little different because we have made it so. But it is not ours to hoard or hold, or it becomes meaningless. You know that?'

'I know that well.'

'He gave me music, and I thought the music was his to give. I loved him, and I thought he was what I needed to be myself. I chose to have my child by him. He was reluctant, but he was my lover, and why should he refuse? It's not such a hard thing to give a woman a child. But just as I thought the music was his, I wanted the child to be his. It wasn't Colin I was thinking about. It was the father of my son. Can you understand that?'

'Not easily. I don't see what difference it could make.'

'To what?'

'To give birth to a child,' explained Emily. 'What has that to do with any man, except in your family, perhaps? But who could be changed by it but you?'

'I didn't care about my family then. I cared about the fiddle player.'

'But he was only your lover?'

'And a musician. That was the thing that confused me. Perhaps he should never have been my lover too. I don't know. When I had Colin, I realised at once that he belonged to my family, and the music belonged to me no more than it did before. In fact it seemed for a while as if I'd put it out of my own reach for ever. I'd learned all I could from the fiddle player, and all the rest of the music in the world was outside my village, out in the world beyond my reach. I couldn't commit myself to my child, knowing that.'

'But my family did. My sister loved him, and she had no child of her own. So we talked about it, all of us. They said it would be better if I went, but that if I did, I must agree not to come back.'

'Why?'

'Because I hurt them all. Can you understand that?'

'It seems to me that you hurt yourself.'

200

'And my village had to take responsibility for that. People don't belong to one another. Only little babies think they are part of somebody else. I wanted the music, you see, but I was afraid of being alone.'

'I can see that that would be a danger to them.'

'I think you know how much. It was for me as much as them. It was obvious that I had to go, and it would be no good trying to come back.'

'So you have been in exile ever since?'

'It doesn't feel like that. Hardly ever. I travelled for a long time in Ireland, then I crossed the sea, and went east. I came to a country that you may know of, called Northumbria. There is an island there, not so different from my home, with a road to the mainland when the tide runs out. I heard of the place as one where people gathered, and there was a great exchange of poetry and music, and eventually I made my way to it. I'd been alone a long time by then.'

'And you found what you were looking for?'

'It was like coming home. I can't explain it to you. But if you can imagine being hungry all your life, not even knowing you were hungry, wandering from village to village always searching, not even being sure what you wanted to find, then coming upon a place full of people, with such a feast as you had never dreamed of, being invited in and given as much as you could take in until you were drunk with it. I wasn't in exile then. I had found my own people, for the first time in my life.'

'But you left again?'

'Not for a long time. But I knew I couldn't stay for ever. What's a performer without an audience? There wasn't any audience there. We were all actors, and so in the end we all had to move on, all but a few, whose place it is. I crossed the sea again, and travelled in countries I had never heard of. I went with a woman who belonged there. She took me to her own village, where I met a musician unlike any I had met before. He taught me the music that I told you of, the new kind of music. New to me, I mean. It was old before the world changed. I don't know if it will mean anything to you but, through Davey, it's my gift to Clachanpluck, though not one most of you will recognise.' Naomi smiled briefly and went on.

'I loved that man. He gave me a priceless gift, and both of us knew it never belonged to him in the first place. I gave him all the love I knew how, and then I left him, taking his music away with

201

me. I had learned how to respect people by then, and that was important too. He was sad to see me go, but I knew I hadn't hurt him, not really. Can you understand what a difference it made to everything, after that?'

'I think I can.'

'I came back to this country, and I kept on travelling. I was happy to be alone, and I knew by then that my music was good, very good. I had nothing to be afraid of, nothing to lose. Wherever I went I could give what I had, and go on. But it was harder to love people. Not that I loved them any the less; much more, in fact. But often I found I'd loved too much. You try to warm a person's heart, and find you've burned them with the flames of it. It was the same old thing, you see. They fall in love with the music, but the music isn't mine, and I'm not the music. It was safer to stay alone. Most often I do, but not in Clachanpluck.'

'He'll be sad,' said Emily. 'But you won't have hurt him, not really.'

'And you?'

'My heart is warmed,' said Emily, smiling at her. 'And then?'

'That's all. There are hundreds of other stories I could tell you, but that's my own. The others are just tracks crossing my path. They have less to do with me.'

'Thank you,' said Emily. 'Thank you for answering my question. You've given me more than I deserved.'

'Nonsense. But it was a bargain. You remember that?'

'Indeed I do.' Emily picked up the potato knife again, and tested the blade against her thumb. 'I'm not as good with words as you, but I'll try.'

'Indeed you are. I wish I could have played it to you instead.'

'You've given me all I wanted,' said Emily. 'I'll try to explain it.'

There was a long silence. Emily drew the blade back over her thumb, and cut herself. 'There,' she said, licking off the blood. 'That's what comes of trying to think.'

'Don't try. Just say what's in your mind.'

'It's been done. It was all written down before the world changed. I have the book.'

'I don't want the book. I want you to tell me.'

'I never thought of finding words for it, before you came. And then I found the book. That showed me that there are enough words for everything, if someone has the courage to use them.

Before that I would have said to you, I can't tell you, there aren't enough words, but that would be like her saying, I can't put down the poem, because there aren't enough letters in the alphabet. I want to find words for you, Naomi, because I love you, and I want you to understand, but I'm not sure that I can choose them right.'

'So the person who made your book was able to choose the right words?'

'That's all. There's no more to it than that.'

'But it's not that easy. There's not that many notes you can play, but more tunes possible than anyone ever dreamed of.'

'I can dream all right,' said Emily. 'You're asking me to bring dreams into daylight. It frustrates me. It's as if you were standing in the forest with your eyes closed, asking me to tell you what I see. I don't know how to tell you that it isn't necessary. You know that I recognise your fear, but why? Why can't you go into the forest for yourself?'

'I don't know how to begin,' said Naomi almost despairingly. 'I don't see what it's all about. I've been into the forest, a little way. It would be easier if it were summer, I suppose.'

'But there is summer. Don't you see that? Don't you know what stories they used to tell, before the world changed? They drove themselves out of their own minds with fear, telling myths of judgment and destruction, of a day when the whole earth would be consumed by fire, followed by darkness and a winter without end?'

'Of course I do. The world had to change. Everyone knows that.'

'But the people never did bring judgment upon themselves.'

'Because the earth heals,' said Naomi dully. '"*The plagues of the people are famine and pestilence, but the Earth has power to heal herself, whereas death is merely a mirror that we hold up to ourselves. The cruelty of the Earth is our salvation, and the promise of the Earth is that we die, and live for ever.*"' She looked up and grinned wryly. 'I was educated as well as you, Emily. They taught me the same things as they taught you.'

'And when you repeat them, you make them sound bitter. I don't understand why.'

'I see it everywhere I go,' replied Naomi. 'Even in your street here. I see broken-down houses, rubble overgrown with weeds, roofs open to the sky. We live among the ruins of forgotten people, and our minds feed upon fragments. I know they were afraid of the wilderness, those people, but I see why. There was too much to lose. I would like to be at home as you are in your forest, but I have something else. I have been given so much out of the past, and I have far too much to lose.'

'They died thinking the whole earth was lost,' said Emily. 'But only because they had lost everything themselves. If the earth were not merciless, she would give up her life for us, and then we would surely die. The village fell into ruin, the houses were empty. The winter was unrelenting, and the promise of summer seemed to be lost for ever.' Emily stood up suddenly and leaned against the stove, letting the warmth seep through her clothes. 'I've talked to Bridget about it most,' she said with an abrupt change of tone. 'About what the change was: whether the earth turned back to her own pattern, because she was after all inextinguishable, or whether the change was only that the people were brought back to her out of their own despair.'

'But there was a change.'

'It happened in Clachanpluck. It could have been any village, perhaps it was. Only we do know this, that the judgment the people had brought upon themselves was at last repealed, and it happened here. Even in the heart of winter, the certainty is always there, and every year it is repeated. However you see it, we are saved from our own hopelessness, or else the earth chooses to turn again. But we have the proof of it. It lies in our own forest, and it is ours to remember and protect.'

'And that is the charge that you hold here?'

'There has to be a connection. The image that I see is only the mirror of myself, but I can capture the substance within it, so far as I am able. If you leave the paths that the people have made, the forest is impenetrable. It has no form; I can see now why it must frighten you. But the paths must still be kept open, and someone has to look through into the earth itself, and realise for the people what is there. We have to know where the summer is, even in the heart of winter, and in the daylight we have to remember that there is still the dark. The earth still turns for us, and we always have the proof of it, in Clachanpluck. But we dare not let go of it, you see that. It must never be forgotten again.'

'Then you . . .?' began Naomi, and stopped. 'When you look for the image of yourself, Emily, what do you see?'

'It's only what you said about the music. I only pass on what I was given. In that respect, it doesn't matter who I am.'

'But it does!' cried out Naomi passionately, suddenly on fire again. 'How can you say that? You are Emily. There never was anyone else like you, you're not just a symbol. You're you, and if you died tomorrow, it would matter. It would make everything different. It would to me, anyway,' she added fiercely.

'Of course it would! I can hold a trust, and not be swallowed up in it. I don't know why you have to be so afraid of it.'

'If you don't know that . . .' Naomi searched for words. 'What about Patrick?' she countered suddenly. 'How can I think of the forest now and not be afraid?'

'Of me?' said Emily, appalled. 'Does that make you afraid of me?'

'Not because of what you did. It was done for me too, we both know that. I am afraid of the way it was done.'

'I did nothing,' said Emily at once. 'But you know the truth as well as I do. If the earth were not merciless, we would all be destroyed. Healing hurts. It's not a soft thing that can be left to time. I will never stand by and see the people condemned. I know too much about the past, and I will pass on what I was given, whatever has to happen to hold it here.'

'You would hold it against me, if necessary,' said Naomi, not questioning, just coldly stating a fact.

'Against myself, if necessary.' Emily relaxed, and came away from the stove, and put her hand on Naomi's shoulder. 'Only it isn't,' she said cheerfully. 'Listen, we could spend all evening thinking of terrible things we might have to do to each other, only I have to make the supper tonight. And I haven't even scraped the potatoes.'

'I'll help you,' said Naomi with an effort.

'You said that before. Please,' said Emily, taking Naomi by the shoulders so she had to look at her. 'Leave it alone. Words are too much to cope with, that's the trouble. You can suggest anything with them. Suppose I smashed your fiddle over your head, what would you do then?'

'You wouldn't,' said Naomi heavily.

'True. So why bother worrying about it? It's only words. We only have a few weeks, you and I, and I want the memory of them to be a gift for both of us.'

Naomi smiled at her slowly. 'What were you going to make besides potatoes?'

'I hadn't thought.'

'I will, if you like. If I'm going to cook, I'd rather do it my own way.'

'It's all yours,' said Emily, picking up another potato.

28

Naomi scrambled up a bare patch of hill between tangled scrub and bracken, and crouched down in the shelter of an outcrop of rock, where a rowan clung above her, branches bent before the wind. The sound of the sea was all around her, waves breaking on a non-existent shore. She pushed her hair back, and stood up straight against the rock, while the wind lashed at her face, defying her to see or think. She moved round the rock with her back to it, so there was a momentary lull, like being suspended in the trough between two waves. Around her the trees were caught in the swell of the wind, gaunt shapes bent and tossed in a current that whipped everything into motion. Gusts of leaves eddied past her, brown and skeletal, torn back to the air from their slow turning back to earth. Naomi stood with her back to the rock in the pocket of still air, like a castaway clinging to a scrap of solid earth. She had never seen the forest as wild as this before. In a way it was easier. There was an element here that was familiar to her.

From here it was possible to look up. Dark clouds were piling above her, blown in from the west, heavy with water from the distant sea. But there was no time for rain, before they were swept away again over the forest, shredded by the wind. A patch of sky appeared, fragile and pale, blue as the sea in summer. Sudden sunlight flooded over her. The trees were alight, tossed into a spectrum of shifting colour, and there was a brightness on her face like a touch of spring. The clouds scudded in again, the sky turned grey as winter, and the forest faded back to the colours of the earth.

Naomi pulled her hood back over her head, and tied it tightly under her chin. Then she pushed off into the wind again. It seized her and tore at her, so that she staggered against it. There was no calm even on the ground; the forest was like the sea in a storm, when the swell breaks so far down that the depths are stirred and shaken out of their timeless quiet.

If anything were hidden here, it would be routed out today. There was no chance of apprehending any secrets within the shelter of the trees, with the silence being torn apart all around her. The place was all motion, all exposed. If only the wind would let her see properly, or hear anything but noise. But she felt at home with it like this. It was alive with sound and movement, and echoed a note out of a past and a place that she had thought lost for ever. Homesickness washed over her, like a freak wave crossing the swell and knocking her off balance. The sharp smell of salt was in her nostrils, and the air seemed wet with white spray.

No, thought Naomi, and stopped in her tracks. The wind buffeted her, mockingly, it seemed, and she dropped to her knees, unresisting. I'm letting myself get in the way, she told herself fearfully. I have made my own way into the forest, and I won't be drowned in my own daydreams. I've nothing to be homesick about now. I am in the forest of Clachanpluck.

The sounds confused her: the crash of water on water, the slow suck of waves across shingle, the shock of sea breaking on rock. No substance anywhere, and salt spray blinding her. Naomi reached out as if seeking the reassurance of the earth beneath her, the solidity of wood or rock, but there was only the sweep of the wind, fluid and intangible, a roar of pure movement that deafened her, whipping itself away from her leaving her breathless, drowning in air. Naomi threw herself against the wind as if it were an enemy, running blindly, trying to force a way up, or out, to find the earth again, solid land or forest.

There was rock in front of her, broken by wind and water. The wind shoved her forward. There was a gap, a brief calm caught between rocks, offering a faint possibility of shelter. Naomi reached out, but her hands met only the darkness, and she fell.

The turbulence was fading above. There was peace beneath it, and a welcome darkness. Slow drift down into depths untouched by storm or winter, quiet far below the surface where shadows drift in the dimness, creatures never seen by daylight eyes, nor heard by human ears. A long descent, forgotten images returning. Rocked by the sea, down in the darkness where there are no more words. Only the music, belonging to a place far beyond words, at the very roots of consciousness. Rhythm of blood in her body, slow circling of the stars, music unheard through all the daylight years behind her. There was nothing left now, only the music, and all the music ever was was the sound of the sea. Rhythm of water, rhythm of blood, the whole music of the world within her. The stars turned, and the sea swelled and retreated, and the long exile was over at last.

But there was form, even in the pit of darkness. Hardness of rock. Rock under her hands, cold rock against her cheek. And the music fading, far away now, distant notes sounding high and cold, inhuman. So cold. The rock beneath her was cold, and the air was heavy with the chill of earth. Naomi stirred, and was conscious of her own body, cramped and frozen, as if she had lain hunched in the dark for a long time. She blinked, but there was still only impenetrable darkness. With a flicker of panic, Naomi half sat up, and put her hands to her eyes, but they were open. There was no music now, only silence of earth, pressing in around her. Naomi reached out, and touched rock. Rock all around her, and the thickness of earth over her head. Terror flooded over her with returning consciousness. Buried alive. The words formed in her mind, sounding unreal, as if she had not thought in words for a long time. She knelt on the bare rock, and stared into the unyielding dark. A dry sob escaped her, and another. Naomi held her breath and forced herself to stop. She sat huddled in a heap, knees clasped to her chest, and tried to begin to think. But the earth was so heavy over her, like a physical weight. And no way out. Thoughts fled from her, refusing understanding. There was only cold rock, and no way out. Naomi covered her face with her hands, and forced herself to think.

There must be a way out. She put her hands flat against the rock before her, and felt her way upwards. It was a solid slab of stone, stretching away in the dark. She stood up slowly, and began to feel her way along it sideways. She reached out with her other hand, and found rock behind her. No knowing if rock met rock, except by feeling her way along. But if it goes round, thought Naomi desperately, I could follow it for ever, and never know. She took off her scarf, and dropped it at her feet to mark the place. Then she felt her way onwards into the dark.

It was impossible, incomprehensible. Naomi shied away from the idea of it, that she should have got here at all. But there had to be a way out. Assuming that she was awake, or alive. Don't think, said Naomi to herself fiercely. Just find a way out.

There was a sound. Naomi stopped, her heart thumping. Perhaps it was only the wind, a faint echo of the gale outside. Or perhaps it was only inside her head, and she had heard it all the time. Naomi held her breath and strained her ears. There was a faint outline of rock, a jagged archway over her head. Naomi stared at it, listening, without taking in what she saw.

It was the ghost of a tune; the heavy air seemed pregnant with it, music just beyond the scope of hearing. A scent of pollen, just distinguishable. Salt and honey, like the smell of thrift in summer at the edge of the sea. And the music was soft as waves breaking on a sandy shore. Pain of longing quickened her, and she ran forward. The lights were all blue and green, shifting and dazzling so she could not see, but the touch of summer was on her skin, and the way through was bright and open.

'Stand still!'

Shocked, she stopped at once, blinded by brightness. The light settled and dimmed. There were walls of rock round her, all dappled with light. Slowly her eyes grew accustomed and were drawn down to the centre of it.

It was only a lamp, after all, a small yellow flame floating in a pool of oil, contained in a plain earthenware dish. Naomi found herself blinking at it stupidly, trying to readjust herself.

When she looked up at last, she had a sharp sense of having been here before. The lamp on the floor, two shadows against the wall, and the music weaving its way between them. Bridget was watching her as she had then, a small straight figure with a grotesque shadow flung against the wall behind her, the same wariness, like a woman who perceives danger. But I am not dangerous, thought Naomi, and the words were absorbed at once. She might as well have spoken them aloud.

Bridget moved at last, and came towards her. There was still a faint breeze on her face, a promise of a way out, but the scent in the air was barely perceptible, subtle as dried herbs in winter.

'You found the way,' said Bridget.

'No. And I don't know how to get out.'

Bridget took her hands. Her hands were warm, and reassuring. Naomi realised that she was deathly cold, and shivered. 'It's this way,' said Bridget, leading her.

It was no distance at all. A few steps, and they were in daylight, and the rhythm in the air resolved itself at last. It was only a waterfall, tumbling over the rocks into a brown pool. The daylight was clear and grey, and the little yellow flame dipped and flickered in the wind, stripped of meaning. Bridget blew it out, and laid the lamp on a ledge of rock beside the waterfall. Naomi gazed round slowly. The trees across the clearing were still tossed by the wind, but over here, in the lee of the rocks, it was calm and sheltered.

Bridget squatted down by the pool, and after a moment's hesitation Naomi sat down beside her. 'Here,' said Bridget. 'You're not faint, are you?'

'No.'

'You look it. Drink this.'

She handed her a small earthenware pot, the sides were cold and damp to touch. Naomi expected it to be water, but it was something stronger, bitter with herbs, but warm as fire in her stomach.

'Thank you.'

Bridget was still regarding her intently. 'Did Emily do this?' she asked abruptly.

'Emily? What do you mean?'

'How did you come here?'

'I came into the forest,' said Naomi, trying to assemble her chaotic thoughts. This seemed as unreal as all the rest; the whole thing was confusion beyond words. 'I never told Emily. Only she made me understand that I was afraid.'

'You came because you were afraid?'

'I'm not used to being afraid,' said Naomi, with a touch of her usual manner.

'I see,' said Bridget, frowning. Presently she said, 'And it didn't occur to you that it was a dangerous time to come?'

'How do you mean?'

'There was a death.'

'I wasn't thinking about that. I was thinking about the forest.'

'It's not different.'

'Have I done harm?'

'I was afraid that you would,' answered Bridget. 'Before, when you first came. You were afraid of the forest. I know the road that brought you here, but I don't know how it was for you to travel it. I didn't think you would find your way here, to be honest, but you have, and you couldn't have chosen a more dangerous time for it. We have to heal what was done. Surely you know that?'

'Is that why you were here?'

'It was just as well for you I was here. Maybe that's reason enough. What's the use of words? You know what you found.'

'Emily tried to give me words for it.'

'I was afraid of that,' said Bridget. 'I think we should go back. I'll take you across in the boat.'

'Boat?'

'Don't you know where you are? The loch is just below us.'

'I started from the crossroads.'

'You don't do things the easy way, do you?' said Bridget, with the glimmer of a smile. 'There was a path for you, if you'd cared to look. But I can take you home by it, anyway.'

29

Fiona removed a piece of toast from the toasting fork and began to spread it lavishly with butter.

'I'll make another bit,' said Anna, 'If you're going to want more.'

'What about you?'

'I'm not hungry.'

Fiona sighed. There was no making everything the same. Anna's room was just the same as ever, warm and comforting around them. There were hangings on the walls, dried grasses in a pot, scraps of wool and other materials, a bowl of puckered apples, useful bits of wood, and a windowsill crammed with plants in pots. No one else kept plants indoors; after all, the forest was full of them, but Anna brought the forest itself into her own place. Autumn leaves still clung to their branch, propped against the wall, and the air was tinged with the scent of dried petals. There was a scuffling and a sucking sound from a box near the fire. No one but Anna would tolerate giving space to a cat and kittens when there were barns and byres outside. Nothing in here was different, only Anna herself, and she was unreachable. Fiona knew what she must try to do, but it was so difficult. Never in her life had she had to give away her own feelings, but it was the only thing left to do.

'Anna.'

'Yes.'

'I hate talking about feelings. But this is important.'

'I don't want to talk about it,' said Anna wearily. 'There's nothing to say. You don't have to make yourself be different.'

'Not that. This is nothing to do with that. I want to say, I need you to come back.'

'Then don't,' said Anna sharply. 'It's no use needing me. I'm not yours. And I shall go.'

'Of course you will. But because of the plants. What's the point of learning if you don't come back?'

213

'I've nothing to come back for.'

'Please,' said Fiona. 'I'm not saying what I think you should do. I'm just thinking about what happens here.'

'I don't want to be here. People live too close to each other. I want to be free of it all, for ever.'

'Well,' said Fiona, hesitatingly. 'Why decide? Suppose you go away, and feel differently after a while? I want you to know you'd be needed, if you came back.'

'Thank you,' said Anna distantly.

'Not for your own good,' said Fiona, annoyed. 'Why do you keep thinking I'm worrying about you all the time? I'm not. It would be an insult if I did. I respect you,' she said stiffly. It was the closest she had ever come to telling Anna she loved her, and she was rigid with embarrassment. 'I'm not likely to treat you like a baby. I think you're very wise, and I need your help.'

'How nice,' said Anna sarcastically, so that Fiona winced. 'Very tactful. But I know you never wanted anyone's help in all your life. So it's no use pretending to be vulnerable. It won't work.'

'Shut up!' said Fiona furiously, sitting up straight. 'I've just been more honest with you than I've ever been in my life, and you think I'm trying to pity you. Well, I'm sick of it! You talk about creeping away from Clachanpluck as though you'd got the plague, and putting yourself in exile as though you'd done any of us harm. And I'm sick of it! What have you ever done? You have every right to insist that it should be different, you know far better than I do what has to be done. How can you walk out and leave me to inherit all this mess?'

'What?' said Anna, astounded. 'What are you talking about now?'

'You won't let me explain. I don't know what to do.'

'This is nothing to do with what happened to me?'

'I suppose everything is to do with everything. But my problem is what's happening to me.'

'Nothing ever happens to you,' stated Anna flatly.

'Well, it has.' Fiona ran her hands through her hair so it stuck up in short spikes round her head. 'How can I explain? Anna, I needed to find you. When you weren't at the ceilidh that night I came here, but no one was here. I needed to talk about it to you. I went home to bed and I was going to come first thing in the morning, but when I woke up it was because the bells were all ringing, and I thought it was too late for ever. I was so confused. To be given such a thing, and the whole world exploding round me before I even had time to think about it. It felt so heavy then, like it was dragging me down into the earth, but then in the forest I took it out, and it seemed to be on fire. Everything was dark and chaotic and I was caught up in what we did, and all the time I was holding it. It's been a burden to me, Anna, and I can't ask her. How can I question her when she's confused and questioning herself? I used to think she knew everything. I dare not ask her. But I meant to ask you, and you were unreachable. I don't know what to do. Perhaps she regrets giving it to me. Aren't I too young? What am I supposed to do, Anna? I thought you'd help me, and you say you're never coming back.'

'Stop a minute,' said Anna, suddenly alert. 'Fiona, start again. I'm sorry, I thought I knew what you were going on about. Start at the beginning. What are you trying to say?'

Fiona looked at her helplessly and shrugged. 'I don't know what to say,' she said. 'But look.' She reached inside her jersey, and pulled something over her head, and handed it to Anna.

Anna took the sapphire and held it up to the fire. Blue splinters of light sparked into life. Anna balanced the jewel between her finger and thumb, and turned it so that the light shifted from one facet to another, like sunlight on blue water.

'It was you that had this in the forest that day?'

'It was me.'

'I never thought,' said Anna. 'I can't think properly about it yet. It was all a nightmare. But I remember what was done. And this. So that was you?'

'It was me.'

'How did you know what you had to do with it?'

'I didn't. But I was more angry than I had thought possible. I'm not sure what I did.'

'One thing you can be very sure of,' said Anna. 'You were distraught, and I was distraught. But your mother was not. Nor Bridget. Nor the rest of them. They knew very well what we were about.'

'I know that.' Fiona glanced at Anna, but Anna was still staring into the heart of the sapphire. 'If it hadn't happened so soon, it wouldn't have been like that. One is meant to understand what one is doing.'

'Yes. But Emily couldn't have known it was going to happen either.'

'She was upset. Something happened when she went into the forest. I followed her, but what I found was beautiful. Like a different world from the rest of you, but more itself than ever. Do you understand me?'

'I don't know.' Anna let the jewel fall, so it swung gently on its chain, and looked round at Fiona. 'So why do you think that you need me?'

'You remember the day we went into the forest, across the loch?'

'Of course I remember.'

'You thought it was like a game. I was quite serious, but it's not the way I would set about it now.'

'What would you do now, Fiona?'

'I don't know. It's quite different. I have been given this. I don't know what to do with it.'

'Why don't you take it into the forest?'

'And if I do that, what will *you* do?'

'What do you think I should do?' asked Anna in her turn.

Fiona was silent, deep in thought, knees hugged to her chest. 'I would go south in the spring,' she said eventually. 'And I'd stay away until I'd found out everything that I wanted to know. And then I would come back to Clachanpluck, where I belonged, and I would take hold of what was mine by right.'

'And where will I find you then, if I do that?'

'In Clachanpluck. Ready for you.' Fiona smiled. Then she turned round suddenly, and hugged her closest friend for the first time in her life.

30

The highest place in the forest of Clachanpluck was the hilltop above the loch. The summit was rough with rock and bare above the trees, so that one could look down upon them as from an island on to the surrounding sea. Within the folds of the forest the village lay enclosed, a glimpse of grey roofs like drifting flotsam. A small thing it seemed from here, a little patch of human material upon the living fabric of the trees. The sun rose and curved across the southern sky, and the shadows shortened. The forest was locked in winter, the trees bare. The day wheeled slowly to its zenith under a pale sun. The hilltop lay open to a sky blue as speedwell, mirrored blue again in the still loch below.

Fiona stood for a long time looking down on to the loch and the valley. The winter weather was all washed out by storms, and everything seemed new. It could be a scent of growing grass in the breeze off the mountains, but perhaps not yet. The whole sky was open, and there was nothing hidden under the naked trees.

She seemed to reach some conclusion, for eventually she turned away from the eastern slopes and went back to the summit. There was a bare slab of rock, lichen-crusted, with the remains of a cairn piled at the top of it. Fiona sat cross-legged at the foot of the cairn facing southwards, her back protected from the northern breeze. To the south there were only hills and trees, and a far horizon with a suggestion of the sea beyond it. No imprint of people, nothing to suggest the world had yet been touched at all. The forest appeared endless, its boundaries beyond compass. There was no colour to it, only grey and brown and black, the colours of dark and winter. But here and there there was after all a touch of green, where the sleeping trees were interspersed with fir, spruce, pine and holly, like sentinels watching over the waiting land.

Fiona undid the top button of her jacket and reached inside. She drew the gold chain over her head, and took the sapphire, holding it in her open hand. It was bright today, reflecting back the blue of the sky from the blue within its depths, like to like. Fiona turned her hand a little, so that new facets woke and sparked another pattern out of the heart of the stone. Then she laid the sapphire on the grey rock before her, and looked over it to the forest.

There is no more fear. There is only acceptance. What I am given is the thing that I must take. In the heart of the winter there is only the birth of the summer, and the promise of the summer is the return of the dark. I have not come to search for anything, for there is nothing that has not always been known. I have not come to take anything, for there is nothing which was not already given. I have not come to seek out the land, for there is nothing which is of the land which is not also within me.

The sun was rising higher in the south, and long rays slanted over the hills. A little higher than it had risen yesterday, not so high as it would rise tomorrow. It was less cold up here than Fiona had expected. She had already been here for a long time, but that was nothing. She buttoned up her jacket again, and waited.

There has been so much pain, and I too have felt it. What I now know can never be forgotten again; there is no returning to childhood. The burden of the past is mine also, and what has happened to my people and my land has happened to me. There has been wrong done, and mourning made for it. Sorrow is a part of me, and cannot be undone.

The forest was deathly silent even for winter. The trees were still, unstirred by any trace of wind. No cloud drifted across the empty sky, and there was no sound of flowing water. The trees seemed to have ceased to dream of summer, but drifted onward into gentle death. The sun hung in the sky like a circle of flame suspended, burning nothing. Fiona watched, silent as the land, and the only cessation of stillness was her own quiet breathing.

There, on the southern horizon. A crack broken in the arch of the sky. A flash of light, too bright. Hands over her eyes, a brightness red as blood. But she was unscathed, out of time. She stood up, hands outstretched to ward off this thing, this end. A cloud of darkness rising, silent. Thick cloud of filth slowly unfurling, a rising shape that pierced the untouched sky. The sun blotted out, and a grey dark. The darkness of the past towering over her, bringing death.

A woman destroyed. 'Fiona,' she said aloud, and found she was lying doubled up, arms curled round her unprotected head. And the dark thing descending while the forest lay open, unresisting, containing no means of defence against that which it did not create.

I saw the sky open. I let my eyes dwell upon what was, or what might be. I have done this. I am responsible for this.

Slowly Fiona lowered her arms, and got up. The shape was becoming shapeless, an unbounded thing, spreading across the paling sky, moving northwards to her own forest. No figment this, no dream. The column subsiding, and the broken sky descending with it, gathering death. Death suspended over the forest, and the forest receptive, uncomprehending.

The circle of space is torn apart, and time is broken. Wrong has been done, or will be done. Despair touches my people like the shadow of a monstrous wing. I have no power upon it. Yet power is invested in me, and in me have they trusted. Who am I against the pain of the whole world, and what can I do that has not already been done?

The nightmare thing hovered and spread, extinguishing the southern sky. There was no wind, only creeping time would disperse it like slow poison smothering the land. It billowed out over the forest, ponderous as nightmare. It touched the farthest trees, and there was no light in the forest, only a greyness that belonged to neither light nor dark. Neither the hope of birth nor the promise of death, only annihilation, and fixity.

Fiona turned away from it in terror and crouched down on the rock. Patches of lichen made meaningless patterns on bare stone, pale colours presaging the spring. The rock was solid as it had always been. The land slept on beneath her feet. There is hope buried in the soil of the forest. Roots go down into the dark and find nourishment, and the bulbs lie quiescent in the cold soil. There is still the forest. If there is hope it lies in the forest, until the forest itself is extinguished and we are left without life.

There was a flower growing at the edge of the rock. In the confusion of hopelessness she saw it, and did not see it. A common enough thing, suggesting nothing. A small spark of yellow piercing the thickening grey air. Tormentil. A flower one would expect to find on the bare summit of a hill. There were more of them dotted in the grass. And violets, dark blue tinged with white. Pimpernel and eyebright. And the smell of thyme on slopes warmed by a mild sun. Thought impinged again, she realised numbly that this thing could not be, and she looked up slowly to the hills in the north.

There was a light after all. It was cool and mellow, and did not hurt at all. A green lightness, like the sun on new grass growing on the forest floor, a soft radiant light that sparkled on spring water cold with earth, and made the windflowers open. It came out of the heart of the forest, the reflection of the sun where there was no sun. There was a stirring of young leaves, and a glint of gold on green, new leaves turning in the breeze, shifting patterns of green and sunlight. Through the leaves the sky was blue and fragrant with the scent of the forest. Fiona raised her head and looked further. The mountains were blue and purple, tinged with summer, and the loch was azure like a summer sky.

'It's not just me,' whispered Fiona. 'There is also the forest, and I am also part of the forest.'

She knelt on the rock and watched. There was a sound of wind through leaves, and the dulcet call of wood pigeons among the trees. The breeze was cool on her face, no longer tinged with ice, but gentle, bringing the smell of the moors with it. She staggered to her feet, her back to what lay southward, and her face turned towards the north.

This is my land, and I will not have this happen.

There was no response, only the breath of summer on her face, and the call of mating birds. This is my land, and I will create a world where this thing shall not be.

Fiona stood quite straight on the rock now, her eyes turned away from the torn world, and breathed in the air of a summer not yet come.

I will create my own village. I will make Clachanpluck, and I will surround it with my forest like the enclosing sea. I will make the forest magical, inviolate, sufficient to itself, impregnable.

Fiona turned a little so that she was facing east. The lowering cloud cast its shadow over the trees at the edges of her vision, draining the world of colour. The village below was still untouched, bright roofs gleaming in the morning air.

I shall set against this thing the people who are my people. I shall call upon the people of Clachanpluck. There will be women and men, and between them they will drive away this nightmare, and I shall see them resolve this fear for ever.

The monster thing drifted further across the sky, then hesitated, as if a breeze had caught it, a clean wind fresh from the northern mountains.

I shall give life to them all. I shall name them, every one. They have all been touched by what is done, but I will not have them destroyed by it. I will name them for what they are and reject none of them, not even the one who had to carry the burden of this with him into the dark.

Fiona turned again, the green forest at her back, so that she could see where the shadow loomed. The greyness was thickening, and the trees faded away into it like the ghosts of the dying. Fiona made herself look southward, and even as she focused upon it again the air began to lighten, and the edges of the cloud diminish, no longer boundless, but contained. There was still a grey threat at the borders of the land, but blue sky arched clear behind her, and the forest was awake and vibrant. She stood on the summit of the hill, with the forest alive around her, creating its own dream.

I will accept what has been handed on to me, and I will allow there to be hope.

31

'I've heard that tune in waltz time too,' said Naomi. 'Listen.'

She raised her fiddle again and played a different version. It was much slower than the way they'd been playing it before, the lilt rising and falling like smooth hills against a blue sky.

'That's not so unfamiliar,' said Davey. 'It's a bit like the tune to a song that we have, but not quite the same. The way we sing it, it goes like this at the end of each part. Like this.'

He played it back to her, and Naomi listened attentively. 'I see. Let me try it.'

Davey played, and Naomi repeated the tune after him. He came in with her then, and the music changed, turning into a duet. Their eyes met, and Naomi led him away into the music, varying it and playing with it, then coming back to it again, so that Davey took the lead and brought the tune back to its beginning, where they finished together with a flourish.

'I like it,' said Naomi. 'Do you know the words?'

'I can never remember words. You know that. Try asking George. He knows all the songs.'

'It doesn't matter. Let's play it the other way again.'

He was very willing. They played it again as a reel, and without stopping Naomi turned it into another reel which Davey didn't know so well. He tried to follow her but lost it, and the tune disintegrated. He lowered his fiddle in mock despair. Naomi grinned at him and carried on, bringing the tune to its proper finish, then bowing to him like a performer ready for applause.

'Failed again,' said Davey cheerfully. 'What do you do that I don't do?'

'Practise,' said Naomi. 'You have to go on until you never forget. What'll you do when there's no one to remember for you?'

The smile left his face instantly, as if a cloud had hidden the sun. There was no way to unsay it. Naomi looked at him in sudden helplessness. 'There's no point,' she said sadly. 'We can only live now.'

'And I do,' replied Davey passionately. 'But it hurts. The more I live now, the more there is to lose. What else can I do?'

'Play music.'

'And then?' he cried despairingly.

'Play more music.' She raised her fiddle again. 'The boat song. Can you remember it?'

Davey picked up his fiddle indifferently. But when she nodded to him he came in with her. He could play this one easily, and there was a poignancy to it that fitted his feelings. Her mood matched his, it was like seeing a reflection of himself, transmuted into something greater. She was weaving his soul out of his body, making him play this. The way she played it was enchanting, tragic, like a spell being woven in a circle round him, binding him more strongly to what he must surely lose. Davey stayed with her until the last lilting notes had died into the silence, and then he turned away, throwing his fiddle on to the bed. 'I can't bear it,' he cried, standing with his back to her. 'I love you too much. How can I pretend differently? What do you expect of me?'

'Music,' said Naomi. 'As you expect of yourself. It's all I have to leave you. I expect you to take it, even if it hurts.'

'Don't you care about anything else?'

'Yes. But the music is what matters.'

'Do you really believe that? Don't people matter too?'

'Yes,' said Naomi again. 'But someone has to go on playing the music.'

'But we have to live too!'

'Of course people have to go on living. That's why the music is so important.'

'Not to me,' said Davey. 'I love you more.'

'And I love you,' said Naomi sorrowfully. 'But what would you have? I can't leave you anything but what I have to give.'

'I wish I could come with you,' said Davey recklessly. He'd said it now, and he waited for her reaction, while time seemed to stand still between them. If she would only accept it. To be free of the past, with all the road before him and her for company. She was his genius, but he could support her, and together they could make

223

music wherever the road might take them, for whoever chose to hear.

'And what would it be like to lose Clachanpluck?' Her question, cold and discouraging, dropped into his thoughts like a splinter of ice. So she didn't want him. He was bitterly hurt, but too proud to give himself away any further.

'I can stand on my own,' said Davey. 'I could take to the road without you.'

'And would you?' The gentleness of her tone belied her. She wasn't fooled. She knew very well he wanted to go nowhere without her. Davey was silent.

'Davey,' said Naomi softly. He dared not look at her. 'I'm not heartless. I want you too. But I chose long ago. I don't belong anywhere, and no one is mine to love for very long. I shan't forget you. But the music is all I have to give in this world. Perhaps it changes nothing, except how people feel. But I think that's important enough.'

'I'm a musician too. I wouldn't take away your music.'

'Is that why you want to come with me?'

Davey said nothing for a while. 'Partly,' he answered at last.

'I've taught you nearly all I know,' said Naomi. 'Soon you'd stop learning from me. Better to part before that happens. I don't have anything else to give you.'

'But you do!' Davey turned and faced her, all on fire again. 'Don't you realise what you are? You're a woman. You're beautiful. You're Naomi, and that's more than all the music in the world. And I love you.'

'Please,' said Naomi. 'Don't tempt me any more. I love you too much already, Davey. It would be opening a box and letting out everything that lurks below the surface. I've brought pain into the world already, and sorrow, and I don't see any end to what I've done. There's no hope I can offer you. Only the music to leave with you. That's what I stayed for, and I didn't pretend it was for anything else. I stayed, knowing it would hurt me more the longer I lingered. I had a debt to pay. Can't you understand that?'

He was listening to her now, as if he recognised something in her words. 'Yes,' said Davey. 'I understand that very well.'

'And having paid it, I shall go. Tomorrow,' added Naomi with sudden decision.

'No!' he cried out.

'Yes,' said Naomi. 'Otherwise,' she paused, and when she spoke again her voice was unsteady. 'Otherwise I won't be strong enough to go on resisting you.'

His face was always so open. She could see conflicting feelings chasing each other like sun and shadow across the hills. Davey himself was all confusion. So she did care. She did love him as much as he loved her. She was as passionate as he was, but for her the music came first. It was what was most lovable about her, the thing he most respected. It was also the thing that shattered his hopes, and broke his fleeting happiness to pieces, this care for nothing but the fulfilment of an ideal. She was wrong, he would never take away her music. And she was right, for if she said yes to him she would cease to be true to herself. He loved her as she was, and wished desperately that she were different.

'Oh I don't know,' said Davey, exhausted, and sank down on the bed.

Naomi sat down on the wooden box by the fire and looked at him. 'It's not tomorrow now, Davey,' she said gently. 'It's tonight. Tomorrow I'll say goodbye to them all and go. But tonight I'm with you. And that'll be for ever. You know that?'

He was crying freely now, but he ignored it. Time was too precious to spend on tears. 'Then I'll take now,' he said, and held out his arms.

She laid down her fiddle and came to him readily. Davey took her in his arms and kissed her without stopping, as if he could defy time, and do it for ever. She gently undid his clothes, and he kicked his slippers off, and undressed her too. Without letting go of one another they rolled over, and Davey pulled the covers over them. It was still light, not yet nightfall. Seconds stretched ahead of him, precious as rubies, minutes and hours beyond price, the whole present which contained everything. He would not sleep; there was all the future to sleep through. Years stretching in the unending cycle, days, nights and seasons, years to grow old and die and be alone for ever.

But now there was Naomi. There was hair the colour of flame against his face, and her alive and present in his arms, untouched by the cold hand of memory. What she was now was what he was, and there was nothing in him that was not given to her. Firelight flamed among the roses, and the fire which was within him met fire. Nothing existing but this, the very centre of the music, still and quick, a sound caught in the web of the moment, a note held forever between two waves of the sea.

There is no dawn and no beginning. There is only where we are.

32

When the villagers realised that Naomi was leaving, they turned out in force to see her on her way. They played music for her, pipes and fiddles and whistles and guitars, played by anyone who could tell one note from another. They played tunes that had been known as far back as memory went in Clachanpluck, and they played her own tunes back to her. The village street was thronged with people, who gathered in a knot outside Emily's house, lining the road to the north up to the very edges of the village. The musicians played, and the people waited patiently for her to come out and say farewell.

Davey didn't join them. He stood at the yard door with her, on the threshold of the house. Naomi was dressed in her travelling clothes again, well-worn brown jacket and red woollen hat, and a new rainbow-coloured scarf trailing loosely over her shoulders, for the day was mild and springlike. She carried her bundle on her back again, just food for a day and clothing for a night, and the fiddle in its case strapped across her back.

'Goodbye, Davey,' she said, looking in his eyes.

He held her to him hard and kissed her. 'Goodbye,' said Davey. 'Fare well.'

She kissed him back very quickly, and strode away from him, disappearing from sight at the gate in the corner of the yard. There was a cheer from the street, and a rousing march struck up, in ragged timing. Davey leaned against the doorpost, his head bowed on his arm. There were footsteps across the yard behind him, and someone touched him on the shoulder. It was his brother. Davey didn't look up, but his hand went up to meet the hand that touched him.

'Never mind it,' said Andrew awkwardly, against the clash of music from outside. 'Never mind it, Davey. After all,' he added, with clumsy comfort, 'she was no kin of yours. No drop of blood related to you at all.'

Davey shook his head, and said nothing.

The street was full of noise and colour. Naomi had never seen it like this. Usually the houses were shut against the cold, silent walls of grey stone, and there were only people in working clothes going about their daily round, hardly stopping to speak to one another, coming from one house and crossing the street to another, doors opening and closing quickly against the weather. There had been little life out in the street itself, little warmth for congregating out of doors. But this seemed the first day of spring, with music and life and colour, people sprung up from nowhere, celebration vibrant in the air, and all for her. Naomi stopped at the yard gate, taking it all in, and grinned at them. Then she stepped down among them, and they gathered round her, making way for her, a trail of children and music following her out of the village. She turned and waved to them all. The sun was shining on the road, and there was blackthorn flowering on the thorn tree by the gate. Naomi danced a few steps to their music, spring sun shining on red hair, and then she turned away from them, facing north, to the road out of the village.

The taggle of children followed her. Alan and Molly were running backwards in front of her, waving her a back to front farewell. Then they fell away, and the last houses were left behind. There was a gate in the hawthorn hedge, leading into a big field. Two women were waiting for her, sitting on the top rung. They jumped down when Naomi came level with them, and walked with her, one on each side, a little way out of the village.

'We'll miss you,' said Bridget. 'You brought us a gift that changed everything. We won't forget.'

Naomi stopped and looked at her, searching for meaning in the polite words. 'Truly?' she said. 'It wasn't so easy for you to have me here. I know that.'

'It was worth it to me,' replied Bridget. 'It's been a hard winter for both of us, but the music is how we live with it. I didn't want it, it made me feel too much. But I took it anyway, and I have to thank you for it.'

'And I have to thank you too, for bringing me back to myself when I was lost.'

'I only showed you the way. The forest is yours as much as mine. I know that now. I've never been far away from here,' went on Bridget, 'but I think that wherever you go, you'll find something which is the same. The forest is always there for you.'

228

'Thank you,' said Naomi, and kissed her.

She turned to Emily, who was standing in the road, the loch stretching behind her, smooth water dappled with sun.

Naomi took her hands. 'One winter is not so very long,' she said.

'I'm glad it proved long enough, for both of us.'

'That's true. I did find my way into the forest, after all.'

'I thought you would, the first time I saw you. It was only a question of recognising what you knew already. Like the music. If I hear it played enough times, I begin to know it. Even the music you gave to Davey.'

'I wish I could have taught it to you. But I've left it with you, and it's yours, as far as it ever can be.'

'You couldn't wish for more. After all, we're not the same. All we do is create worlds for ourselves, I suppose, and when one touches another, there's a tension between one image and another. But the images we use reflect the same thing.'

'I love you,' said Naomi. 'I may not come back, but it makes a difference. I won't forget.'

'And I love you,' said Emily. 'And that is always so.'

They held each other. A small breeze stirred the new grass at the roadside, and a scrap of cloud dimmed the sun for a moment, then drifted on into an empty sky. For a moment their eyes met, and then they parted quickly. Bridget and Emily turned away, and walked back along the road past the loch to the village.

The strains of music were dying away in the distance behind her. The road to the north was wide and open, skirting the still water. There were hills ahead, and more hills, and beyond them all a ridge of mountains, their summits still white with winter snow. But down here in the hedgerows the grass was fresh and green, and bright buds were opening on the hedges. No touch of frost now, but flakes of white at the roadside, snowdrops tough as gossamer, and between them aconites like sparks of scattered fire. There was a blackbird singing in an alder, his feathers preened and polished to a shining black, beak yellow as a candle flame. And bluetits in new plumage, dipping and hopping among the briar-strewn hedgerows. The sky arched over her, blue as sapphire in the first heat of the sun, and the road stretched away ahead of her, limitless, weaving its way into the north, finding new ways and making connections, bringing together every village in the world.